Case for Three Detectives

MACBETH: 'Twas a rough night.

LENOX: My young remembrance cannot parallel
      A fellow to it.

Re-enter Macduff

MACDUFF: O horror! horror! horror!
      Tongue, nor heart, cannot conceive, nor name thee!

MACBETH and LENOX: What's the matter?

MACDUFF: Confusion now hath made his masterpiece!
      Most sacrilegious murder hath broke open
      The Lord's anointed temple, and stole thence
      The life o' the building.

Case for Three Detectives

By

LEO BRUCE

Academy
Chicago

First printing: August, 1980
Second printing: November, 1982

Published by Academy Chicago
425 North Michigan Avenue
Chicago, Illinois 60611
All rights reserved.

Printed and bound in the United States of America.

Library of Congress Cataloging in Publication Data

Croft-Cooke, Rupert, 1903–
    Case for three detectives.

    I. Title.
PZ3.C8742Cas 1980 [PR6005.R673] 823'.912 80-17976
ISBN 0-89733-032-3
ISBN 0-89733-033-1 (pbk.)

Case for Three Detectives

CHAPTER 1

I CANNOT pretend that there was anything sinister in the atmosphere that evening. Nothing of the sort that is supposed to precede a crime. Nobody walked about looking furtive, no whispered quarrels were interrupted, no mysterious strangers lurked near the house. Although afterwards, as you may imagine, I went over the events of the day again and again in my mind, I could remember nothing which might have served as a warning, nothing at all extraordinary in anyone's behaviour. That is why the thing came as such an abominable shock to me.

I remember, of course—I have good cause to remember—that we discussed crime over our cocktails. But we discussed it in general terms, and how could one have guessed that there was any relevance in the discussion? And I could not say for certain who had brought up the subject. Perhaps if I could have done so, if anyone could have done so, it would have helped us later to understand. For that discussion was relevant, appallingly relevant, in a very special sense. As you shall see.

But at the time—well, at the Thurstons' week-end parties, crime might be discussed, or religion, politics, the cinema, or ghosts. Any topic of general interest which arose was sure to be pretty well threshed out. That was the kind of party which the Thurstons gave, a party at which everyone talked a great deal, shouting opinions which he would afterwards have denied, and trying to shout them as cleverly as possible. I do not mean that it was all rather self-conscious and arty, like those awful parties in London at which women with unpleasant breath advocate free love and nudism. But at the Thurstons' conversation was enjoyed, and not treated as a tiresome stop-gap between dinner and bridge.

Dr. Thurston himself was no conversationalist, though he enjoyed listening, and could put in an incentive phrase now and again. He was a big, bespectacled man, rather Teutonic in appearance, and in manner, too, for he showed a jolly German simplicity and sentimentality to everyone. He liked pressing his guests to food and drink and cigars, with booming emphasis. He had been the local doctor in that Sussex village, till he married, and although he no longer practised he had kept on the house, because he liked it, and allowed the new practitioner to build afresh. It was understood that Mrs. Thurston had money; at all events they had been very well off since their marriage, and entertained a great deal.

She, too, was amiable, most amiable, but not very intelligent. Although I stayed with the Thurstons many times, and must have spent hours in the same room with Mary Thurston, I cannot recall a single sentence that she uttered. She was stout, and spent a great deal of money on her clothes, a big, blonde, rather painted woman, easy-going and quite unpretentious. I can see her clearly enough, even if I cannot remember words of hers, beaming round on us all, filling quite a wide arm-chair, giggling like a girl at flattery, obviously overflowing with kindness. 'The Goddess of Plenty' someone once called her, aptly enough, for as a hostess, from the practical point of view, she was supreme. The food was really exquisite, the house beautifully kept, and Mrs. Thurston had that important gift—a memory for drinks. She was a good woman.

Whoever may have started discussing crime, it was Alec Norris who did most of the talking, though he pretended to be contemptuous of the topic.

"Crime?" he said. "Can't we talk about anything else? Don't we get enough of it in books and films? I'm sick to death of this crime crime, crime, wherever you turn."

Dr. Thurston chuckled. He knew Norris, and knew why he spoke so bitterly. Norris was an unsuccessful writer of novels very different from murder mysteries—rather intense psychological books, with a good deal of sex in them. Dr. Thurston saw his chance of making Norris excited.

"But *is* it crime in those books?" he asked. "Crime as it really happens?"

Norris might have been a diver on a spring-board. He hesitated for one moment, blinking at Thurston, then he plunged. "No, I'm damned if it is," he said. "Literary crime is all baffling mystery and startling clues. Whereas in real life, murder, for instance, nearly always turns out to be some sordid business of a strangled servant girl. There are only two kinds of murder which could baffle the police for one second. One is that committed by a man with a victim who *cannot* be missed—like the recent Brighton murder. The other is the act of a madman, who murders for the sake of murder, without another motive. No premeditated murder could puzzle the police for very long: Where there's a motive and the victim's identified, there's an arrest."

He paused to swallow the rest of his cocktail. I was watching him, thinking what an odd-looking fellow Alec Norris was—narrow in head and body, with a bony face in which jaw and teeth, cheek-bones and forehead protruded, while the flesh seemed to have shrunk till it barely covered the skull.

Another guest spoke then. Young David Strickland, I think it was. "But an arrest doesn't always mean a verdict of guilty," he said. "There have been murderers so desperate that though they knew beforehand they would be suspected and probably charged, they took the chance. They were clever enough not to provide enough evidence."

9

I did not look with much interest towards Strickland, for I knew him quite well. He was younger than any of us, a thick-set fellow, fond of sport, particularly of racing. He was apt to try to borrow a fiver from you, but bore no malice if it was refused. He was some sort of protégé of the Thurstons, and Dr. Thurston sometimes spoke to his wife of him good-humouredly as 'your lover, my dear'. There was nothing in that, however, though I could imagine Mary Thurston helping him out of difficulties. Nothing of the gigolo about young Strickland, a hard-drinking, gambling type, fond of smutty stories.

Alec Norris brushed aside his interruption. "The police will find the evidence, when they know their man," he said, and returned to his condemnation of detective fiction. "It's all so artificial," he said. "So unrelated to life. You, all of you, know these literary murders. Suddenly, in the middle of a party—like this one, perhaps—someone is found dead in the adjoining room. By the trickery of the novelist all the guests and half the staff are suspect. Then down comes the wonderful detective, who neatly proves that it was in fact the only person you never suspected at all. Curtain."

"Have another drink, Alec?"

"Thanks. But I haven't finished yet. I was going to point out that it has become a mere game—fox and hounds between readers and novelist. Only readers are getting clever nowadays. They don't suspect the obvious people, as they used to. But if the novelist has a character who wasn't at all the sort of person to have done it, they may just wonder, by analogy. Every one of the minor characters has been used. It has turned out to be the family lawyer, like you, Mr. Williams. The host himself, like you, Thurston. The young friend staying in the house, like you, Townsend," he glanced in my direction, "or like you, Strickland, or like me. The butler, like Stall, the Vicar, like Mr. Rider, the housemaid, like Enid, the chauffeur, like yours—what is his name?

—or the very hostess, like you, Mrs. Thurston. Or else it has been a total stranger who doesn't appear till Chapter Twenty-two, though that I call cheating. In fact, each of us has been overworked."

He had us smiling rather uncomfortably now. "Yes, what I said is true," he ended rather peevishly. "It has become a game, a mere game like chess, this writing of murder mysteries. While in real life it is no game, but something quite simple and savage, with about as much mystery wrapped round it as that piano leg. And that's why I've no use for detective fiction. It's false. It depicts the impossible."

Sam Williams answered him. Williams was the Thurstons' lawyer, and I had met him several times at their house. He was one of those very clean, pink-and-white, cigar-smoking men, whom you see swinging a patent-leathered foot in the corner of a first class railway-carriage. He had thick white hair, always beautifully brushed, a young man's figure, and an open face. He dressed well, and moved smartly. He had the reputation of being a first-rate solicitor, and I had consulted him more than once.

He said now—"That may be so. But I enjoy the game. It has, as you say, become far more subtle lately, and no one can guess the murderer till the last few pages. But after all, we expect fiction to transcend life, and a murder in a book to be more mysterious than a real one."

Just then Thurston, who always mixed the cocktails himself, rang for some more gin, and Stall, the butler, answered the bell. I had never liked Stall, and had I been playing what Norris called 'the game of mystery', Stall would have been my first guess. There really was something sinister about his lean bald head, and narrow eyes, and silent movements. But he was an excellent servant.

Mary Thurston stopped him, as he was leaving the room, "Tell Fellowes I want to speak to him, will you?" she said, and added to her husband, "It's about those rats, dear.

I'm sure I've heard them again. I think they're in the apple-room. He must do something about it."

"Well, don't let him put poison down in case T'ang gets hold of it." T'ang was Mary Thurston's Pekingese.

"No. A trap would be best," she said, and went out into the hall to speak to Fellowes, the chauffeur.

It was a Georgian house, simple and dignified in architecture, with the flat front and four-square look of the period, rows of long and dignified windows, and high carved ceilings. But I was not altogether surprised to hear that Mrs. Thurston had heard rats. I remember thinking it rather silly, but not unlike her, to mention it in front of her guests.

Not that the interior of the house gave the impression of possible rats, or even of mice, it was too well kept and well cleaned. It was only its age which made them seem possible to me. Its rooms were light and centrally heated, its inside walls painted in cream, with vivid water-colours hung on them, its floors parquet, while it had a luxurious array of deep settees and arm-chairs, with gay soft cushions in them, to distract the eye from the reproduction furniture. I remember its air of conventional warmth, light and luxury, as that of a very expensive hotel. In fact, that is what it was all rather like—a good hotel. Nickel taps running hot water in your bedroom, reading-lamps to switch on wherever you were sitting, drinks whenever you wanted them. Most pleasant for a week-end, but rather an insipid background for a longer stay. That's as near as I can get to a portrayal of it—it seems so long ago, now, that we were all there.

"One more!" Dr. Thurston was begging us, as he went round with the cocktail shaker. "Just half of one!" And we had our glasses filled up.

"You seem to have a down on writers of crime stories," said Williams, across the hearth to Norris.

"Only because their books conform to type."

"Have you never thought of writing a crime story yourself?"

The question seemed to startle Norris. "I? No!" he said. "If I ever did anything of the sort it would be a study of the state of mind in a criminal. It wouldn't be a blasted drawing-room game of clues, and false clues, and alibis; tricks of time and place and method and motive, which have no relationship with real life. I might try one day to depict a man's agony as he made up his mind whether or not to commit a murder. And his agony afterwards . . ." he added slowly.

"But surely," Williams said, "Dostoievski did that for all time, didn't he? In *Crime and Punishment*, I mean?"

"Nothing is done 'for all time'," said Norris sharply; "every murderer is a little different from the rest. Though your crime writer doesn't seem to realize it."

Just then the first gong sounded, and we rose to go upstairs to dress. Williams and Norris were still talking as we left the room, though I followed no more of their argument.

I must have been the first, I think, to reach the hall, and I found Mary Thurston finishing her instructions to the chauffeur. Fellowes was a rather good-looking young man of thirty or so. He had one of those keen intelligent faces, with frank eyes and a good profile, which seem to occur often enough among the mechanically-minded of his class. He was well built, too, and standing stiffly in his uniform he made his mistress, in spite of her clever clothes, look rather flabby.

He left her as we emerged, and when Mary Thurston turned towards us, I noticed that she was flushed, and seemed to be controlling emotions such as one would scarcely have thought would be aroused by a discussion of rat-traps. However, she smiled to us, and preceded us up the wide staircase.

CHAPTER 2

I HAVE said that nothing sinister happened during the earlier part of that evening, and it is true. But there was one small incident which I thought, even at the time, was odd. It was not in the least sinister, and might even, at another time, have been thought rather comic.

I dress very quickly. I have never been able to afford a man-servant capable of looking after my clothes, and consequently am accustomed to doing everything myself. I must have been the first to finish changing, and left my room to go downstairs within fifteen minutes of the time when the first gong had been rung.

The house, I have explained, was Georgian, and so simple in plan that one could take it all in at a glance. There were three storeys, and on each floor the corridor ran from end to end of the house, with doors to right and left of it. My own was at the east end of the corridor, and Mary Thurston's at the west end, while young Strickland, I knew, had the bedroom next to hers. Her husband's room was opposite to hers.

I had reached the top of the stairs, and was about to descend, when I noticed that the door of Mary Thurston's room was being opened. Thinking that she, too, had by some means effected a quick change, I waited for her. But it was Strickland who began cautiously to emerge. When he saw me standing there he made a clumsy effort to return to the room, but, realizing that I had seen him, he seemed to think better of it, and walked out as boldly as possible. He even gave me a brief nod as he entered his own room.

I went on downstairs wishing that I had not paused, since it might have appeared that I was spying. It was embarras-

14

sing, too, to have seen that. And I found myself wondering what might be the relationship between these two, the ageing, stout, motherly woman, and the thick-set, hard-drinking young gambler. Whatever it might be, it was not a love-affair, of that I was certain.

Downstairs I found the Vicar, who, I gathered, had been invited to dinner. I was a little dismayed to find him sitting beside the fire in the lounge, for I realized that I should be alone for some little time with him. He sat bolt upright on a straight-backed chair, his hands on his bony knees, and his eyes—after he had greeted me—blinking solemnly at the fire.

I had met Mr. Rider before, of course, and never without embarrassment. This little, wiry, staring man was quite out of place in the Thurstons' cheerful house—in more senses than one a skeleton at the feast. His very appearance made him inappropriate. He was bald, and his cheeks were yellow, and his collars too large for his thin neck. His clothes were always untidy, and sometimes rather soiled, for he was a bachelor and depended on a village woman for service in his draughty Vicarage. But it was his stare which used to make me uncomfortable. He had a trick of fixing his eyes on one, then apparently forgetting himself, so that for perhaps five or even ten minutes, one remained under scrutiny. He had dark, round, surprised eyes, in deep sockets.

His reputation was unusual, too. His puritanism was ferocious. Towards those of his parishioners whose way of living was supposed to be lax, his attitude was merciless. A number of stories were current in the district of his un-compromising warfare against what he called 'sins of the flesh'. It was said of him that once, meeting a pair of rustic lovers walking in the fields on a Sunday afternoon, he had lectured them so severely that they had actually untwined themselves (a feat which would not have seemed easy to anyone who had observed the complications of circling arm, yielding waist, knotted fingers, and clutched shoulder), and hurried home, guiltily isolated. He had preached violently at an unfortunate farmer's wife who had come to one of his services with a dress cut a trifle lower at the neck than was customary, and his manner when he was obliged to conduct marriage services was supposed to be unwilling and curt.

At the Thurstons' he usually spoke very little, unless he was roused, and I gathered that he was invited out of kindness, for neither the Doctor nor May Thurston believed that he had enough to eat at the Vicarage.

I made one or two attempts to converse with him but was answered only by absent monosyllables. Suddenly, however, he turned to me.

"Mr. Townsend," he said, "I want to ask you a question."

The tone in which he said this was strange. His voice was hollow, almost fierce. There was no apology in it. It was as though he were going to give me a chance to defend myself against some serious imputation. Then he seemed to grow distant again. He stared into the fire.

"You may," he said at last without looking at me, "you may be able to put my mind at rest. I hope you can." I waited. Then abruptly he turned to me again. "Have you noticed anything in this household? Anything going on which should not go on? Anything . . . improper?"

I thought of David Strickland, secretively coming out of Mary Thurston's room. But I smiled, and said cheerfully, "Good Lord, no, Mr. Rider. I've always considered it a model household."

He was so quaint and eccentric that I forgot to blame him for the indiscretion of his query. You could blame him no more than you would blame a child for discussing his hosts' concerns. But I was greatly relieved when just then the door opened, and Sam Williams came in, so that the talk became more natural.

Dinner, I remember, was a cheerful, almost an hilarious meal. We all ate with real enjoyment and Thurston was excited about some hock he had bought at an auction sale of a neighbouring estate. Stall handled it with reverent efficiency and it was certainly excellent.

It was irritating, though, when Mary Thurston had left us, to have the Vicar sitting morosely at the table, primly refusing the port, and making it impossible to talk more freely than we had done in the presence of our hostess. Not that the conversation after dinner at the Thurstons' was ever particularly crude—it was not. But young Strickland could tell stories nimbly, in spite of his rather weighty character, and perhaps it was just because Mr. Rider was there that I for one was peeved by the silence forced on him. I was relieved when someone suggested bridge, though neither Thurston nor I were particularly fond of cards.

Several of us were tired that evening. I was not at all surprised when quite early young Strickland got up and apologetically proposed to go to bed. He had got up very early that day, he said, and felt fagged out.

"Whisky and soda before you go?" suggested Thurston from the card-table.

But Strickland unexpectedly refused. "No, thanks awfully," he said, "I really think I'll turn in right away." And he nodded to us, and left the room.

I did not notice the time then, but I have since calculated from later events that it was about half-past ten.

The next to get up was Alec Norris. He had threatened to break up the game at the end of the next rubber. He had been playing with Thurston, Williams and me, while the Vicar and Mary Thurston had been talking with some intentness where they sat together on the settee.

"You would like to join the game, Mrs. Thurston," the

17

Vicar said, "and it is quite time I started to walk home."

"It's not very far, Rider," Thurston remarked politely, though I don't think anyone was sorry.

"No. I shall go through the orchard. Be home in five minutes " And protesting his gratitude for a pleasant evening, he took himself off.

We did play one more rubber, but it was not very successful, for Mary Thurston was a poor player, and Sam Williams, who was her partner, was inclined to take his bridge seriously. And we finished it just as the clock' in the hall struck eleven.

"No," Mary Thurston said, "no more, really. I'm making poor Mr. Williams miserable. Besides, eleven o'clock is my bedtime."

That was quite true. Like a little child, Mary Thurston had her fixed hour for retiring, and if she stayed up beyond it, did so always with a sense of guilt. I could remember her often enough in the past standing up when she had heard that chime, kissing her husband, and bidding us good night with an ingenuous, even rather babyish smile.

She left the three of us, Williams, Thurston and me, to pour ourselves out a very welcome whisky.

Looking back on that night I remember with gratitude that from then until the . . . until the tragedy, I remained with the other two. None of us stirred from the room. Our staying there talking saved us, as you will see, from a great deal of interrogation and unpleasantness. Once I remembered a letter which I had left in my overcoat pocket, and thought for a moment of fetching it. I actually crossed the room and opened the door, but fortunately at that moment Williams asked me some question which it interested me to answer, and I went no farther. I have cause enough to be glad of it.

Before leaving us, Mary Thurston had turned on the wireless, and though none of us was exhilarated by the efforts of a popular dance band to provide entertainment for Great Britain, we did not actually turn it off. It made an uninteresting undertone to our conversation. Since I was on my feet, however, I thought of switching it off, and should have done so before sitting down. But I paused to answer Williams's question, and it was during that pause that we heard the first scream.

So much of the subsequent enquiry depended on time, that I should like to have been able to fix this precisely, but I can do no more than say that it must have been at about a quarter past eleven. I had closed the door again, and was returning to the other two by the fireside.

Now you must know I have no wish to chill your blood or emphasize the gruesome aspects of this affair. But I do ask you to imagine the effect of that interruption. We were in the cosy firelight of an autumn evening, quietly sipping our whisky, in a cheerful friendly house. We knew each other and the household well. There had been nothing to arouse even the faintest presentment of evil or misfortune. We were normal English people in a very ordinary house. And suddenly, from just over our heads it seemed, came that long, horrifying woman's cry of terror. It was the shock of it which seemed to stun me. Not the actual sound or its implications, but the sudden shock.

Almost before we had jumped to our feet there was another, and a third followed it, but the third was the most hideous of all, for it died slowly out of our hearing. By that time we had made for the staircase. Thurston was first. "Mary!" he shouted, and in spite of his weight he bounded upstairs like a frightened boy.

CHAPTER 3

I DO not know how many seconds it took us to reach the door of Mary Thurston's room. But that it was seconds, and not minutes, not even one minute, I am certain. At the door stood Alec Norris. But the door was locked.

At first we threw our shoulders against it. Then Williams, pressing first the top, then the bottom of it, shouted, "Bolted! In two places. Smash the panel in, Thurston."

Thurston was still heaving his weight blindly at the door, and it was I who picked up a solid wooden chair which stood on the landing, and drove it through the upper panel. And through the jagged gap I caught a glimpse of the room, and of something in it which was horrible, and yet which gave me none of the astounded shock which the screams had given me. I suppose they had made me expect it. For what I saw was the dim outline of Mary Thurston's face on a pillow which was more crimson than white, and I knew at once that she had been murdered.

Before we could enter, however, it was necessary to smash in a lower panel as well, for the door was tall, and, as Williams had said, bolted at top and bottom. I myself leaned through the broken woodwork and pulled back those bolts. And lest it should be doubted later, let me say quite clearly now that each was driven home securely. Indeed, it took me several seconds to get the lower one back at all.

When I had done that, and while I was standing up to turn the handle, Thurston pushed past us into the room. And as he did so I became aware that we had been joined by two others. My whole conscious attention was concentrated on the room before us, so that it was only as it

20

were from the corner of my mind that I perceived Strickland standing there beside us, and Fellowes on the staircase which rose from beyond Mary Thurston's door to the second floor. At what moment they had arrived I did not, do not, know. But I am certain that neither was there when we had first reached the landing, and that neither had appeared when I stepped back to pick up the chair. In other words, neither was on the scene within a minute of the screams, though both had arrived soon after that.

And now we were peering in at that doorway. We stood there, the four of us, as though we had been warned to respect the room. We stood, and saw what we saw, and watched Thurston's movements.

There was only a reading-lamp alight in the room, but it was not too heavily shaded for us to see the whole interior. Across the bed lay Mary Thurston, fully dressed. But it was the pillow on which her head lay which drew our horrified stare, the pillow and her throat. For the pillow, as I had already seen, was stained hideously with scarlet, and across her throat, her fat white throat, there was a still ghastlier scar. But once again I do not wish to be unnecessarily harrowing. It is sufficient to say that when Thurston told us in a choking voice that she was dead, we did not speak or move, for we had known what his words must be.

Sam Williams kept his head. "Don't move," he said to us who stood in the doorway. "He must be in there." And he reached for the light switch, and snapped it down. This, however, had no result, and I was conscious of a slight relief. Any further light on that scene would have been too merciless.

But I think it was the fruitless click of that electric light that turned my attention from the realization of Mary Thurston's death, to the necessity of discovering her murderer. In the agonizing seconds during which we had stared at what lay on the bed, I had thought how dreadful, how tragic, as though it had been an accident. But when

Williams pressed the switch and the room became no lighter, something woke me to see that this . . . this horror was human work, and that its agent must be discovered.

Still, it could only have been two or three minutes at the most after the time of the first scream. By no means could the murderer have escaped.

"Stay in the doorway, Townsend," Williams said again, and began to search the room.

I stood with Strickland and Fellowes behind me, watching him. He crossed first to the window, and peered out, and up and down, then went to a large cupboard, built into the wall beside the fireplace, and searched it quickly. I saw him look up to the roof of it, and down in the farthest recess. He crossed to the fireplace, and briefly examined it. He looked undei .he bed, and at the mattresses; he opened a wardrobe.

"The window again," I shouted suddenly. Though there were two windows in the room, only one of them was made to open, and towards this Williams hurried again. It is true that I had already seen him look out of it, but some instinct had made me beg him to do so once more.

"Impossible," he said. "There's a twenty-foot drop. And," he looked out again, "ten feet to the window above."

Williams continued his search as though oblivious of Thurston, who was standing beside the bed. Very low sounds like buried sobs came from him, and he did not move. Presently Williams had finished his first investigation.

"If there's any place of concealment in that room," he said, "it is a specially constructed one."

That was true enough. I had been eager to point out any possible space left unexamined by Williams, if he gave me an opportunity. I suppose that the hunting instinct is still strong in us, and though I never moved from the door my eyes and mind were occupied with the search. There was nowhere left to probe in the room itself.

"Fellowes, help me move this carpet," Williams said suddenly. "We'll leave nothing to chance."

They pulled up the carpet and examined the floorboards. They looked over every foot of wall space. They re-examined the cupboard, the floor of the cupboard, and the upper part of it. The bed was a single one, light, and high above the floor. They scrutinized the boards beneath it. They went again to the fireplace, as though to see whether it might not conceal a means of escape. They moved the furniture and looked behind it.

Williams was white, and his teeth were clenched as though he were repressing emotion. "It's unbelievable," he said to me; then, in a lower voice, "It's unnatural." And I was inclined to agree with him.

By this time, or during this time, we had been joined by Stall. Norris and Fellowes both said afterwards that he had arrived before Williams had first pushed up the window, but I did not notice him come. He was, incidentally, the only one of us, apparently, who was already in pyjamas. He wore an ugly woollen dressing-gown, and seemed to be shivering, though the evening could not have been called cold.

Presently Williams, whose lawyer's mind was best equipped for the situation, said, "We must get a doctor. And the police. There's no point in staying here. Better search the grounds. I'll telephone."

Then Thurston joined us. "Have you 'phoned, Sam?" he asked. His voice was low and tired. "Doctor? And everything?"

"Just going to," said Williams, and patted his arm.

And then—perhaps you will be shocked—the first thing we did was to have a stiff whisky. Williams poured one out for Dr. Thurston, who had sunk into a chair in the lounge, and gave one each to Fellowes and Stall. Alec Norris's teeth rattled on the rim of his glass as he drank. Strickland had not spoken yet, but drank greedily.

"Look here, Townsend," said Williams, "you take Norris, Strickland and Fellowes and make a thorough search of the grounds."

"Certainly," I said, though I had little hope of discovering anything. But I felt I could no longer bear the atmosphere of that house. The thought of Thurston, the rotund and cheerful, looking puffy and drawn, and Alec Norris with his white face and thin trembling frame, was too much for me. The man I most respected was Williams, who never lost his head, and handled the hideous situation admirably.

In the hall were Fellowes and Stall, and we decided to take the chauffeur with us, leaving Stall in case he should be wanted.

"What about the women-servants?" I asked. "Do they know?"

It had struck me that it would be cruel to let Enid, the young parlourmaid, go into that room unprepared.

"Yes, sir. The parlourmaid was upstairs while we were at the door, and I sent her down to the kitchen," Fellowes said.

"Well, stay with her and the cook," I told Stall. "And don't let either of them leave the kitchen."

"Very well, sir," said the butler.

We had just arranged our routes when Williams called me from the little cloakroom off the hall to which he had gone to telephone for the police. "I think the 'phone's out of order," he said, "or the wires have been cut. I can't get an answer, anyway. Better tell Fellowes to take the car and fetch Dr. Tate and the Sergeant at once. As quick as he can."

"All right."

"I'll have another try at this thing. But it seems pretty dead," he said, returning to the cloakroom.

So Fellowes went off to the village, and Strickland, Norris and I out into the grounds. We had decided that Norris was to go round by the stable-yards, Strickland was to make an outer circuit, in the remote hope that he might find someone, or something, among the trees which would help us. You will understand that we had little confidence in this chase of ours into the open air. But the fact that Mary Thurston's door had been bolted, her windows inaccessible, and her room empty, already seemed to us so fantastic and inexplicable that we no longer behaved, or tried to behave, logically.

I could realize little more than that a murder had been committed by some means which seemed to me almost supernatural. I was so much distressed, and so much at a loss, that any course of action which had been suggested to me as likely to capture the murderer would have done as well as this mad rush into the grounds. If Williams had told me to search the garage, or the village church, or to take a train to London, I would have obeyed as readily. I had to do something. When I remembered that poor, kindly, stupid woman who had always been so gently foolish and free from any sort of malice, lying as I had seen her, I was eager enough for work which might avenge her. So that I did not wait to calculate the chances of any success for Norris, Strickland and me in the garden. I ran out blindly.

I had snatched up a powerful electric torch which lay on the hall table, and after a general look round the house I went to the gravel path which ran beyond the wide flower-bed that was under Mary Thurston's window. It seemed to me that here, if anywhere, I might find something, some . . . (the word had already come into my mind) clue. And I was not disappointed. I found two objects which, if they were not clues, were at least, I thought, connected with the crime.

The first lay far out on the tennis court, fifteen yards or more from the house. It was a broken electric-light bulb.

As soon as I saw its fragments gleaming on the short grass, I stopped to pick them up. But before my hand touched them, I paused. I suddenly remembered all I had read of crimes, and their discovery. Finger-prints! And I thought with a shudder that I had been projected by this affair into a new and frightening world, in which investigation, cross-examination, and the discovery of finger-prints took the place of the more normal events of my previous life.

The other object was even more relevant. It was the knife with which the murder had been done. When I saw it lying on the wide flower-bed under the window, I was surprised. And yet, as it was afterwards shown to me, I ought to have been prepared for greater surprise if it had not lain there. For where else should it be? Wherever the murderer was at that moment concealed, it must have been his first care to rid himself of his weapon. And since the weapon was one which would easily be identified, he did not care how soon it was found, provided it was not found on him. He had done the obvious and the safest thing—he had dropped it out of the window as soon as he had committed his crime.

So there it lay, and my torch even revealed a wet blood-stain on it. But once again I knew better than to touch it. I left it lying there, and decided to return to the house to report my discoveries.

As I stood up I saw Strickland hurrying towards me. "Not a sign of anything," he said. His voice was a little thick, but he seemed cool enough. His nature was perhaps too bovine to be easily stirred.

I showed him the knife, and he whistled.

"Poor old Mary," he said, looking down at it.

I did not like the mixture of conventional regret and familiarity in the remark, and said sharply, "You were fond of her, weren't you?"

"Yes," said Strickland, making no attempt to move, or

to take his eyes from the knife. "Lend me that light a minute," he added.

He held the torch near to the knife, then stood up. "It's one of those blasted Chinese things from the hall," he said. Then thoughtfully, "That'll keep suspicion in the household."

I was not listening very carefully, for another thought had occurred to me.

"What about footprints," I said, "supposing that anyone *did* get down from that window by any means?"

It seemed a remote hope, but then so was everything else. Very carefully we examined the flowerbeds for several yards left and right of a line from Mary Thurston's window to the ground, and from the wall to the very edge of the bed. But the ground was quite undisturbed. Slowly Strickland and I walked along to the front door together. We met Norris coming from the opposite direction.

"Seen anything?" I asked him.

He said "No" very quickly, and led the way into the house.

CHAPTER 4

As we came in we met Dr. Thurston coming downstairs. He stopped and looked at us fixedly. Then he asked sharply—"Where have you been, you three?"

I told him we had been searching the grounds, but almost before I had finished speaking he had walked on dazedly into the lounge. He sank into a chair and seemed to take no further interest.

Williams, who was standing by the mantelpiece, called me aside, and I told him what I had found. He nodded. "It's almost a relief," he said.

"What? That the knife is found?"

"Well, in a way. I had almost begun to doubt whether there would be a knife. Whether there would be anything so . . . prosaic."

I glanced aside at his face. He seemed calm enough, but his wording was so odd that I asked him again what he meant.

"Look here, Townsend. I haven't a scrap of superstition in my nature. I believe in facts. But I'm going to admit to you that the mildest word I can use about this is uncanny. I don't mean just because we found Mary dead behind a bolted door. I've heard of that sort of thing before—with quite a normal explanation. But damn it, when you consider this . . . the door was bolted. Within two minutes of the scream I looked out of the window. Within two minutes everyone in the house was accounted for. And yet I am certain that there was no way out of that room. I examined every inch of it. What in the world can be said? Someone did it. A hand held the knife. There could be no tricks of suspension. I tell you it affects me as if I had actually seen something impossible—like a tree growing visibly or snow falling on a hot day. It . . . it really frightens me."

'Frighten' was the last word I should have expected from Sam Williams. And yet when we were discussing the whole affair on the following day he said that he distinctly remembered using it.

"In what way?" I asked, for my mind was stupefied.

"Well, how *can* the brute have escaped? This is not a matter of detection. I haven't the slightest hope of anything Scotland Yard can do. It's . . . it isn't human, Townsend."

I think those words of Williams, the level-headed, sceptical lawyer, disturbed me more deeply than anything else. And because I more than half agreed with him, I contradicted most flatly.

"Oh, rot," I said, "there'll be some perfectly simple explanation."

"My dear chap, how *can* there be? Unless the man had wings."

The vision which this aroused—a dark, murderous creature like a giant bat flapping away from the house— was too fantastic. "No, no," I said; "don't get side-tracked into nightmare. There must be a means of escape from that room."

"Shall we look again, then?"

"Oh, I don't . . ." The thought of what lay there made me sick and miserable. I must have a literal mind, for it was the actual . . . body, which was most distressing to me, while for Williams, unexpectedly, the doubts and fancies were worse.

"Come on," he said. "Better than sitting here, thinking."

We went upstairs again, and reached the broken door. But as we opened it we both paused in astonishment. The body was no longer alone. Kneeling beside the bed, his face buried in his hands, was Mr. Rider, the Vicar. When he realized our presence, he looked up. And the expression on his face was unforgettable. It was like the agony on the face of a martyr in a primitive religious painting. His cheeks were bloodless, and his lower jaw dropped as though he had lost the power to control it.

"Rider! How did you get here?" asked Sam Williams. His voice seemed to me to have a note of suspicion in it.

The Vicar slowly stood up. He moved stiffly as though he had knelt for a long time. "Get here?" he repeated, not seeming to understand the purport of the question. "I arrived a few moments ago."

"Where? How?" The sharpness of the lawyer's voice surprised me. Could he still be thinking of his winged man?

"I don't understand you," said Mr. Rider slowly, and it seemed to me that he spoke the truth. "I came to the front door," he added.

"Who showed you in?"

"Stall, the butler."

Williams hesitated. "And you came straight up here?" he asked at last.

"Yes." He looked down at the bed again. "Poor soul! Poor soul!" he said. "I hope she will be forgiven." Then he added in a lower but it seemed to me more fervent voice, "I hope we all may be forgiven."

Sam Williams looked at him closely. "Mr. Rider, do you realize that this was a most savage murder? And that the murderer has not been traced? Can you tell us anything that will help us?"

The man was in great distress. I could see that he was trembling. "She died . . . a sinner," was his reply, at which Williams made a sound of impatience. "But then . . ." said Mr. Rider, staring at us, "we are all sinners, aren't we? All of us." And he almost ran from the room.

Williams and I stood as though listening to his footsteps pattering quickly downstairs.

"What do you think?"

"What can one think?" I said; "the man's mad, of course. But whether he had anything to do with it or not, I can't even guess."

Before we could start once more that meaningless search which Williams had proposed, we heard the car draw up to the front door. Fellowes had returned, bringing the local doctor and Sergeant Beef, the village policeman.

There was little enough for the former to do. He soon joined us downstairs, but before saying anything he went over to the crumpled figure of Thurston, and said, "Look here, Doctor, I'm going to order you to bed. We're going to do everything in the world we can for you, and it won't help us for you to stay here. Now be a good chap . . ."

Thurston rose, as obedient as a small boy.

"Stall!" Doctor Tate was a friend of the household, and knew the servants' names. "Go upstairs with your master, and see he has everything he wants."

Dr. Thurston turned at the door to bid us good night, and when I remembered his loud and cheery greetings and leave-takings I was deeply moved by the wretched little smile he gave us.

"It must have been a powerful stroke," Dr. Tate said when we were alone. "About thirty minutes ago, I suppose?" It was now a quarter to twelve. "It's hard to tell precisely. Somewhere between eleven and half past, anyway. Who did it?"

It did not seem to have occurred to him that we were mystified. I suppose he thought that an act of such violence in a familiar household could scarcely have been done without instant discovery. When we explained it all to him, he was, of course, incredulous. "But . . . but . . ." he began.

Williams interrupted him. "I know," he said curtly, "it's incredible. But you see it has happened."

The police sergeant joined us. We scarcely looked up as he came in. He was a big red-faced man of forty-eight or fifty, with a straggling ginger moustache, and a look of rather beery benevolence.

"I've made my examination of the body," he announced in a heavy voice, such as he probably used for giving evidence in Court, "and I've formed my conclusions," he added.

"You've what?" snapped Williams.

"I said, I've made my examination of the body, sir, and the bloodstains, and the instrument. And I've formed my conclusions."

This was almost comic relief. "You mean to say you think you know who did it?" I gasped.

"I didn't go so far as to say that, sir," admitted Sergeant Beef, "but I've done all that's necessary for to-night."

"You had better get in touch with Scotland Yard as soon as possible," I told him, feeling somewhat irritated by the stolid self-importance of the man.

"That may not be necessary," he replied ponderously.

Dr. Tate, who knew the local reputations only too well, said sharply, "Don't be ridiculous, Beef. This is quite evidently not a case for you. And I very much doubt"—he turned to us—"whether even Scotland Yard will be able to solve it. But there must be no delay in sending for them. No delay at all. I for one could not stand by and see time wasted which might be valuable in tracing the murderer. You had better ring up from here."

The Sergeant remained unmoved. He blinked his red eyelids. "I know my duty, sir," he replied.

Dr. Tate grew angry then. "I suppose you've been in the Red Lion all the evening?" he said. "Well, I tell you now that unless this matter gets proper investigation without delay I shall go to the Chief Constable at once."

"You must do as you think proper about that," said the policeman, "but in the meantime I must ask that none of these gentlemen leave the house. I'll tell the servants the same. I'll be up in the morning to . . ."—he tapped a large note-book—"to ask some questions."

"That, I believe, is the usual thing."

"Very well, then, gentlemen, I may take it that you will all be here to-morrow? Perhaps I'd better just have your names."

And slowly, painfully, he began to write our full names and private addresses in his large book. It was an exasperating ten minutes. But at last he finished, and went out into the kitchen, apparently to collect the names of the staff.

Presently we heard the front door slam, and knew that the eye of the law was no longer on us. Yet none of us moved. Williams turned to Dr. Tate.

"What do you know of Rider?" he asked.

"Rider? He's a hard-working chap. But I sometimes wonder if he's quite sane. He has a monomania, anyway. Purity. He really does the most unbalanced things when purity's called into question."

Suddenly I remembered the curious question he had asked me before dinner, and repeated the gist of it.

"Just like him," exclaimed Tate. "He probably suspected something absurd, or something quite trivial."

"What I don't understand," said Williams, "is how he came to be beside Mary Thurston's bed, within half an hour of the murder. He left to go home long before eleven, and the Vicarage is only just across the orchard."

"Could anyone have telephoned to him?" asked Strickland.

"Impossible. The telephone's out of order. Wires cut, probably."

"Then he can never have gone home," I said.

Williams rang the bell. "We'll ask Stall," he said. "Rider old us that he let him in."

Stall came into the room. I felt at once, looking at him, that he was on his guard. He glanced from one to another of us, as though wondering whence the attack would come.

"Oh, Stall," said Williams, "did you see Mr. Rider out?"

"On which occasion, sir? When he first left the house, before Mrs. Thurston had retired, I saw him out."

"I see. When did he return?"

"It must have been ten minutes or a quarter of an hour after . . . the discovery, sir."

"For whom did he ask?"

"For Dr. Thurston, sir."

"And did you show him into the lounge?"

"No, sir. It was just then that the parlourmaid was took 'ysterical, sir. Very 'ysterical, she was. And I was 'urrying back to the kitchen. I left Mr. Rider to go into the lounge himself. I did not see him again, sir."

"He said nothing to you beyond asking for Dr. Thurston?"

"No, sir. Nothing. But he seemed agitated, sir."

"I see. You go to his church, don't you, Stall?"

"Yes, sir. I sing in the choir. Bass, sir."

"Thank you, Stall. You'd better get to bed now."

When the door was closed we exchanged glances, as though each wanted to see what the others thought of it.

"Extraordinary—about Rider." I said after a moment. But no one answered. So much was extraordinary. And so very extraordinary.

Leaning back in my chair I began considering each of the men who were in that house separately, as a possible murderer. It was not a pleasant occupation, for there was not one of them to whom I wished evil, or whom I had hitherto really disliked. But as each one presented himself to my doubt, I was faced again and again by the same blank wall. How had he got out? Those two bolts—I had pulled them back myself. Whoever had done it, if natural laws existed still, had left that room during the few moments

34

it had taken us to run upstairs and break down the door. but how? How? I felt as though the doubt would lead me to madness. There was *no* way out of that room.

At last we decided to turn in. But when we were standing, waiting for someone to lead the way out of the room, young Strickland said a rather tactless thing to Alec Norris.

"Well " he said, "it seems that already your theory about murder has been proved to be wrong."

I had forgotten all about that conversation. over the cocktails. The recollection gave me a start. But the effect of the remark on Norris was quite unexpected. He answered in a high-pitched voice, shrill with hysteria.

"Yes," he said, "I *must* have been wrong!" And he began to utter a laugh, which was low at first, grew louder and higher, until Williams, who was standing beisde him, struck him across the mouth.

Norris stopped at once. "I'm sorry," he said.

"I'm sorry, too," said Williams. "But it's the only thing to do with hysteria. Couldn't have you waking the household. It's long past midnight."

CHAPTER 5

Quite early the next morning those indefatigably brilliant private investigators who seem to be always handy when a murder has been committed, began to arrive. I had some knowledge of their habits, and guessed at once what had happened to bring them here. One had probably been staying in the district, another was a friend of Dr. Tate's, while a third, perhaps, had already been asked to stay with the Thurstons. At any rate, it was not long before the house seemed to be alive with them, crawling about on floors, applying lenses to the paint-work, and asking the servants the most unexpected questions.

The first on the scene was Lord Simon Plimsoll. He stepped out of the foremost of three Rolls-Royces, the second of which contained his man-servant, whose name I afterwards learnt was Butterfield, and the third, a quantity of photographic apparatus. I happened to be outside the front door at the time, and heard him address his man. I was at first a little startled at his idiom, for it reminded me of a dialogue I had heard in a cabaret between two entertainers whose name I believe was Western, and it took me a few moments to believe that this was his natural mode of speech.

He handed me a cigar of superlative quality, and invited me to 'spill the beans'. This I did at some length. I told him in detail of the incredible mystery which confronted us, and the insoluble problem of the murderer's way of escape. When I had finished, he sighed.

"Another of these locked-door cases," he said with palpable ennui. "I was hopin' it might. be something new, what?"

But he came into the lounge, and glanced about him.

·You say it happened in the room above this one. No footprints outside, I suppose?"

"No," I said, pleased that I had shown enough professional acumen to have looked for them last night. Then I led him to the scene of my search. He glanced cursorily at the shattered light bulb, and noted the place in which I had found the knife, stepping back to glance upward at the window. Then he stooped to examine the flower-bed, but without disarranging the crease in his beautifully cut trousers. Finally he stepped back again and remained quite motionless, staring up at the windows above him.

As he did so I examined this young man. I had heard of him first some ten years ago, and was surprised to find now that he appeared no older. But perhaps among other secrets he had discovered that of changeless youth. The length of his chin, like most other things about him, was excessive. But I liked him, because from the moment he arrived at that house the somewhat macabre atmosphere of the previous evening was dissipated. His cheerful and inquisitive nature seemed to discourage any morbid dwelling on the horror of Mary Thurston's death, and to induce everyone, whether bereaved or guilty, into a pleasant and eager state of curiosity.

I know that for my part from the time when I met Lord Simon I ceased to remember the ghastly moment when we had first looked into that locked bedroom—I even forgot more than a perfunctory duty of mourning. I became wholly absorbed in the fascinating problem which confronted us. And I have gathered that this is the experience of most people intimately connected with a murder which a first-rate private detective or criminologist is investigating.

"Now, which of those windows did you say?" asked Lord Simon when he had finished the tune he was humming.

I explained to him as fully as I could what will be obvious from the accompanying plan, for Williams and I had already ascertained the uses of the upper rooms.

"You say it was a windy night?" he asked dreamily when I had finished.

"Yes. Fairly."

"You could hear the wind when you were in the lounge?"

"Well, yes. These trees round the house . . ."

"Quite. And when you were standing at the door of the room watching Williams search it?"

"Now I come to think of it, yes."

"Good. Let's go upstairs."

We walked towards the front door, and Lord Simon paused to speak to his man. "Butterfield," he said, with apologetic hesitation.

"Yes, my lord," said Butterfield, suavely of course.

"Take some photographs. And telephone to the dowager Duchess and the Ex-Queen that I shall not be lunching with either of them."

"Very good, my lord."

"Oh, and—Butterfield?"

"Yes, my lord?"

"Have you got the Napoleon brandy in the car?"

"Yes, my lord."

"Excellent."

We re-entered the house, and started to go upstairs. I was determined to remain with Lord Simon while he was investigating. His care-free manner, which evidently concealed great astuteness, interested me enormously. I was wondering what discoveries he would make in the fatal bedroom, what he would find that we had missed. But when I reached the door of it, he stopped.

"This is the room," I said.

"What room?"

"The room where it happened."

"Indeed? Let's go a little higher up, shall we?"

I reflected that criminologists are nothing if not unex-

1. Window of Stall's room.
2.   ,,   ,, Fellowes' room.
3.   ,,   ,, Apple-room.
4.   ,,   ,, Box-room.
5.   ,,   ,, my room.
6.   ,,   ,, Strickland's room.
7. Window of Mary Thurston's room.
8. Window in Mary Thurston's room which did not open.
9. }
10. } Windows in lounge.

pected, and led the way to the floor above. The boxroom, which we entered first, filled Lord Simon with enthusiasm.

"I love old box-rooms," he said. "Don't you? Never know what you may come across when you start pokin' about in them."

His eye travelled round the room. There was little enough to see—a number of old trunks, a pair of rusty skates, an array of slightly mildewed boots, and a moth-eaten leopard-skin rug.

"Fascinatin'," he said, and crossed to the window. This, with its stone mullions, seemed to occupy his attention for longer than I could understand, and he glanced languidly from it to the beams above.

"And now we're going to do something very Scotland Yard," he drawled. "Yes. Definitely Scotland Yard. But necessary. We're going to examine the contents of these boxes."

"Really," I began. "I don't know whether Dr. Thurston . . ."

But Lord Simon smiled disarmingly, and I remembered that criminologists are exempt from such trifling considerations. "Come along," he said. "There's a good chap,"

I helped him to turn out the boxes. One contained only odd bits of material, stray scraps of lace, pieces from ancient dresses which poor Mary Thurston had probably stored "in case they might come in useful." I did not care for this, as it brought the dead woman vividly back to me with all her stupidity and good-nature.

"Like bein' a beastly Customs officer, isn't it?" said Lord Simon, disdainfully plucking out a disused petticoat.

I nodded. We had soon finished that box, and after replacing its contents, turned to the next. This smelt more strongly of camphor, and proved to be an undisturbed mausoleum of Dr. Thurston's cast-off suits—old morning coats, and a dinner-jacket of antique cut. We went through the remaining boxes with the same thoroughness, but came on nothing which appeared to interest Lord Simon.

"Disappointin'," he said. "We must try the apple-room."

When we entered it the apple-room appeared to me even more barren of possibilities than the box-room, but Lord Simon seemed to like the place.

"Rippin' smell, stored apples," he remarked, drawing it in through his chiselled nostrils.

The fruit had been laid out on the floor, each apple separated from its fellow to prevent the spread of any infection. But a clear passage, about a yard wide, had been left from door to window. Lord Simon stood looking down at the crimson and yellow rows, then stooped to pick up a Cox's Orange Pippin.

"Recently crushed," he said, and took a bite from the undamaged side of it.

Then his eyes were alight again, and he became unaffectedly active. He took off his pale grey overcoat, and hung it carefully behind the door. His handsomely tailored jacket followed it, and he stood in his shirt sleeves fumbling with a pair of Asprey cuff-links.

An unpleasant thought occurred to me. "You're *not* going to move all these apples, are you?" I asked.

"Rather not," he returned. "Just a lucky dip, that's all." And he picked his way among the fruit to the water-tank which wheezed stertorously in the corner.

Breathlessly I watched Lord Simon. Would he discover another corpse? I knew he had a penchant for that sort of thing. But surely he would not blindly plunge his arm into the water if that was what he sought. No, I could see by his face that he had found whatever he had anticipated. And presently he began to draw it out—a length of very thick rope.

He laid it on the floor between the apples, as tenderly as if it had been a child. There was a great knot at one end

41

of it and an iron ring at the other. It must have been about fifteen feet long.

"Exhibit A," he said. "Undoubtedly Exhibit A. Ever seen it before?"

"It looks as though it came from the gymnasium."

"Gymnasium? You never told me that there was a gymnasium."

"I did not see that it could have any bearing."

"No, no. Of course not. Yes, certainly this rope comes from the gymnasium. At any rate, it has been used for climbin'."

"But . . ."

"I never could climb a rope at Eton. Could you at wherever you were?"

"Yes," I said rather shortly.

"Well, let's go down. I think it's time I . . ."

"Viewed the body?" I suggested.

"Exactly," said Lord Simon. But before he left the room he examined the stone frame of the window very carefully, as he had done that of the box-room.

We came down the narrow staircase, and I tapped at the door of the room in which the tragedy had happened. It was Sergeant Beef's voice which bade us come in. My knowledge of these situations was sufficient to tell me just what sort of greetings to expect between these two, and I was not disappointed.

"Mornin', Beef," said Lord Simon gaily.

The Sergeant seemed to be suffering from the effects of his visit to the Red Lion last night.

"I shouldn't 'ardly 'ave thought you'd of bothered with a little case like this," he said slowly. "It's all plain sailing."

"You find it so?" asked Lord Simon.

"Yes. Of course I do. Why it's . . ."

"What are you doin' there, Sergeant?"

"Just 'aving another look at these bloodstains," said Beef sulkily.

Lord Simon turned to me. "The police love blood," he said. "Surprisin', isn't it?"

The Sergeant did not appreciate the joke. Very soon there was silence in the room, as Beef and I watched Lord Simon at work. He went with sure-fingered efficiency over every object in the room, tapped the walls once or twice, and examined the fireplace.

"No means of escape," he observed.

Sergeant Beef guffawed. "Surely you wasn't expecting to find one, was you?" he asked.

"No, Sergeant," said Lord Simon quietly. "Oddly enough, I wasn't."

Next he went to the wardrobe, and after poking about, rather rudely I thought, among a number of Mary Thurston's coats, he pulled out two old parasols.

"Going out in the sun, and afraid of your complexion?" asked Sergeant Beef, with heavy satire.

"No. Just interested," said Lord Simon, scrutinizing them carefully.

At last he put them down, and started a stupid game with the long curtains. He pulled one over a little way, then pulled it back carelessly, two or three times.

"Nice curtains," he said, releasing them.

Finally he returned to the dressing-table, and to my surprise stooped over it, and applied his nose to a point near the mirror. In a moment he was sneezing violently.

"Disgustin'," he said. "I'm glad you hadn't noticed it, Sergeant. It's most unpleasant. By the way, who in this household takes snuff?"

"I know that Stall does," I told him. "I saw him once on the landing when he thought no one noticed him."

"Oh," said Lord Simon dimly. "Well, I'm going to get some lunch."

It was barely twelve o'clock, so I guessed he had some other purpose in leaving us just then. But I accompanied him downstairs and towards the hall door.

Just before I opened this for him he stopped and glanced at a little window beside it, which looked out from the front of the house. "Do you happen to know whether these curtains are drawn at night?" he asked me.

I was unable to tell him, but Stall, who was passing at that moment, said, "I am afraid they are usually forgotten, my lord. It is the parlourmaid's place to draw them, but they seem to get missed."

"Drawn last night?"

"I believe not, my lord."

"Thanks," said Lord Simon to Stall, and thereupon ambled off.

CHAPTER 6

As the three Rolls-Royces were disappearing down the drive, I became aware of a very curious little man, who was on all fours beside the flower-bed in which I had discovered the knife during the previous evening. His physique was frail, and topped by a large egg-shaped head, a head so much and so often egg-shaped that I was surprised to find a nose and mouth in it at all, but half expected its white surface to break and release a chick. I recognized him at once and approached.

"M. Amer Picon, I think?"

"Yes, *mon ami*. The great Amer Picon," he amplified, glancing up for a moment from his operations.

"My name is Townsend," I told him. "Can I help you at all?"

I had had an opportunity of watching one great criminologist at work, and was pleased by the prospect of seeing another.

"But certainly you can help me," he exclaimed. "I shall be *enchanté*. I have just this minute arrived."

"Then you don't know . . ." I began, eager to tell him what we had already learned.

But he interrupted me. "I know all that you know, *mon vieux*, and per'aps a leetle more. *Oho, tiens, voilà!*" he ended not very relevantly.

"But pardon me, *m'sieur*, that is impossible if you have just arrived. I have been with Lord Simon Plimsoll this morning, and he has made some important discoveries."

"Plimsoll? That *amateur des livres?*" he scoffed, with more command of French than I had previously credited him with. "And what has he found? The rope, I suppose?"

"How did you know that?"

"How did I know? But am I not Picon? Amer Picon? *Tiens!* These are not problems. There are problems enough. But such as you mention are not problems. And where was the rope? In the water-tank, I presume?"

"Well, yes it was. Did someone tell you?"

He stood up indignantly. "Tell me?" he said. "Do I need to be told? Where else *could* the rope be, I should like to know?"

I was unable to answer that, so I remained silent. Apparently M. Picon was sorry for his brusqueness.

"*M'sieur*, you must excuse *Papa* Picon. He is troubled. Yes, even he. *Allons.* Let us go to the garage."

"To the garage?" I repeated.

"But naturally. Where else should we go?"

And he set off on his short legs at a great pace. The garage was at the end of the house opposite to that of Mary Thurston's room, and on the farther side of a yard. Across this the little man stepped resolutely, and did not hesitate till he came to the space in front of the garage door. Here we found Fellowes, his legs in rubber boots, applying a powerful hose to the Thurstons' Austin car. He turned to say good morning to us, but did not cease his work.

M. Picon watched him for some moments, then said, "*Mon ami*, why do you clean again and yet again what is already spotless?"

Fellowes seemed somewhat confused. I had never known him to show any surliness before, and was surprised to notice his attitude to my eccentric companion.

"Is it that you wish to appear busy, eh? You do not like the—what you call?—the cross-examination? Have no fear. The time for questions has not come yet. Now, I look a little, no more."

Rather unwillingly the chauffeur smiled at that. "Well, it's quite right I don't like being questioned," he said. Who does?"

But Picon took little notice of his reply. The chauffeur's sleeves were rolled almost to the shoulder, revealing a pair of very muscular arms. And on one fore-arm were tattooed several devices. These had attracted Picon's bird-like attention. Presently he walked up to Fellowes and seized his wrist with both his little hands.

"Forgive," he said, and began to examine the tattoo-marks.

Personally I could see nothing unusual in these, in fact they seemed to be the conventional markings. There were two hearts entwined and pierced by an arrow. There was a Union Jack. And there was an irregular pattern of stars.

"Anything wrong?" asked Fellowes, quite good-humouredly, as he waited patiently for Picon to finish.

"*Voyons. Voyons,*" said the little man, and we left Fellowes to continue his work.

As we were walking back to the house, a detail reoccurred to me which had hitherto escaped my memory.

"Monsieur Picon," I said, "you say that you already know everything that I could tell you. You are mistaken. I have just remembered a detail which I have mentioned to nobody."

"Indeed, *mon ami?* And what is that so important detail?"

"Well, of course it may have nothing to do with the crime. But I think it ought to be known, now. Yesterday evening, when I had dressed before dinner, someone came out of Mrs. Thurston's room. A man."

"Yes?"

"Do you think it may be important? Because unless it helps your investigation, I do not wish to mention his name."

"Anything may help."

"Very well. I'll tell you. It was David Strickland. When he saw me he tried to get back into the room, but it was too late."

"Indeed? *Voilà!* Strickland, the young man in the room next to Madame Thurston? The young man of the gambling, no?"

I nodded.

"Then we go and make a little visit to the room of Mr. Strickland. *Allons.*"

"You can, *m'sieur.* You are an investigator. But I shan't go and poke about in someone else's room."

"As you will," said M. Picon.

So I found myself once again standing where I had been in those ugly moments on the previous night, while the small detective went into Strickland's room. I wondered where the occupant was. As we had passed the lounge I had heard voices, and guessed that Williams, Norris and Strickland had gathered there. Dr. Thurston had not appeared to-day, and we understood from Stall that he intended to stay in his room unless he was urgently wanted. I was glad of that. It seemed to me that the bizarre form of treasure-hunt which was going on in the house would bring little enough comfort to a bereaved man.

Stall told us that his master had thought of everyone, and sent down instructions that we were to ask for everything we wanted, and apologies that we should be kept here against our wishes. It was typical of him that he did not forget his manners as host even in the stress of those days.

I soon grew impatient. I did not like standing where the broken panels of that door faced me. I wanted to get downstairs to the others. But it seemed a long time before the diminutive detective reappeared, and when he did so, he did not emerge wholly from the door, but holding it ajar with his foot, called me over to him.

I was startled to see that in his hand was a diamond pendant.

"*Vite!*" he whispered inevitably. "Look! You know this, is it not?"

48

"Yes," I said. "It was Mrs. Thurston's."

"*Bien*. Wait." he whispered, and again disappeared into the room.

When he came out he was calmer.

"What does this mean?" I asked.

"It means that a diamond pendant which belonged to the dead lady is in the suitcase of Mr. David Strickland."

"That proves he is the murderer, then?" I asked quickly.

"Not such hurry, *mon ami*," he returned, brushing a speck of dust from the lapel of my jacket. "It may prove just the contrary. I say it *may*. And now for the chauffeur's bedroom."

The places chosen for visits by these remarkable investigators had ceased to produce in me any emotion of surprise. So that once again—though I was tired and hungry—I climbed the upper staircase, and indicated to Picon the door of Fellowes's room.

I had always admired this little man, and it was exciting to watch his jumpy enthusiasm. But I was astonished at the interest he had already shown in Fellowes. I could not believe that the frank-looking chauffeur had anything to conceal beyond a local love-affair or two. But I respected Picon and his genius too much to put in any remarks to this effect.

He had left the door of the room open, and I could see him hopping from place to place among the simple and well-ordered furniture. Everything in the room was scrupulously tidy, and the man's clothes had been folded and put away. Picon seemed to find nothing to hold his attention for some time, until, on a small table by the bedside, he saw a copy of the *Daily Telegraph*. At first he glanced casually at this, but then something on the front page seemed to catch his eye, and he began to look through the paper very carefully.

At last, when he had reached the back pages, he began

to cry *"Tiens!"* and *"Voilà!"* and make other un-English sounds.

"What is it?" I asked.

He came across to me. "You see?" he said excitedly, and indicated some pencil markings in one of the advertisement columns.

I bent down to examine these, and found that they came under the heading of 'Licensed Premises, Hotels and Restaurants for Sale.' I knew better than to express any surprise, but I could gather nothing from this.

"There!" cried Picon, "the little link. *En avant!* Piece by piece. Oh, it is not an ordinary matter, this."

"I'm glad you think that," I said, for I had been disappointed at Lord Simon's bored description of it as 'another of these locked-room cases.'

"No, no. By no means. What is your so English expression? The plot thickens, eh? This paper is three weeks old!"

And he danced back to replace it. As we went downstairs I ventured to ask if he had a theory.

"Not as you might say a theory," he replied. "All is dark. But see, what is that? A little light! Slowly it grows stronger. And soon *Papa* Picon sees all. All!" he added, and I hoped he was right.

At last we came to Mary Thurston's bedroom, and found Sergeant Beef deep in an arm-chair by the window.

"Ah, the good Bœuf!" cried Picon, with a Gallic flippancy which I did not altogether like in the presence of the dead. "On guard, eh? Is it permitted to look about?"

"You can 'ave a look round," said the Sergeant. "But nothink's to be touched, sir."

"*Bien.* And what for do you wait so patiently, Sergeant?"

"Me? Oh, I'm just waiting for the warrant to come through. I've made my report."

Picon could not help smiling. "Waiting for the warrant,

eh? That is good. You know, then, who is guilty?"

"Course I know. It's as plain as the nose on your face."

Picon turned to me. "What is your English expression? He is out for blood, eh?"

It was the Sergeant's turn to smile. "That's just about it," he said.

Picon took some time to examine the contents of that room. And as he did so I thought that his examination was made not because he expected to find evidence there, but because the man was by nature thorough, and would not attach himself to a theory until he had made sure that there was nothing to contradict it.

"And now, Mr. Townsend, will you oblige me a moment? Will you go down to the lounge, turn on the wireless, and return here?"

I began to obey rather unwillingly, wondering what Thurston and the rest of them would think of the sound of music in this house. I made a hasty explanation to Williams, Norris and Strickland, who were in the lounge, and did as Picon had asked.

"Thank you," he said when I returned. "And now the light grows stronger."

Thinking that I understood what he meant, I said, "You need have no doubt about our hearing Mrs. Thurston's scream, Monsieur Picon."

"You heard that?" he asked slowly.

"Of course I did."

Then he said an extraordinary thing. "Do not be too sure, M'sieur. The human ear is a curious organ. Sometimes it hears what is not there to hear. And sometimes it fails to hear what is."

After that, which I interpreted as a piece of deliberate mystification, he too hurried down to the village, probably in search of lunch.

CHAPTER 7

THE gong sounded for lunch, and when I reached the dining-room I was not at all surprised to find that we had been joined by a small human pudding, who was introduced as Monsignor Smith. When he had deposited a number of parcels and hung a green parasol on the back of his chair, he beamed round on us, and refused the soup.

There seemed to be a general, and most understandable, desire to avoid the topic which occupied most of our private thoughts. But perhaps it was some subconscious reversion to his far-fetched ideas of yesterday evening which caused Sam Williams to speak of flying, and the progress of flight, gliding, and the making of midget aeroplanes.

"Why, I've actually heard that an American has risen from the ground and moved through the air with wings," he said, "and without sharing the fate of Icarus."

The little cleric was staring out of the window through the thick lenses of his spectacles. "But there are so many kinds of wings," he murmured; "there are the wings of aeroplanes and of birds. There are angels' wings, and"— his voice dropped—"there are devils' wings." Then he nibbled at a piece of bread which he had been crumbling.

We were silent at once. My acquaintance with all of this remarkable man that had been made public, led me to look for something in his words which would turn out to have some bearing on our problem.

"But there is flight without wings," he went on, "more terrible than flight with wings. The Zeppelins had no wings to lift them. A bullet has no wings. A skilfully thrown knife, flashing through the air like a drunken comet, is wingless, too."

This was too pointed for Alec Norris, who began to talk hastily of motor-cars. And because these had little place in Mgr. Smith's life, his work being done on foot and in places where motor-cars were not welcome, he became silent again.

Presently the talk was interrupted. Young Strickland made a sudden exclamation, and turned to Stall. "Look!" he said.

A spider had fallen from the ceiling, or from the flowers, and was beginning to crawl across the table. The butler stepped forward, picked it up, and bore it to the window in his fingers. The little round-faced priest beside me was watching him absently. Suddenly he jumped up.

"Oh no!" he cried. "No!" And his voice was plaintive, distressed, and at the same time startled.

He ran across to the window, threw it open, picked up the spider, and dropped it on to the flower-bed.

"Why, whatever's the matter?" asked Norris. "Didn't Stall kill it?"

Mgr. Smith paused before answering. Stall had left the room, and closed the door. "I wish he had," moaned Mgr. Smith. "I only wish he had!"

We exchanged glances. What could he mean? One would not have suspected him of a hatred for spiders, or for anything else for that matter. He was too mild and benevolent to hate. Besides, if it had been hatred for the insect which had made him run across the room, why hadn't he crushed it? Why had he released it so carefully into the garden?

"Are you a nature-lover, Monsignor Smith? Have you made a special study of the Arachnidæ?"

"If you mean spiders," he said, "I know only two things about them. And those are the things which everyone knows. They kill flies. And they hang on threads."

The rest of the meal was rather difficult, for childishly innocent as this man seemed, he had, as I already knew, a knack of saying the most disturbing things.

I began idly wondering as to what unanticipated place he would ask to be conducted when lunch was over, but even so it was a surprise when he came up to me and asked if I could show him the village church.

I expostulated, of course. "Do you think," I ventured to ask him, "that we ought to waste time examining an old building while this problem is to be solved? It still presents such difficulties . . ."

"Yet what can we do with our difficulties better than take them to the Church?" he asked blandly, and we set out.

In the churchyard we met the Vicar. He greeted me with his quick nervous smile, and I introduced Mgr. Smith. The two seemed to have much to talk about, and I agreed to wait while the Vicar showed my new acquaintance the beauties of the old building.

I must have been sitting on the low wall in the pale autumn sunshine for ten minutes, when Mgr. Smith bundled out of the building, evidently under some great stress. His clothes were slightly muddy, I noticed as he came forward, and his thick boots dodged in and out rapidly.

"He called it a wash-basin," he cried; "there is not a moment to be lost. Don't you realize he called it a wash-basin?"

I was getting so used to this sort of cryptic excitement that I expressed no wonder, but strode beside the breathless little man towards the Thurstons' house.

"A wash-basin," he murmured. "His very words."

Suddenly Mgr. Smith stopped in the centre of the path. "Why!" he said quite loudly, turning his glasses towards me, "why, of course!" After a moment he went on. "We must go to the gymnasium," he said.

"The gymnasium?"

"Yes. At once. You say one rope has been found?"

"Yes. *The* rope."

"One of the ropes," he replied absently.

"Are there two, then?" I asked, feeling as though I were Alice.

"I'm afraid so. If there was only one, it would be better. It would be much better. But I'm afraid there are two. And yet—who can say? One rope makes a noose."

The gymnasium had been built by Thurston's predecessor, an enthusiast for physical fitness. It stood beside the garage, a long white building. Since it was entirely modern in architecture, and made no attempt to ape the crusted red brick of the house, it had been discreetly set out of sight of even the bedroom windows.

It was not used, nowadays, by the Thurstons themselves, or their friends. None of us were physical culturists. But strolling that way one morning during a previous visit, I had heard some movement in the place, and had looked in to see Fellowes, the chauffeur, in a position on the parallel bars which would have been thought impossible to anyone but a contortionist. I had asked him then whether the gymnasium was used at all, and he said that Dr. Thurston allowed the local boy-scout troup to gather there once or twice a week. He, Fellowes, did not like this scheme, because the boys made so much noise, and had been known to run about the grounds afterwards.

When we entered it now it was very silent, and had that empty gloom which haunts schools and churches when no one is in them. One missed the crowd that should have been in that place.

Little Mgr. Smith was gazing up to the roof like an idle shepherd boy watching clouds. And I looked up to see what held his attention. Two hooks, of the reinforced kind used for the fixing of gymnasium apparatus, were in the crossbeam, but no rope hung from them.

"You're quite right," I said, "I remember now. There were two ropes. The man who built the place, so Fellowes told me, had them fixed so that he and his friends could have races. And they're gone."

Lying along the wall was a ladder.

"Strange place to keep a ladder," I commented. But Mgr. Smith did not wait to answer. I realized afterwards that he had gathered at a glance that the ladder had been brought in to enable the man who had removed the ropes to get them down.

It was he who led the way into the house, and up the stairs to the second floor—stairs which I was beginning to know too well. He bustled briskly into the apple-room, and scarcely troubling to pull the black cloth from his arm he plunged his hand into the water-tank. A moment later a second rope, similar in every respect to the first, lay dripping beside it on the floor.

Then Mgr. Smith sat himself plumply down on a wooden bench and said nothing for a long, long time. Dusk was already beginning to fall outside, but in the apple-room there was still light enough for me to see his round features, with a look of great and fearful wonder on them. The sun went down in crimson and yellow, like a vast battle between two armies on the hills of Spain.

And presently Mgr. Smith said: "Have you never thought what vile things men have invented for the killing one of another? And to what use they have put inventions already evil, like gunpowder and gas? But neither gunpowder nor gas, neither pistol nor poison, is as terrible as the instrument which this murderer chose."

"I should have thought it was a very ordinary instrument," I ventured. "A knife."

"You are speaking of the weapon, only. I was thinking of more than that."

"You mean, he had an accomplice?"

"I mean he had seven."

"Seven," I almost shouted, for this obscure suggestion startled me.

"Seven devils," he said, and rocked himself to and fro sadly.

"But, Monsignor Smith," I said, "what is the distinction between the weapon and the instrument? Surely you are playing with words?"

"That is too perilous a game for me to play. I would sooner amuse boys with a bomb which they think is a ball, than confuse men with a word which they believe is a warning. The instrument may yield the weapon as the guillotine dropped the blade."

"But then—if you understand it all . . ."

"But I don't!" cried Mgr. Smith. "I know the weapon, and I think I know the instrument. But I have yet to be sure of the murderer."

The apple-room was almost dark now, and I felt that it must be tea-time. I stood up to see whether it would move him. To my relief Mgr. Smith rose too.

"You are right," he said, "there is evil in this room."

He seemed to be no longer in a hurry, but thumped downstairs prosaically. As we came into the lounge to join the others I could hear him murmuring softly to himself, and half-turned to catch the words.

"King Bruce, King Bruce," he was whispering mystically.

CHAPTER 8

IN a deep arm-chair beyond the circle round the tea-table, Lord Simon Plimsoll was extended, with a cigar between his long fingers and a book in his hand.

"Nice copy, this," he commented; "it's the Aldine Plato. I've never seen the 1513 edition on vellum before. Aldus and Musurus did it together, you know, and dedicated it to Leo X. He was so tickled that he renewed the privileges granted to Aldus by Alexander VI and Julius II. Your friend must be a bit of a collector?"

"I believe he is."

"Do a bit myself," said Lord Simon.

I thought this was modest when I remembered some of the books with which his collection had been credited.

"So I have heard. In the meantime I've got some news for you."

He continued to turn over the leaves of his book while I told him of M. Picon's discovery of the tattoo marks on Fellowes's forearm.

"Interestin'," he conceded, "but not very helpful. We want to know who did the murder, not who thought of it."

Rather disappointed, I tried him with the story of the jewels in Strickland's bedroom, and the marked newspaper on Fellowes's table. But to both of these he nodded and said, "Very likely. Very likely."

It was when I came to the second rope which Mgr. Smith had found that he jumped to his feet.

"Another rope?" he said. "That's awkward. That throws everything out. Unless . . . ." He paused. "Look here, Townsend, give me a hand, will you? I want to take one of those ropes to the gymnasium."

Though it meant yet another climb to the second storey, I could not very well refuse. Soon we had dragged the thing across the garden, and Lord Simon, delicately poised on the ladder, had hung it in its original place. He descended, and standing back to the door, looked fixedly at it.

"It's all right," he said, as we left the gymnasium. "Quite all right. I might have known it would be." And he pulled gratefully at his cigar.

The muffins were cold when we got back, but I knew better than to think food was important while there was investigation to be done. Why, I have known people, after murders, to go whole days without eating.

Thurston still had not appeared, but I understood that he was to be present at the enquiry that evening. I was thankful that he had kept out of the way all day. My knowledge of these situations, gathered from some study of them, taught me that we were all behaving according to the very best precedents, but I could not help feeling that a man who had just lost his wife might not see it that way. I had learnt that after a murder it is quite proper and conventional for everyone in the house to join the investigators in this entertaining game of hide-and-seek which seemed wholly to absorb us. It was not extraordinary for there to be three total strangers questioning the servants, or for the police to be treated with smiling patronage, or for the corpse to be pulled about by anyone who was curious to know how it had become a corpse. But when I thought of the man to whom the tragedy would be something more than an entrancing problem for talented investigators, I really wondered how these queer customs had arisen.

All three of our distinguished visitors, I noticed, kept very much to himself, or at least remained at some distance from his rivals. Lord Simon, having satisfied himself that the rope was, as he put it, all right, had settled down again to his

Aldine Plato. Mgr. Smith was discussing mediæval art with Alec Norris, and M. Picon, after rearranging the cups which had been laid haphazardly on the tea-table, sat isolated near the fire.

The time had come, I thought, for stock-taking. The three great investigators, not to mention the police sergeant, had all begun to form theories, and since I had as much evidence in my hands as they had, I did not see why I should not do the same.

However they might differ in the details of their research, they had all been interested in the rope, or two ropes, which had been discovered. Yet I could not see how those ropes could have been used. What made them impossible was that we had been so prompt, so very prompt, in breaking down that door. If the murderer had escaped by climbing a rope he would have murdered Mary Thurston, crossed to the window, climbed out on to the sill, closed the window after him, climbed the rope and drawn it up after him, all during the few moments it had taken us to run upstairs and break down the door, for certainly a rope against that window would have been visible, and probably it would have swung against it noisily. But even if neither was the case I could not believe that the rope could have been drawn up before Sam Williams crossed to the window to look out for it.

And then, even suppose that it could have been, who was there in the house who could have done it? I have explained that before even we had started to break the door down, Norris was with us, and Stall, Strickland and Fellowes had all appeared within a few moments—too few moments for any of them to have climbed a rope, entered by the upper windows and come down to join us. That left only the Vicar, the cook and the parlourmaid as possible rope-climbers. It was safe to exclude the two women from suspicion of this feat. As for the Vicar, we had Stall's word that he had admitted him some time after the crime. But more final than that was the fact that if he had murdered Mary Thurston and escaped by climbing the rope, he would either have had to climb and enter the upper window as we were coming upstairs and breaking in, or have delayed his climb. In the first of these cases he would certainly have been heard or seen entering the apple-room by Stall and Fellowes, who were on that floor at the time, or his rope would still have been dangling, and he on it, outside the window when Williams had opened it.

No, on the whole, I was inclined to discount the whole of the rope theory. I will concede a great deal to human agility, but not the quickness of action that would have been necessary in this case.

There remained some of the more subtle possibilities, or half-possibilities, which I remembered had turned into successful theories in other cases of murder behind locked doors, and for these everyone was in some way suspect. In my consideration up to this point I had ignored all questions of psychology, and had not been swayed by my knowledge of the characters of people concerned. In my heart, for instance, I could not suspect Fellowes or the Vicar of murder, but I had included them as suspects so long as the facts made it possible for one of them to be guilty. And so now, as I considered the wilder enigmas of time, as opposed to those of place, I excluded no one.

I could not see, for instance, how either Williams or Thurston could be guilty, since I had been with them continuously from the time Mary Thurston had left the room, to the time of the scream, and had not lost sight of them even after that until the discovery of the corpse. And here an ingenious theory half-presented itself, to be contradicted at once by irrefutable fact. For if I had not seen that terrible figure on the bed in the moment of breaking in the panel, and if there had been no light in the room, it might have been conceivable—however far-fetched—that Thurston himself could have walked into the room in front of us and murdered her in our presence without our suspecting him. He could have arranged something in the room which would have given her a severe fright to cause those rending screams, and so have had an alibi. I was rather proud of having thought this out, and seriously considered using it as a plot for a murder story. But in this case it did not fit. The light in the room had not been strong, but it had been quite sufficient to show me the revolting sight on the bed as soon as I had broken the top panel, and quite sufficient for me and Williams to have seen every movement of Thurston's when he entered the room first. He had simply crossed to his wife, placed his hand on her heart and told us that she was dead.

Ingenious though I considered this, I was a little ashamed of dragging Thurston into my theories, until I realized that everyone must be considered suspect by the real investigator. There was Williams himself, for instance. Was there any imaginable means by which Williams could be implicated? Was there any trick of time or place such as I had learned to look for in my study of criminal investigation as it is publicly understood, which could connect Dr. Tate or even the Police Sergeant with the murder? Or the parlourmaid? Or the cook? I knew better than to dismiss any of them as quite obviously innocent. If I had learnt nothing else from my study of the methods of the three great men sitting near me, I had learnt this, that they would eventually pick out the one person I had not suspected. So I followed the simple plan of suspecting everyone. I was determined not to be surprised.

But the maddening fact remained that, suspect how I would, I could find no adequate reason for connecting anyone in that house with Mary Thurston's murder, and my suspicions were nothing in the end but the most humiliating little attempts to believe that those I disliked, such as Norris and Stall, had been responsible, and that those I liked, such as Williams and Fellowes, had not. Which, I recognized, was a method owing nothing to deduction.

And yet—well, someone had done it. It was not suicide. A woman does not scream three times and then cut her own throat with a gash which a doctor attributes to a very powerful man. And that someone would be discovered. That, too, was certain enough. I had never known a case in which any one of these three investigators was concerned end with the mystery unsolved, let alone a case in which all three of them had taken up. And if the clues discovered had taught them so much that Lord Simon Plimsoll was calmly looking at a book, and M. Picon restfully peering into the fire, and Mgr. Smith discussing mediæval art, then surely I could learn something from them?

The ropes, the tattoo marks, the marked advertisements, the snuff, the fact that the Vicar had called something a wash-basin, the jewels in Strickland's room—why, I asked myself, did these mean so much to the great brains near me, and so little to me? Because, I told myself, these men were investigators, while I was a mere observer. But I wished, how I wished, I had a theory, just as they had.

Never mind. In a few moments now the cross-examination was to begin, and no doubt that would make everything clear.

CHAPTER 9

WHEN tea was cleared away Strickland and Norris tactfully left the room, for it had been understood that only Thurston, Williams and I were to be present during the enquiry. It must have been about five o'clock when Sergeant Beef was shown in, and nodded to us, rather in the manner of a man who thinks that he must be on the defensive. Doubtless he felt somewhat out of place. With his raw red face and thirsty moustache he looked as though he would have been happier in the local public bar. However, he did not push himself forward, but taking the most upright chair he could find he drew out his enormous black note-book, and waited.

Then Thurston came in. I had not seen him since the previous evening, and looked anxiously towards him while he was being introduced by Sam Williams to each in turn of the three investigators. He looked yellow and very wretched, but he managed to force a feeble smile as he shook hands.

"I don't want to be in the room while you gentlemen enquire into this . . ." he said slowly, "so I thought I would come down first and give you all the information that I can. And if you want to see me again about anything when you have made more enquiries, I will do my best to help you. I appreciate the efforts which you are making to clear this up."

"We all sympathize very deeply," said Lord Simon, his voice becoming quite sincere. I liked him for that remark.

Thurston nodded. "I'll tell you all I can," he said, "and there is a certain amount of . . . family history which you must know. I have discussed the matter with Mr. Williams, who besides being my lawyer is an old friend, and we both agree that you should hear it."

The silence was broken by a movement from Sergeant Beef. Rather tactlessly, I thought, at this point he pulled open his note-book and made ponderous preparations to write in it.

"My wife had been married before," said Thurston, and I started. "I will tell you the story, so far as I know it. She was the only daughter of a Gloucestershire parson." His voice stumbled, but he went on. "I never knew her parents, but I gather that they were very hardworking, rather severe people, devoted to their daughter. She was brought up in a manner which even in those pre-War days would have been considered strait-laced. But she was quite happy, though that may seem strange to the present generation. She worked, as her mother did, in the parish, and learnt then, perhaps, to practise the unselfishness which was hers by nature. Indeed, who could imagine her anywhere as being anything but happy and unselfish?"

There was a tense but sympathetic silence. At last Dr. Thurston went on. "A visitor to the parsonage was a rich, local land-owner, a man very much her senior, who had made a fortune in Birmingham and had recently retired to a Gloucestershire manor. He had lost his wife some years previously, and after he had met Mary a number of times he—in the old-fashioned way—sought permission of her father to ask Mary to marry him. The parson consented, but his wife raised one objection before the matter was mentioned to Mary. For this man, in his late middle-age, seemed in every way a desirable husband, except for the fact that he had a son."

"Oh my Lord!" whispered Lord Simon Plimsoll.

"Mary had never seen this son, and to the best of my knowledge never did see him. The boy had already got a bad name for himself—or at least so her first husband said. He did not live with his father in Gloucestershire, and it was understood that he was abroad—though whether he was a mere lad sent on a training ship, or a grown man in the colonies, I do not know. Only his very existence rather perturbed Mary's parents, which is perhaps why she heard even so much of him as she did. Suppose he should return, and cause trouble between Mary and her husband? Suppose he should fall in love with Mary? You must imagine that her parents were simple people whose ideas on such matters were drawn largely from the sentimental novels of the day.

"At all events the difficulty was talked over, and dismissed. You will gather some of the selfishness and unconscious brutality of such arrangements in those days, when I tell you that, so far as I can make out, it was arranged between Mary's parents and her husband that the son should be kept out of the way. He was given an allowance, I believe, and Mary once told me that the last that was heard of him for a long time was that he was thought to be in America. But even then she wasn't sure if it was not Australia."

Thurston was speaking very slowly and thoughtfully. It seemed that he had nerved himself to this recital, and was determined to get through it. But it was easy to see that he was suffering.

"They were married for ten years," he continued, "and I think that they were fairly happy together. Mary certainly never realized the faults of her first husband. Or of her second husband either, if it comes to that. She was not a woman to find the faults in any human being.

"During the early years of their marriage, Mary lost both of her parents, and one of the few really considerate things her husband did for her was to leave the district of her first home, and move to a house about a mile from here. I first met them when I attended him for influenza, not long after they moved. Then the War came, and Mary's stepson came home to serve, and did so with some distinction. But even when he was on leave he was not asked down to his father's home. Occasionally Mary's husband went up to town to meet him, and spoke rather more kindly of him at this period. But she never met him.

"After the War, the son, like so many sons who had fought, was again a problem. A few years on a private allowance abroad, followed by three or four years of war, do not represent the ideal training for a citizen. He was not a bad boy, but he was a difficult one. He had the normal vices, slightly pronounced, and I don't think he ever cared much for his father. He was put unsuccessfully into a number of jobs, and sent to a number of places. But he had a way of turning up again in London. Not an unusual case, I suppose.

"It was after his father had sent him with some finality to Canada that the old man made his will, and in the circumstances I suppose it was fair enough, though not very generous to his son. The young man's small allowance was to be continued, the rest of the fortune was to provide an income for Mary during her lifetime, and, should she die before the son, it was to revert to him. Actually I do not believe that Mary was very much older than her stepson, but she never seemed to her husband a young woman, because in his self-centred view she was his wife, and to be regarded as about his own age. It was not therefore quite such an unfair arrangement in his mind as it may seem to you. He expressed the hope, in his will, that should his son ever inherit the money he would by then have learnt its value."

Again he paused. "You will understand that it is not very pleasant for me to go over all this. But I want to make things as easy as possible for you. And whether it has any bearing on the matter or not, you might feel you had to find it out for yourselves, and so waste time. But I have nearly finished now. I attended my wife's first husband in his last illness. She and I were thrown together a great deal at that time. And those of you who knew her will not be surprised that we were married within a year of her becoming a widow."

Williams murmured something, and Dr. Thurston shifted uncomfortably in his chair. "And now I must touch on something even more intimate," he said. "My wife had an income of nearly two thousand pounds a year. My own income, apart from the practice which I then had, was considerably, very considerably, less. I am not going into all the complications which follow when a poor man marries a rich woman. But there are points I must explain. First of all, I myself was an interested party in a will of my uncle's, by which I was then expecting shortly to inherit a sum of money rather larger than my wife's fortune. This sum actually came to me about six months ago. It was delayed by some legal difficulty. Secondly, it might be as well for you to know how our private finances were arranged. My wife retained her income absolutely in her own hands, but at her own wish she met all the expenses of this house. My own private expenses were few, and my small income amply sufficed for them. Since I have inherited the sum I have mentioned, however, I have not allowed my wife to to use her money for anything but herself. The rest of the details, such as her own will, you may learn from Mr. Williams."

The investigators were looking up now. It was M. Picon who spoke. "And the stepson?" he queried.

"Has never reappeared. My wife used at one time to worry about him a great deal. She felt that she had taken away what justly belonged to him. She even went to the extent of advertising for him, but without result. You can imagine how concerned she was over anything like that. She was a very generous woman."

Lord Simon Plimsoll spoke rather uneasily. "You won't mind, Doctor, if we ask you one or two questions?"

"By all means."

"What was the name of Mrs. Thurston's first husband?"

"Burroughs."

"And the village where she was brought up?"

"Watercombe, near Cheltenham."

"And no one has any idea what has happened to this young man?"

"I certainly have not."

M. Picon broke in. "So that, *hélas*," he said, "he might be dead?"

"It is possible," said Dr. Thurston.

"Or, on the other hand, he might be in this house," said Lord Simon.

Dr. Thurston smiled very faintly. "I don't think that is likely. You see, I know everyone here."

"Yes, Doctor. But suppose—of course it is the merest supposition—suppose that this young man had by any chance reappeared. How long, for example, have you known Townsend?" And he glanced without apology at me.

"About three years."

"And Strickland?"

"Rather longer."

"Do you happen to remember how you met Strickland?"

"My wife met him. In town, I believe. She had a good many friends. She asked him down here, and I liked him. Always have done. Irresponsible fellow, but a very good sort!"

"Then Norris, Doctor?"

"Well, he also came here through my wife. I know where she met him, though. It was at the Bagleys, about six miles from here. They make some pretensions towards being literary, I believe, and often have fellows like Norris staying there."

"Then again, the chauffeur. How did he come into your employ?"

"My wife engaged all the servants. She was far more

69

practical than I am in such things." He paused. "But really, you know, Lord Simon, if you're supposing that my wife's stepson could have been in the house, masquerading as one of our friends or employers, I must tell you that I think the idea is too far-fetched. The fellow disappeared years ago."

Lord Simon smiled. "You mustn't mind me, Doctor," he said, "I was born inquisitive."

M. Amer Picon had been moving about in his chair in a most restless way, and now spoke impatiently. "*Monsieur le docteur*," he said, "you will forgive Picon. He may seem—what you call—impertinent. But there is a little question, difficult to ask. Yet it is necessary. You permit? A thousand thanks. It is this. Do you remember if ever your so unfortunate *Madame* seemed to have something concealed from you? Oh, I mean nothing of—what you say?—a guilty secret. Some little thing, which she might have concealed as one hides a Christmas present before Christmas, perhaps?"

Dr. Thurston took this quietly. He seemed to appreciate the dainty way in which Picon had put it to him. He was silent for nearly a minute, then he said, "Only once. I *do* remember such an incident—but it is a long time ago; soon after we were married. Your speaking of Christmas presents reminds me, because it was just before Christmas, and I accounted for it at the time in that way. I thought it was a little ingenuous secret such as she loved, connected with a gift for me. But when Christmas came I could not see that it had anything to do with her gift. But I never attached any real importance to it."

Picon could scarcely wait. "Yes, yes, *Monsieur le docteur?*" he said.

"One afternoon I came into her room and found her sitting at the little bureau she always used when she had any letters to write. She had not heard me come in, but when she saw me she looked very startled, and quickly tore up the envelope she was writing. I can give you no idea how innocent such behaviour made her seem. No really deceitful person could have blushed and been so confused as she was."

"But is that all?" queried M. Picon anxiously, "you read nothing that was written?"

Dr. Thurston looked wistfully towards him. "If I tell you I read a man's name," he said, "you must not let your imagination start working. You must believe me when I tell you that my wife was incapable of carrying on anything like an intrigue. The mere thought of it, to anyone who knew her, is absurd. But it was a man's name that I read on that piece of paper, and I can tell it you. It was Sidney Sewell."

"Just the name? You saw no more?"

"That was all. But really, you should attach no importance to it. Ask Williams here. He knew my wife. Whatever significance the matter had·it did not mean that there was some clandestine love-affair in her life."

There was a sympathetic murmur of assent, and Williams said something to the effect that it had never been doubted.

Thurston rose painfully from his chair. "And now, gentlemen, is there anything else you wish to ask me?" He looked so exhausted and wretched that even had there been any further questions to put to him after his very lucid narrative, I doubt if they would have been broached just then.

"Very well, then," he said, "I'll say good night. I have told Stall to give you anything you may want." With evident relief he left the room.

Lord Simon turned to Williams. "There can be no doubt about that will?" he asked, "the stepson will inherit?"

Williams nodded. "Yes," he said, "I have always understood that it was like that. I was not the old man's lawyer. But that was his will."

"Looks pretty bad for the stepson, whoever he is," I observed.

But Mgr. Smith blinked at me gently. "You mustn't

71

say that," he observed. "The fact that it is a piece of parchment does not mean that it is a piece of prophecy. You are like so many of these modern thinkers. Because it was a new Will you want to turn it into an Old Testament."

"What is more of moment," said M. Picon, turning to Williams, "is the will of the lady herself. What can be said of that?"

Rather unexpectedly Williams smiled. "Mrs. Thurston," he said, "was in some ways a very ingenuous person. As Mr. Townsend here will tell you, her great pride was her house. She devoted her life to making it comfortable. And she had an idea by which she hoped to get very good service. She got me to draw up a will leaving her personal belongings to her husband, but all the money of which she might die possessed was to be divided equally among such employees as were with her at the time of her death. This was, of course, after her husband had come into his own fortune."

"But," I said, "since she had only a life interest . . ."

"Exactly. That was the idea. She never had very much money in her possession at any time. She received her income quarterly, and spent it, or gave it away. So that what the servants would receive was the sum actually to her credit in the bank at the time of her death. That would be about the amount normally left to servants. But of course they were not to know that. It was common knowledge among them that Mrs. Thurston was rich. And certainly the plan seemed to work, for she has not changed the staff since then."

"In other words it was a trick," said Mgr. Smith.

"I should hardly call it that," snapped Williams.

"And tricks can work both ways," reflected the little cleric. "If you try to make anyone an April Fool after midday on the First of April, the joke rebounds on to you."

"I can see no joke," said Williams.

"Nor I," said Mgr. Smith, "I see no joke here at all."

CHAPTER 10

WHEN Dr. Thurston had left us the atmosphere of constraint which had been noticeable in his presence was at once dissipated, and everyone seemed to return with some relief to the excitement of the chase. Bereavement, on these occasions, as I have often noticed, is a bore; detection is what matters. So that the enquiry was taken up with gusto.

The first person to be questioned was the mechanic sent by the telephone service to repair the wire. He had found it cut clean through where it passed outside the window of the little cloakroom on the ground floor. He seemed an intelligent young man, eager to add his quota of suggestions.

"There was a pair of little clippers, like you use for pruning rose-trees, lying on the window-sill," he said. "I should think more than likely it 'ud been done with them. All anyone had to do," he explained enthusiastically, "was to shove open the window, lean out, and snip! the telephone was out of order."

"Have these so important clippers been examined?" asked M. Picon. "Perhaps the good Bœuf has seen whether there are finger-prints on them?"

The Sergeant cleared his throat, and looked a trifle uncomfortable. "I didn't 'ardly think it worth while," he admitted, "seeing as I know oo'd done it."

M. Picon gave vent to a guttural gallicism, but Lord Simon drawled, "My man Butterfield has looked at the beastly things. No finger-prints."

The mechanic was not to be excluded. "Ah, but I tell you what," he said, leaning forward knowingly, "there was a pair of old gardening gloves there beside them. Whoever cut that wire could have pulled 'em on"—he gave an appropriate gesture—"cut it, and taken 'em off again."

"*Voilà!*" said M. Picon ironically.

"It would be more to the point if you could tell us when the Exchange discovered that the line was out of order."

"I can tell you that. It wasn't till this morning. There was no call for this house last night, and no one came down to report it till ten o'clock to-day."

"Do you know who came then?"

"Yes. The chauffeur."

M. Picon glanced up again. "And the last time the telephone was known to be in order, what was that?"

"I understand that there was a call at about six o'clock yesterday evening. That was the last."

"Thank you very much." Sam Williams dismissed the young man with a friendly nod.

"Puzzlin'," commented Lord Simon. "Very puzzlin'."

"I don't see why," I could not help replying. "The mechanic sounded to me as though he was right. Clippers, gloves . . . all handy."

"I didn't mean that," returned Lord Simon. "But why did he bother to do it? What was the point of delayin' communication with people outside? There were plenty of people in the house . . ."

Sergeant Beef cleared his throat again, and prepared a volley of his heaviest sarcasm. "P'raps it doesn't occur to your Lordship, that being a murderer 'e might 'ave been afraid of the police?"

Lord Simon smiled coldly. "I am bound to say that didn't occur to me," he retorted, lighting a new cigar.

Sergeant Beef grunted. "Such things *'ave* been known," was all he said.

"What you forget," murmured Mgr. Smith, "is that there is one thing at least in common between the man who decides to be a murderer and the man who decides to be a monk. It is that each leaves his fellows, and for ever.

And nothing that either does to effect that isolation is to be marvelled at. This, too, they have in common—each finds at last a cell. So that while one man cuts an acquaintance, this other cut a telephone wire. And that is all there is to it."

There was silence for a moment, and I glanced about me. The lounge itself was as cheerful and normal as it had been at this time yesterday, when we had sat about, airily discussing the literature of crime, instead of the actuality. But the vividly miscellaneous people now gathered here gave it an atmosphere of unreality, almost of the macabre. Lord Simon, showing an inch of delicate silk sock on his outstretched ankles, certainly might have been one of the Thurstons' guests, but the little cleric, bundled untidily into a small, wooden-framed arm-chair, belonged not at all to this conventionally luxurious background, and Sergeant Beef, scribbling industriously in his note-book, added an almost sordid touch. Little M. Picon, upright near the fire, and stooping forward to brush the ash from the grate each time it fell there, was birdlike enough to have perched for a moment here before fluttering to some other gathering, though his excessive foreignness made him exotic in our very English surroundings.

There was an intentness about us all which certainly had not existed yesterday, and every question that was asked now seemed to hang in the air like a rocket waiting to burst. It made the cross-examination of the people who followed almost unbearably tense. In fact as time went on I began to feel that each question was not the mere flash of a rocket, but was a shaft of savage lightning which one of the investigators released. Then the insufferable pause. Then the rumbling thunder of a reply.

They looked harmless enough, these three, the languid young man, the benevolent priest, the chirpy foreigner. But they were aware of things at which we could not guess, they asked questions that we did not understand, they carried the fear of the unknown in their faces and in their words.

So you must picture us, sitting about that room. Williams and I genuinely on tenterhooks, Sergeant Beef stolid and a little sulky over his note-book, and the three investigators, who were accustomed to this sort of thing, calm, but deeply interested.

A chair had been set near the middle of the room, and each of those whom we were to question took it while he was with us. It had been set in a position that allowed the light to fall fully but not conspicuously on its occupant.

After the telephone mechanic had left us, the next to enter was a cashier from the neighbouring bank at which Mary Thurston had kept her account. It was Sam Williams who had arranged for his presence, for he, with his logical and legal mind, having perceived that he himself could not give the investigators much information, had spent the day in doing all he could to help. He had summoned everyone whose evidence might be in the least bit interesting and arranged for their introduction to the conclave. I could not help feeling how much more practical this had been than my own efforts to discover the murderer.

Before anyone could speak to Mr. Kingsly, the cashier, he himself addressed us. He was a colourless man in his forties, dapperly but inexpensively dressed in grey. I saw Lord Simon suppress a shudder when he noticed a large garnet in his necktie.

"Well, gentlemen," Mr. Kingsly said in a prim but determined voice, "I have both the Manager's and Dr. Thurston's permission to give you what information I can. What do you wish to know?"

"'Ow much 'ad Mrs. Thurston got in the bank?" asked Sergeant Beef rather coarsely. It seemed as though he felt it incumbent upon him to ask some sort of question.

Mr. Kingsly coughed. "Her account was very considerably overdrawn."

This produced an astounded silence, until Lord Simon said, "Well, well. Much drawn out lately?"

"The day before yesterday, that would be Thursday, Mrs. Thurston arranged to overdraw to the limit that we could allow. She drew in cash the sum of two hundred pounds."

"In little small notes?" queried M. Picon excitedly.

"In one-pound notes," said Mr. Kingsly.

"Two hundred one-pound notes. What you call peculiar, is it not?" went on Picon.

"It might be for many of our clients. Mrs. Thurston had been in the habit lately of drawing out quite large sums in just such denominations."

"I thought so," said Beef. "Blackmail, I'll bet."

M. Picon looked pained. "The good Bœuf is a little direct," he explained to Mr. Kingsly. "But is it not possible?"

"It was not for me to question the uses to which our clients put their money," replied the cashier priggishly.

"You say she had been doing this pretty regularly?" asked Lord Simon.

"On five occasions. The sums varied from fifty to two hundred pounds."

"When was the first occasion?"

"About three months ago."

"And did she always come in person to draw these sums?"

"Always."

"Otherwise there was nothing remarkable about her account? Nothing worth mentionin'?"

"Nothing at all. It was quite regularly conducted."

"Were you actually at the bank when Mrs. Thurston came down to draw that two hundred pounds?"

"I was."

"You actually handed it to her, perhaps?"

"I did. That is, after she had been in to see the Manager. He instructed me to cash her cheque for that amount. I have since learnt that she wanted a rather larger sum, but that we were unable to arrange it."

"And now—this is really important. At what time did Mrs. Thurston leave the bank?"

"It cannot have been many minutes before three o'clock."

"Certain?"

"Absolutely."

"One other little point, Mr. Kingsly," said Lord Simon. "Do you happen to remember whether at any time the name Sidney Sewell appeared on your books? I know, of course, that it would be the merest chance if you remembered it, but I should like to know whether Mrs. Thurston was in the habit of making cheques payable to a Mr. Sidney Sewell."

The cashier sniffed almost imperceptibly. "That, of course, I cannot say. But if the matter is of importance to your . . . researches, I will find out to-morrow whether that name appears."

"Thank you. I should be most grateful."

"There is no other point on which I can enlighten you?" His use of the word 'enlighten' struck me as characteristic. It carried in it a suggestion of all the self-importance of men whose life is spent with matters of money. He was probably convinced that the answer to our problem was to be found in the books of his bank.

Lord Simon glanced round enquiringly, "No. I think that is all, thanks," he said, and Mr. Kingsly left us.

Sergeant Beef sucked his moustache. "So she was being blackmailed, was she?"

Williams turned on him. "That is a wild assumption,"

he snapped. "She might have had other reasons for drawing money in that way."

"What other reasons?" asked Beef truculently. "Only bookmakers and people as are being blackmailed want it like that."

"I knew Mary Thurston well," said Williams, "and I am certain that there was nothing in her life for which she could be blackmailed. She was a good woman, essentially."

"If she was being blackmailed," I said, "why did she show no sign of it? She was always quite cheerful—one might say care-free."

"A very brave prince also bore blackmail," (it was, of course, Mgr. Smith who was speaking), "and bore it lightly."

Lord Simon answered this somewhat impatiently. I already knew that in his methods he was nothing if not practical, and had little sympathy with such utterances. At any rate," he said, "we shall probably know before the end of the evening whether or not Mrs. Thurston was being blackmailed, and if she was, why, and by whom. So surely we might leave the point. I am far more anxious to know something of her stepson, and the identity of Mr. Sidney Sewell."

Sergeant Beef sighed. "Can't see no reason for you to get on to that," he said. "'E 'ad nothink to do with the murder, 'ooever 'e was."

Lord Simon ignored this and said—"By the way, Beef, have you had any new-comers to the district lately? Anyone you've thought worth watching?"

Sergeant Beef hesitated. "I don't know as I ought to say anythink about that. But I suppose you gentlemen's to be trusted. Well, there is a certain individual as I've been told to watch. Mills, 'is name is. Working at the local 'otel. I understand it was Mrs. Thurston got 'im the job."

Lord Simon sat up. "Really, you might have mentioned this before, Beef. What age? "

"Round about thirty."

"What does he do at the hotel?"

"Porter 'n' boots."

"And why have you been instructed to watch him?"

"Oh, 'e'd got a bit of a record. Couple of stretches, I understood. Cat burglary. But nothink against him for over a year." He looked defiantly at Lord Simon. "Now make a murderer out of 'im," he challenged.

"It's certainly illuminatin'," he said. "Most illuminatin'."

Mgr. Smith's spectacles flashed vacantly. "Red lights are illuminating too," he sighed to the ceiling.

CHAPTER 11

So here we were with a new suspect, but his introduction did not seem to have produced much effect on the three investigators. This, I reflected, accorded with precedent, for investigators in these cases are never, by any chance, to be taken by surprise. Mgr. Smith had smiled blandly as he had answered Lord Simon, while M. Picon, who had remained silent for some time, now started assiduously to rearrange the fire-irons. Only Lord Simon himself, who was always painstaking and thorough, seemed to have taken much notice of the fact that a Mr. Miles, a competent cat-burglar, was working in the district.

Before anyone else came into the room, he lifted the telephone receiver and asked the manager of the local hotel which was his porter's night off. The manager appeared to feel no astonishment at this sudden query from a stranger, for we heard Lord Simon thank him with drawling civility, and watched him replace the receiver. He turned calmly to us. "Last night, Friday, of course," he said.

"But naturally," pouted M. Picon, while Mgr. Smith nodded absently.

"He was back at ten-thirty, though," said Lord Simon.

"Are you ready for the next person to be questioned?" asked Sam Williams.

There was no dissent, so that the lawyer rang the bell, and the cook came into the room. I had never seen her, though I had often felt kindly towards her, and was not a little disappointed to find that she was not the ample, beaming woman whom one expects to find happily tasting sauces in a cheerful kitchen, but a spare, grey-haired person with glasses, in appearance not unlike her predecessor, Mr.

Kingsly. Her face, however, seemed to me to be not so much uncharitable, as I had at first supposed, as competent. I should have said, after scrutinizing her, that she was extremely good at her job, but like most artists, somewhat at sea in alien surroundings.

Lord Simon seemed to feel this, for he smiled reassuringly. "Oh, Miss Storey," he said, and it was typical of him that he had troubled to find out her name, "sorry to drag you up here, an' all that. And I'm sure everyone staying in the house will be the loser by your leavin' the kitchen just now. Your fame has reached us."

"There's no dinner this evening," said Miss Storey, glad to remain among familiar topics as long as possible; "the Doctor said you wouldn't be done in time. Cold buffet when you want it."

"I see. Well, you won't mind if I ask you some of my dam' silly questions, will you? I'm famous for 'em."

"Well, I don't see what *I* can tell you, I'm sure."

"Funny thing. People never do. But you can tell me for one thing how long you've been with the family."

"Longer than anyone else on the staff. Over four years now."

"You like being here?"

"If I hadn't I wouldn't have stayed. I never took any notice of that silly idea about the will. I used to tell them all they was fools to listen to it. It was just a bit of stupidness of the missus's. Poor thing—she used to think she was so clever with anything like that. And now look what it's done for her!"

"You think her death had something to do with that will, then?"

"I'm not saying it did, am I? I know nothing about it. I was downstairs at the time, and only heard the screaming."

"Did the other servants take the will serious y?"

"Well, they did and they didn't. We all used to talk

about it, of course. It was a funny thing, when you come to think of it—us knowing all that money might come our way if anything was to 'appen to her. But none of us wished her any harm if that's what you mean. None of us didn't."

"You speak for the others, too, then?"

"No one can live morning, noon and night with people and not know something of what's going on in their heads, replied Miss Storey. "I wasn't overkeen on any of them, and I'm not going to say I was, and there was things I didn't approve of. But I know very well it wasn't none of them as did it. So if you're trying to put it on to them you're mistaken, that's all."

"We're trying to come by a spot of truth," said Lord Simon.

"I'm glad to hear it," snapped Miss Storey, almost before his sentence was finished.

"Did you approve of Stall?"

"I'm not going to discuss the other servants, sir. I've made up my mind to that. I'll give you what information I can, but beyond that my opinion's my affair."

"Quite right. Will you tell us, then, at what time Stall went up to bed yesterday evening?"

"As soon as ever he'd taken the whisky into the lounge. Couldn't have been later than half-past ten. He complained of a headache, and Enid, the parlourmaid, said she'd be up if anything was wanted, and he popped off to bed."

"You're sure he went to bed?"

"How can I be? He took his alarm-clock, as he always does, and left the kitchen."

"Saying good night?"

"He did to Enid. Him and me wasn't on speaking terms."

"How was that?"

"Oh, nothing to mention. Something to do with the soufflé."

"Just so. Then you and Enid remained together in the kitchen. What about the chauffeur, Fellowes?"

"He was there, too. I never approved of the arrangement, and I told Mrs. Thurston a dozen times, but there it was. Fellowes comes in for his supper every night about nine, and stays in my kitchen smoking cigarettes till all hours."

"But hang it all, where else was he to go, Miss Storey?"

"That's not my look-out. There's the village down the road. But I didn't like it."

"Well, there you were, the three of you. Who left the room first?"

"Enid did, when she heard Mrs. Thurston go up to bed."

"Oh, you could hear that from the kitchen, could you?"

"Not if the door had been shut you couldn't. But Enid would keep it ajar last night."

"Did she appear to be listening for something?"

"She and the chauffeur, yes. Once I got up and put the door to, because of the draught. But she soon had it open again."

"How did you account for that?"

"Oh, it was nothing very unusual. She always used to go up when Mrs. Thurston did. She was fond of her mistress, I will say that for her, and used to follow her up to see if she wanted anything."

"We know that that was at eleven o'clock. How long did Fellowes stay with you?"

"Not more than a minute or so, because I remember him looking up at the clock and remarking on it."

"On the clock?"

"No. On the time. 'Hullo,' he said, 'it's past eleven.' And he got up and went upstairs."

"Did you look up at the clock?"

"I can't say I did. But I know it wasn't many seconds after Enid had gone."

"At any rate, you saw neither of them again until after the screams?"

"No."

"Which did you see first?"

"Enid. She came rushing in to say they were breaking down the missus's door."

"That would be within two minutes of the scream?"

"Yes."

"What had you done in the meantime?"

"Me? I was froze to the spot for a minute. Well, all alone in this old kitchen, which is creepy enough at the best of times, and then to hear someone hollering out like that. I'm not one to be frightened, but I ask you. When I'd pulled myself together, I heard the gentlemen running upstairs, and as soon as I'd got the door open I saw Enid come tearing down with her eyes popping out of her head."

"Then?"

"Well, then, some time later, down comes Mr. Stall, looking like a ghost in his dressing-gown. And then Fellowes comes running down and says he's sent for the doctor and the police. I heard him start the car and drive off. For about ten minutes, I should say, Enid sits there silent. Then all of a sudden she goes into hysterics, and Mr. Stall runs out of the room saying 'e was after brandy. He comes back for a minute, we gets Enid a bit calm, then he goes away again, to see to things as he called it."

"Good. You've got it all admirably clear. You saw no one else that evening? None of the guests?"

"No."

"I'm afraid I've been very inquisitive. But I can't think of any more questions to ask you."

Suddenly M. Picon turned round from the fireplace. "A little moment if you please, mam'selle," he said. "You will tell Papa Picon what you call 'a thing or two', no?"

Miss Storey seemed to wonder for a moment whether

this was the sort of opening favoured by old gentlemen in railway-carriages, or a genuine request for information, so she remained non-committally silent.

"The young man, the chauffeur. He called your attention to the clock perhaps?"

"Not exactly that. He just said it was past eleven, and that he must go."

"He did not say why or where?"

"No. But he had a rat-trap with him."

"Ah yes. The trap for the little rat, *n'est-ce pas?* And where would he be taking that?"

"The apple-room, I suppose. Mrs. Thurston was always complaining she could hear them over her head."

"Always complaining, is it not, to Fellowes?"

"Yes."

"And tell 'im to place the trap, no?"

"I suppose so."

"And now the girl. Did she tell you perhaps where she was when the screams were heard?"

"Oh yes. She was in Dr. Thurston's room, turning back the bed."

"And the chauffeur, you saw him no more that night?"

"Not to speak to."

"I thank you. I thank you also, mam'selle, in anticipation, for the cold buffet," he added with characteristic courtesy.

"That's all, then?" asked Miss Storey.

Instinctively we turned to Mgr. Smith, but he was apparently asleep.

"Monsignor Smith . . ." Sam Williams called him.

"Oh yes. Dear me. I'm afraid I was dozing. I was going to ask you about a bell. The front-door bell. Did you hear it last night, Miss Storey?"

"When?"

"When the girl had hysterics?"

"Can't say I did. But then—I might easily not have, even if it had rung a dozen times. She was in convulsions, as you might say. I had no time for listening to bells."

Mgr. Smith resumed his sleepy posture, and Miss Storey left us.

"I can certainly believe in that lady's cookin'," commented Lord Simon; "accuracy and discretion seem to be her strong suits."

"She is no lover of romance, your Mademoiselle Storey," admitted M. Picon. "I wonder whether perhaps she had cause to dislike romance—a certain special romance. *Voyons*. We shall see as the time continues."

I could not resist a query to Mgr. Smith. "You were thinking . . .?" I said.

"I was thinking about bells."

"Campanology, perhaps?"

"No, electric bells. Marriage bells, maybe. Or even . . ." his voice sank, "even muffled bells."

Whereas I, just then, was troubled with many new doubts. Why did Miss Storey dislike the rest of the staff? Of what did she disapprove? Why had Fellowes called her attention to the time when he left her? And was it a coincidence that at the moment of the screams Enid, Fellowes, Stall, Strickland and Norris had all been, presumably, upstairs, while Miss Storey herself had been alone in the kitchen with no one to establish her alibi, and Mr. Miles, that new and rather sinister person, had been enjoying, somewhere in the district, his 'evening off'?

CHAPTER 12

STALL came in deferentially and seemed embarrassed when he was told that he might sit down. He had no sooner done so than Sergeant Beef rounded on him with deplorable crudeness.

"'Ere," he almost shouted, "'ave you been blackmailing Mrs. Thurston?"

Stall stirred uneasily. Surely even Beef could have expected only one answer to the question. "Certainly not," was all that the man wisely said.

"Well, it looks very much like it," went on the insuppressible Beef. "Very much like it. She's been drawing out big sums in small notes, and I don't know who else could 'ave been on to 'er if it wasn't you. Why don't you own up, now?"

Such crass methods evidently helped Stall to reassure himself. His composure returned and he faced the Sergeant. "I don't think I need answer such a question," he said. "It's ridiculous."

"Oh no, it's not," Beef went on, while I could see that the three investigators, whose delicate wits were outraged by all this, had become impatient. "Oh no, it's not. You're one of the 'ypocritical sort, Mr. Stall. Sing in the choir, you do, instead of coming down to the local. I'm more than 'arf convinced that you've been up to something in the blackmailing line. Out with it now, what 'ave you done with that two 'undred quid you 'ad off of Mrs. Thurston?"

"If you've quite finished, Beef," sighed Lord Simon.

"Oright, you 'ave a go at 'im. You'll see if I wasn't right."

There was evident relief when the Sergeant returned to

his note-book, and Lord Simon, leaning back in his chair, began a more tactful sort of cross-examination.

"Of course you knew of Mrs. Thurston's will, Stall?"

"Oh yes, my lord."

"And what did you think about it?"

"Very gratifying, my lord, that Mrs. Thurston should have considered us in that way. But not a matter to be taken very seriously."

"And the other servants?"

"Very similar ideas, my lord. If I may say so, domestic servants to-day are more highly educated than in former times, and not likely to be deceived by anything quite so ingenuous."

"Really. Yet ingenuous or not, the bally thing was there, wasn't it?"

Stall shrugged. "I had scarcely troubled to consider it," he said.

"I see. Were you and Fellowes friendly? You know, pals, pals, jolly old pals, if you'll excuse my low-brow idiom?"

"Your lordship can afford to use slang. No, we were in no sense friends. It could hardly be expected that in my position I should fraternize with a young fellow of that type."

"What type?"

"The chauffeur has been to sea, my lord, if not worse. He is a very blunt-spoken young man, whose history has not been altogether reputable, I believe."

"Whereas your own?"

"My references go back over many years, my lord, and I believe are unimpeachable."

"It must have taken you those many years to cultivate your manner, Stall. It is the most perfect thing of its kind I've ever come upon."

"Thank you, my lord."

"Was there anything else you didn't like about Fellowes?"

"I disapproved of his familiarity with the parlourmaid."

I noticed M. Picon at this point making patterns furiously with match-sticks. He was evidently much excited by the turn the examination had taken.

"Was it very noticeable?"

"I believe they went to the length of considering themselves engaged to be married."

"Was that so very wrong? After all, Stall, we're all young once. Spring in the air, and what not."

"Unsuitable, however, in members of the same staff, my lord."

"Did Mrs. Thurston know of it?"

"Certainly not."

"Would she have minded, do you think, if she had done so?"

At this point there was a noticeable pause, and watching Stall I could see him glance with real hostility towards his questioner. The last question had sounded so commonplace that I could not understand this.

"I am not in a position to say, my lord," he returned at last.

"There is nothing else, in fact, that you can tell us about the household, which might help us?"

Stall paused again. "I think not, my lord."

"There was nothing you had noticed which, for instance, would have displeased Dr. Thurston?"

Again that uncomfortable pause, and a shifty side-glance at Lord Simon. "No, my lord."

"It's a very great pity, Stall, that when you learnt that charmin' way of talkin', you did not at the same time get in the habit of speakin' the truth."

"My lord . . ."

"You know to what I'm referrin', don't you?"

I respected Lord Simon at that moment. He was so mercilessly, so icily, calm. One felt all the reserve of experience and introspection that lay behind his foppish manner. He was watching the wretched butler with a cold and detached stare, and I could see perspiration on Stall's narrow forehead. Several times the butler tried to avoid his eyes, and to speak, but it seemed that the young man was too strong for the older one.

"I have an idea," he admitted in a low voice.

"You know that between Mrs. Thurston and the chauffeur was something which . . . shall we say, ought not to have existed?"

Williams broke in, "Really, Plimsoll . . ."

"Forgive me. Jolly old murder will out," Lord Simon reassured him. "Never mind what it was, Stall, you know there was something?"

"I had my suspicions."

"And you were paid for keepin' them to yourself?"

At last the man pulled himself together. His stage butler's manner seemed to leave him and he turned angrily to Lord Simon. "That's not true!" he said. "It wasn't that!"

"Suppose you treat us to an inklin' of the truth, then?"

"I had given Mrs. Thurston my notice," he said slowly. "I was to leave at the end of a fortnight."

"Why?"

"Because . . . because of what you've just said. She, and the chauffeur. I wouldn't stay in a place where that was going on. I'm a respectable man."

"Well?"

"Leaving meant losing my share of the will. Or what I would have got if she'd gone first. So Mrs. Thurston, of her own free will, decided to compensate me."

"For your share of the will which you didn't take seriously?"

"Well, since I had to leave through no fault of mine, Mrs. Thurston did not wish me to lose."

"So she paid you several sums in single pound notes?"

"She gave me what compensation she saw fit."

"I think you'll be bally lucky if you get less than five years' incomparably hard labour, Stall. Even if that's where your troubles end, my lad."

Oddly enough it was at this point that Stall's self-confidence seemed once more to return. "For accepting a present from a lady on leaving her service, my lord? I hardly think so."

"For blackmail," said Lord Simon briefly. "Your witness, Picon."

The little man sprang nimbly to his feet, scarcely able to contain himself. "You have said that between the chauffeur and the parlourmaid there was what you call a romance, is it not?"

Stall looked contemptuous. "If you like to put it that way."

"They were attached to each other, these two?"

"Oh yes."

"And between the chauffeur and madame, also a little *rapport, n'est-ce pas?*"

"I don't know what there was. There was something."

"Then the parlourmaid, seeing her lover has some understanding with her mistress, is she not jealous?"

"Oh, she knew which side her bread was buttered." It was strange how Stall's grand manner had gone since he had been exposed. He was defiant now, natural, and a little crude.

"Her bread? Pardon me, but what has to do with it the bread and the butter?"

"I mean she knew what suited her own convenience. She didn't want him losing his job just then."

"*Bien.* So she allowed him to flirt, as you say, with madame?"

"I'm not saying she liked it. But she had to put up with it."

"You take a cynical view, Monsieur Stall."

"I've seen enough to. She with her rats! What else did she want but to talk to him?"

"Ah. That is *interessant*. So the trap for the little rat, it was a bluff, then? An arrangement? A *rendez-vous?*"

"That's what it comes to."

"*Voilà!* Now we are marching. So that last night when madame told the chauffeur to set the trap, she meant for him to come and speak with her?"

"Shouldn't be surprised."

"And the girl, she would know that, too?"

"I don't know about that."

"Then—as to this little gift, which madame so kindly and so of her free will made you. When did you receive that?"

Once again it seemed that Stall had been touched on a painful spot. He did not answer.

"Yes?" encouraged M. Picon gently.

"I'm trying to remember."

"But surely, *mon ami*, one does not receive two hundred pounds every day. Is it so ordinary that you have already forgotten?"

"Who said anything about two hundred pounds?"

"Was that not then the sum?"

Stall looked sulky. "I don't know. It was a bundle of notes. I haven't counted it yet."

"*Voilà!* A truly disinterested man! But come, my friend, when did you receive this?"

This time his answer came pat. "On Thursday afternoon."

"At what time?"

"Just after lunch."

"On Thursday? The day before yesterday?"

"That's right."

Lord Simon heaved a despairing sigh, but M. Picon left the point.

"What then did you do after leaving Miss Storey so abruptly last night?"

"Went to bed."

"Direct to bed?"

"Yes."

"You were in bed when you heard the screams?"

"Yes."

"And you came straight down to the floor below?"

"Yes."

"In the meanwhile, you heard nothing?"

"No."

"Your room is next door to that of the chauffeur, I think?"

"That's right."

"Did you hear him come to bed?"

"No. I had a headache and wanted to sleep."

"Do you sleep with the window open?"

"No. Closed."

Lord Simon groaned. "So unhealthy," he murmured.

But just then I received a shock of surprise. So, from all appearances, did Stall. For M. Picon snapped an extraordinary question at him. "*Where did the screams come from?*" he said, looking straight at the butler.

"Come from? What do you mean?"

"Just *précisement* what I say. You heard the screams from your room. Where did it seem to you that the scream was made?"

"I . . . I hadn't thought of it. I was half-asleep. I just heard three screams."

"But where? Where?"

"Why, from Mrs. Thurston's room, I suppose."

"You suppose! But of what value to me, Amer Picon, is what you suppose? You are sure that they came from Mrs. Thurston's room?"

Stall seemed bewildered. "Well . . . I hadn't thought of it."

With an impatient foreign sound, M. Picon turned away from him.

"Forgive my chiming in," said Mgr. Smith. "But a man may chime in as a bell may chime out. And did a bell chime out, Stall?"

"When?"

"When the girl was having hysterics?"

"Oh, then. Let me think. Yes. The front-door bell. It was the Vicar."

Mgr. Smith was silent, and after a moment Sam Williams signed to the butler to leave.

"Our most illuminatin' witness to date," commented Lord Simon.

"He has certainly thrown some light on the subject," said M. Picon.

"And the bell which did not ring may be its curfew," soliloquized Mgr. Smith.

CHAPTER 13

IT was at this point that the 'cold buffet' promised to us by the competent Miss Storey was produced. Stall wheeled in two butler's trolleys, and supplied us with food as urbanely as if he had never thought of shouting back his indignant denials a few minutes earlier. His manner was once more impeccable—such a word as blackmail might never have assailed his lobeless ears.

The food, too, was excellent. I remember eating three lobster patties with as much gusto as if poor Mary Thurston herself had been there to press me to another. And with them I had a drink of which I am extremely fond, though gourmets tell me that it should not be thought of at a time when one is eating—a stiff whisky in a large tumbler, filled to the brim with soda-water.

I could see Lord Simon shuddering at this. "My dear old boy," he could not help saying, "that's death, you know. Absolutely bally death."

"It's never done me any harm," I grinned. I had realized that I was expected to be something of a fool—to catch the last finesse in an investigator's work one had best be that.

"And I suppose you'll smoke a cigar on top of it?" he breathed, as though it hurt him.

"I've every intention of doing so."

"Then God help your stomach. What do you think of the case—so far?"

My conclusions, it must be owned, were at this point a trifle confused. And when under Lord Simon's kindly glance I tried to express them, they really did not sound very helpful. I was sure enough on one point—that Stall knew more than he had admitted. Otherwise, why had he lied about the time at which he received the money? On Thursday, he had said, but a few grains of his snuff were still on the dressing-table when we examined it. The dressing-table had a glass top. In a house as well cleaned as this one, it would have been impossible for it to have escaped Enid's duster on Friday morning. But why should Stall have lied? Surely he could not have committed the murder, for he had been outside that locked door almost as soon as we were. But then, so had everyone else.

At this point I saw a faint smile stretch the aristocratic lips above the Jack Hulbert chin.

"Everyone?" said Lord Simon.

"Well, everyone except the Vicar and the new suspect, Miles. On the whole, I think it is probably one of those two, though I don't see how it can have been the Vicar, or where was he when we broke into the room? And however clever a cat-burglar Miles was, how could he have climbed in or out of that window? And if he by any means used one of those ropes to get in at the window above, how had he escaped notice, and got out of the hotel after ten-thirty? Besides, what motive could he have?

"Confusin', isn't it?" said Lord Simon.

I plunged on. I wondered about the cook. She was a determined sort of a woman, evidently with strong prejudices. And she had no alibi at the time of the murder. Or Norris. What about Norris? No one had seemed to pay much attention to him. He was on the scene pretty quickly. But then—that might be in his favour. After all, he couldn't have come *through* the door, and he hadn't had time to come round. Or Strickland? He slept next door. That was suspicious, surely. But he had come out of his room within so short a time. And there was no ledge along which he could have climbed. Then there was Fellowes. A violent sort of a chap, and as it appeared now, a bit of a Don Juan. An affair with Enid, and something of the sort with Mary Thurston.

"In fact," said Lord Simon, "you suspect everyone?"

"Well, that's what it seems like. Though I don't see how any of them could have done it, really."

"What about that stepson?"

"Oh yes," I returned ingenuously, "I was forgetting that. Well, there again, there are several possibilities. I thought at first it was Strickland. But I'm not so sure now. Why shouldn't it be Norris? Or Fellowes? Or Miles?"

"Or even you," said Lord Simon quietly.

"Well, it doesn't happen to be me," I returned, not caring much for the remark, "but I see what you mean, of course."

"At any rate, you find it all pretty puzzlin', what?"

"Of course I do. Don't you?"

"I have my moments of lucidity," said Lord Simon, "but there's a lot of information I'm hankerin' after still." He turned aside. "By the way, Beef!" he called across the room.

The Sergeant's mouth was full of rabbit-pie, but he made some answering sound.

"Have you looked up the record of our next witness—Fellowes, the chauffeur?"

The Sergeant swallowed so violently that his throat seemed to distend like a chicken's. "Record?" he said. "What record?"

"The criminal record, of course," said Lord Simon, who seemed to enjoy discomfiting the Sergeant.

"Didn't know 'e 'ad one," said the latter sulkily.

"There! It's a good thing I have Butterfield with me. He was able to discover that Fellowes did a stretch of eighteen months in prison four years ago, for burglary. Violent sort of business, I gather."

"Can't know everything," mumbled Sergeant Beef. "And it 'asn't got nothink to do with the case, anyway," he added.

Lord Simon shrugged. "Beef of the evening, beautiful Beef," he murmured.

I moved across to M. Picon. The little man was munching happily, and quite elated. I could not remember him enjoying a meal before this, and was delighted to see the colour rising to his bovine cheeks.

"Whatever else that Mademoiselle Storey may be," he said, "she is an *artiste*."

I hesitated to explain that with that term in our mixed language he had accused her of activities on the music-hall stage, and nodded appreciatively.

"Are you beginning to get the hang of this affair?" I asked.

"Get the hang?" He laughed outright. "That is a good phrase! But it is not *Papa* Picon who will 'get the hang'. *Pas du tout!*"

"I mean, do you understand it yet?"

"I will tell you. I see more light. But what is that? A mote. A black spot. All is not unclouded. But *allons*, *mon ami*. All in good time. I, Amer Picon, have said so. And, presently, you will say—'Ah, why have I not seen that?'"

"That's good. But tell me, Monsieur Picon, what did you mean by asking Stall where the screams came from? I thought that was such an extraordinary question."

"An idea, no more. Just a little idea. Quite small. Quite little. But, *voyons*. We shall see. Sometimes even Amer Picon has an idea, no? Very childish, very simple, perhaps. But still an idea."

And that was all I could get out of him. Mgr. Smith, on the other hand, talked quite readily, though I could not call him informative. Finding myself plunged into this role of enquiring and credulous fool, to whom the great investigators would voice their conundrums, I resolved to make the best of it, and see whether he would add to my bewilderment, or elucidate it.

"It's simple enough so far as it has gone, but like all mysteries, it has not gone far enough. Don't you see that that is what is always puzzling—the case half-stated. the character half-formed? The were-wolf was the most terrifying creature in mythology because it was half a man. The centaur was a horror because he was half a beast. The trouble with most modern thought is that it is half-hearted . . "

"But, Monsignor Smith," I interrupted, fearing that he might continue in this strain all the evening, "who do you think it was that actually used that weapon?" I thought my question was as direct as it could be, and must succeed in securing as flat an answer.

"Oh, that's easy enough," came the calm reply. "But we are trying to discover who killed Mrs. Thurston."

"Then . . . then you don't think she was killed with that little Oriental knife?"

"I am sorry, but I'm afraid that she was, yes."

"Well, then?"

"What really puzzles me is the two hundred pounds."

"But surely there's no mystery about that. It was about the maximum which could be got out of poor Mary Thurston just then."

"And since that sum was drawn and paid, why did not the front-door bell ring? I would like it to have rung. A bell may sound for a man's passing, but it may save his soul."

"How do you know it didn't ring?" I asked him. "After all, the cook wasn't sure. She said the girl was having hysterics, and she might not have noticed it. It may have rung, for all you know."

He blinked at me with solemn interest. "That's true. Yes. I believe you're right. The bell might have rung to tell those in the kitchen that someone was outside. On the other hand, it might have rung to tell them that someone was *not* outside!"

I could not feel that this sort of speculation, brilliant though doubtless it was, could help me much towards deciding on the identity of the murderer, and left Mgr. Smith to his glass of red wine and oatmeal biscuit.

More out of sympathy than anything else I crossed to old Beef. The investigation, so far as it had gone, had evidently given him a splendid appetite and an enviable thirst. He had made the most of them, but although the supply of food and drink had been lavish and varied, I fancied that he would have been more at home in his usual seat in the public bar.

"Shouldn't be surprised if this didn't upset me," he said, referring to a plate of trifle he was finishing. "Bread and cheese and pickles is my supper, generally speaking."

"And very nice, too," I admitted. "Well, Sergeant, what do you think of this investigation?"

"Think of it? Blarsted waste of time, that's what it is. I 'ad a darts match to play to-night," he added regretfully.

"But we've got to find the murderer," I reminded him.

"'Aven't I told you I know 'oo it is?" he said, growing quite crimson with impatience. "It's as plain as a pikestaff," he added.

"Then why don't you arrest the man—or woman, without further delay?"

"Why not? Because these 'ere private detectives can't mind their own business. Pushing their noses in at Scotland Yard! When I made my report I was told to wait till they've had their say. Well, I'm waiting. Only I wish they'd 'urry up about it. With their stepsons, and their bells, and their where-did-the-screams-come-from. Why, they *try* to make it complicated."

"I'm bound to say, though, Beef, it doesn't look very simple to me."

"No, sir. But then, you see, *you're* not a policeman, are you?"

To which piece of stupid self-importance I made no reply.

CHAPTER 14

FELLOWES seemed to have changed from the smart and well-mannered chauffeur who had met me several times at the village station. He sat in the chair offered to him, with his head bent forward, so that when his eyes rose to meet those of his questioner he had an almost lowering appearance. He looked sullen and on his guard. I was disappointed in this, for I had somehow hoped that he would prove to be innocent, and I felt that he was making a bad impression on the investigators.

For the first time I allowed a purely psychological or instinctive kind of speculation to work. Was this the kind of man who could have murdered Mary Thurston? Could I picture him doing it? Was it in his nature to do it?

I had never observed him closely when his hat was off until now. I could not help admitting that his square, straight forehead, and the low line where his thick hair began, suggested something brutal about him. Yet there was also in his manner an air of carefree and sailor-like good nature which seemed to contradict that. On the whole, I felt that if he was guilty, it had been with some extreme provocation, if such a thing were possible. He had not murdered with a mean or a greedy motive, if he had murdered at all.

Lord Simon had begun quite chattily. "Know a bloke called Miles?" he asked.

Fellowes glanced up quickly. "Yes," he said, with enquiry in his voice.

"Known him long?"

"Some years."

"Got into a spot of trouble with him, didn't you?"

"Good God. Are you going to rake that up?" growled Fellowes.

"Can't help it. Sorry to pull out the bally skeleton, and all that. But it can't bc helped. When did you see Miles last?"

"This morning."

"See him yesterday?"

"In the afternoon, yes."

"Where?"

A long pause. "In the village." It was evident that Fellowes meant to give absolutely the minimum of information necessary.

"By appointment?"

"No."

"Where did you spend yesterday afternoon?"

"I had to meet Mr. Townsend at five-five."

"And before that?"

"I was free."

"What did you do?"

"I was running in the car engine. She's just been rebored."

"Anyone with you?"

Very decidedly Fellowes said, "No."

"You've been a sailor, haven't you, Fellowes? Life on the ocean wave, and all that sort of thing?"

"I was in the Merchant Service for a few years."

"Had a pretty tough life, one way and another?"

He grinned. "I suppose you'd call it pretty tough."

"Ever seen anyone killed?"

"Saw a boy eaten by alligators once. Crossing a river it was, on the East Coast."

"And so what with such hair-raisin' experiences and a spell in chokey, you can reckon to be pretty hardboiled?"

"Is that your way of tying this thing on me?" asked Fellowes truculently.

"Just one of my dam' silly questions," said Lord Simon, recrossing his legs. "And now tell me something more interestin'. What was there between you and Mrs. Thurston?"

This question seemed to produce a greater intensity in the atmosphere. Sam Williams looked up, and watched Fellowes keenly, while even Sergeant Beef seemed interested.

"Oh, that . . ." prevaricated Fellowes. "Well, nothing really."

"Nothing at all?"

"Well . . ."

"Come along, man. You're not going to pretend to be bashful, are you?"

"It wasn't anything to speak of. I suppose she'd taken rather a fancy to me."

"Entirely unreciprocated by you, of course?"

"How do you mean?"

Sergeant Beef came manfully to the rescue. " 'E means was you, or was you not, carrying on with the lady?"

Fellowes's answer was an odd one, and seemed to be the result of genuine embarrassment. "Not more than I could help," he said.

"Did it worry you?"

"A bit."

"Why?"

"Well, Dr. Thurston was all right. I didn't want anything like that."

At this point I respected Fellowes. I felt that I could see in a moment all that had happened. Mary Thurston, indulgent, stupid, affectionate, having her little romantic *affaire* with this good-looking rather piratical young man. Nothing serious, of course. But she liked him about her. Liked his opening the door of the car and arranging the rugs for her. Probably gave him things, and expected little attentions such as young lovers show. Altogether rather like one of those stout and wealthy English and American women you see in Majorca with a youth attached to them.

"There was nothing else that worried you about it?"

"Only . . . when she wanted me to stop talking with her . . ."

"As she did last night?"

"What do you mean?"

"I mean, she complained of hearing rats in the apple-room, and told you to set the trap."

"That's right, she did."

"And did you set it?"

"Yes."

"Did you talk to her?"

"No."

"Why not?"

"Because . . . when I got to her door, I heard someone in there talking to her."

"Who was it?"

"I don't know. A man."

"Did you hear anything said?"

"No. I didn't stop to listen. I went on upstairs and set the trap."

"What time would that have been?"

"Soon after eleven."

"How do you know?"

"Looked at the kitchen clock."

Whether it was the result of mental rehearsal, or honesty, or slick lying, I don't know, but I noticed that Fellowes gave his answers promptly and clearly. He scarcely ever paused.

"And having set the trap?"

"Went to my bedroom."

"Undress?"

"No. Took my coat off."

"Then?"

"Then, after a bit, I heard the screams."

"Nothing else? Nothing before that?"

'No.'

"Keen on a bit of P.T., aren't you, Fellowes? Gymnastics, and what not?"

"Yes."

"When did you go in the gymnasium last?"

"Not for about a week."

"You didn't know, then, that the ropes were missing from there?"

"No." The answer was sullen and quiet.

"In fact you know nothing more at all—nothing you want to tell us?"

"No."

"But, my friend . . ." It was M. Amer Picon who broke in now, unable to repress himself any longer. "You have told us nothing—nothing at all to the point. There are many questions which you can, as you say, clear up. For instance, what did your young lady, your fiancée, think of Madame Thurston's so kindly attention to you?"

"What young lady?"

"*Allons*, my friend, you need not affect an air quite so innocent. The parlourmaid, Enid."

"She? I don't see why she need be brought into this."

"Everyone, *tout le monde*, who lives in this house is brought into it. What did she say?"

"She did not much like it." Again he spoke in a deep sulky voice, without excitement, without any elaboration of the blunt fact.

"So she knew well that something was there?"

"She knew that Mrs. Thurston used to talk to me."

"And she was jealous, perhaps?"

"No. Not jealous. She knew there was nothing in it."

"With her mind she knew, with her heart she doubted. The woman is like that, *mon ami*. You had, perhaps, known this young lady a long time? Before you came to this house?"

"Yes."

That surprised me—I scarcely knew why. I suppose because I had assumed that they had met and fallen in love while both were in the Thurstons' service. But I admired M. Picon for thinking of other possibilities.

"Before you first knew Miles?"

"No. Soon after."

"*Bien.* A trio, I perceive."

Fellowes did not answer.

M. Picon seemed irritated by that, and his next question was asked quite fiercely. "You climb pretty well the rope, *n'est-ce pas?*"

Fellowes looked him full in the face. "Yes."

"And you have thought of taking a little public-house, I think?"

This astounded the chauffeur. "What's it to do with you? Can't I have my own affairs without their being poked into? And suppose I had?"

"Suppose you had, then I should like to know from where had come the money for so interesting an enterprise."

"Can't anyone save a bit without being suspected?"

"Perhaps. Perhaps. And now would you tell me something else equally *interessant.* Who entered first the service of Doctor and Mrs. Thurston, you or Enid?"

"She did."

"And obtained for you the job which you now have?"

"She told Mrs. Thurston I was out of a job. Anything else you want to know?"

"Please. One other little thing. Quite little, but very important. You have told us that yesterday afternoon you were nowhere near the house. You were driving the motor-car because it must be driven slow for a time after the mechanical reparations. That is so?"

"I was running her in, yes."

"To prove that, would you perhaps be so good as to tell me something which would, as one might say, establish

the alibi? Show that you had been away from here? Someone, perhaps, you spoke to? Something you noticed?"

Fellowes did not look up for a while. I wondered whether
he was indeed searching in his memory for the information
demanded, or whether he was doubting the advisability of
giving it. M. Picon's tone had been suave, but there was
such an interested hush in the room while the chauffeur
hesitated that it really made one feel that there might be a
sinister significance behind the innocent query.

Presently Fellowes said, "Yes. I can tell you something.
I noticed that the flag on the church tower at Morton Scone
was at half-mast'.'

M. Picon jumped.

"You did. That is very interesting.'

Then Sergeant Beef broke in again. "That's right," he
said. "It would 'uv been. The doctor over at Morton Scone
oo'd been there twenty years died yesterday morning."

"Indeed? That is more interesting yet. Thank you."

And the extraordinary little man sat down, his cross-
examination ended.

It was scarcely necessary to appeal to Mgr. Smith this
time. Frankly, I was disappointed in this one of the great
three. He seemed to have lost all interest in the proceedings.
Of course I realized that the case was not fraught with the
phenomena to which he was accustomed. No tall strangers
with Homeric beards and black cloaks were here, no un-
common or alliterative surnames, no ghost which turned
out not to be a ghost, or supernatural things which became
more harrowing when they proved to be natural, no ruins,
no artists, no Americans. Still, it did not seem to me to be
such an uninteresting crime as all that. I did not see why he
should show quite such boredom. For now from the black
bundle in the arm-chair was coming a sound quite regular,
distinctly audible, and not very polite. Mgr. Smith was
snoring.

CHAPTER 15

IF the chauffeur had been uncommunicative, the girl who had been described as his fiancée made amends for him. She seemed to have a great deal to say, both on the subject of her life and his before they had entered the Thurstons' service, and on the events of yesterday. Little questioning was needed to elicit from her a great deal of information which the investigators may or may not have required.

She was a handsome girl. I was annoyed with myself, as I looked at her now, to think how unobservant I had been in the past. Perhaps I could blame my upbringing a little, but I'm afraid that I had not until now been very much aware of her as a human being. I had seen her often enough, of course, on the many occasions on which I had stayed in the house. But beyond a cheerful good morning when I had passed her, I had paid little attention to her.

With her thick brown hair, and rather liquid brown eyes, she might have had an insipid face, were it not for the almost puckish tilt of the nose, and humorous mobile mouth. She looked intelligent, and full of character, attractive, but also determined. She was a young woman, I was sure, who would not shrink from a desperate act if it was a necessary one. On the other hand, she would be capable of loyalty, I thought. An interesting face, and an interesting creature.

The story she told in answer to Lord Simon's tentative questions about the past was an unexpected one. She had been born in Soho, the daughter of a Greek mother and an English father. Her father kept a newspaper shop, and 'did a bit for a bookie', but when she was about twelve he had come home one day to say that a certain race gang was out for his blood, and that he had to disappear. She had never known whether the story was true, or merely an excuse for him to leave her mother, but at all events he had gone, and none of them had seen him since.

He left his foreign wife, the shop, Enid and her brother, then a lad of fifteen. The mother had been quite incapable of keeping the shop going, since she could not even write English. Within two months their stock was seized for arrears in rent, and the three of them moved into one room.

Sergeant Beef interrupted at this point in his official capacity. "One room?" he asked.

Enid sniffed. "There was a curtain down the middle of it," she said, and continued her story.

According to her own account she had then appeared to be at least sixteen years old, and soon got a job for herself as a domestic servant to a couple who kept a small sweet and tobacco shop in Battersea. She left her mother, and it was perhaps typical of the circumstances in which she had been born and raised, that she now had to admit that she had never seen or heard of her mother again. She went back once, a month or so later, to the address where she had left her, but the Greek woman had owed two weeks' rent and had disappeared during the night-time. "The only thing I got from the people in the house," said Enid, "was a box over the ears when they found that I wasn't going to pay the rent that was owing."

But, in her own words, she 'kept herself decent'. She soon left the Battersea shop, where she had been overworked and 'treated like dirt' and found employment with a young married couple. And as time had gone on she had moved from place to place, endeavouring always to 'better herself'. By this she explained that she did not merely mean getting better wages, but finding a job with more educated people from whom she could learn how to behave.

Her ambitions seemed to have been entirely social.

'Upwards' to her meant nearer refinement. And I felt, as she talked, that she had let nothing stand in her way in that pursuit. A new expression came into her face and her voice as she spoke, a grating hardness which surprised me. This mixture of English and Mediterranean blood, I thought, could be a dangerous one. But I tried to keep an open mind.

Her meeting with her brother, five years after they had separated, was rather dramatic. They had seen and recognized one another at a dance-hall. And with her brother, on that night, had been Fellowes.

Her brother seemed to have plenty of money, but he gave her no explanations. He said he was working—'electrical work', was his only description—and he did not encourage her to ask questions. He, too, had left their mother, or at least she had left him when she had got work in the kitchen of a Greek restaurant. So that the brother and sister had become two of those detached individuals, such, presumably as one hears besought in S.O.S. messages to return to a dying parent.

She wrote her address on a piece of paper for her brother that night, but she did not hear from him, or of him, until some weeks later when Fellowes had called to see her. He had then told her that her brother was in gaol for burglary. She had realized at once, she said, that his prosperity had not been due to any isolated act, but that he was a professional criminal. While he had been in prison, she had seen a good deal of Fellowes, and we gathered that 'an attachment' soon existed between them. He admitted having helped her brother in several 'jobs', but had been quite ready to promise her to have nothing more to do with the life.

When, however, her brother had come out of gaol, he and Fellowes had become, as Enid put it, 'very thick again', and as a sequel to that friendship they were both arrested and given terms of imprisonment. But it was not, Enid hastened to explain, in the nature of Fellowes. Her brother had a strong character, and had led him into it.

"In spite of his promise to you?" put in Lord Simon.

"Well—he was out of work," was Enid's defence.

When he came out, however, as he did nearly a year before her brother, who was by now regarded as an habitual criminal, she had been able to help him. She had already got her job with the Thurstons, and, by appealing to Mrs. Thurston, and telling her the whole truth, she had persuaded her to engage him as a chauffeur. For nearly three years, she assured us, he had been as straight as a die, enjoying his job, and saving his wages.

"Until, of course, your brother reappeared?"

"That made no difference. My brother hasn't done anything wrong since he's been out."

"I can believe in one reformed criminal," said Sam Williams, "but two are hard to credit."

"Well, it's true, anyway," said Enid. "My brother . . ."

"Respectively employed as porter at the local hotel . . ."

"Yes. He's gone straight. And why shouldn't he? He's got a decent job. Twenty-five bob a week, and tips, besides his keep. Mrs. Thurston got it for him, and she knew all about him. You ask the Sergeant whether he hasn't gone straight."

"No complaints so far," admitted Beef.

"Then I wonder why Fellowes didn't mention that Miles was your brother."

"Did you ask him? Why should he tell you what he isn't asked? It's not his nature. He'd rather say too little than too much."

The end of her story was soon told. She and Fellowes had decided to get married, and to start in a little hotel of their own. It had always been her idea. And each of them had saved some money. There was that will of Mrs. Thurston's, but of course, she took no notice of that. Why,

Mrs. Thurston might have lived another thirty years. And she didn't mean to spend all that time in domestic service. Not she.

At this point the suspicion in my mind left the other people who might have been involved in the murder of Mary Thurston, and became for a time centred on this trio. It seemed to me almost too much of a coincidence that two men and a woman, all of them more or less sprung from the criminal classes, should have been on the spot, without having been involved.

I could not see, of course, how they could have done it, for I could not yet see how anyone could have done it, but I felt that one or two, or all three of them, were guilty. And I do not deny that I was sorry. I should have liked to have felt that the story told by the girl was true. They had all had to fight for existence. I had caught some glimpses of that fight—the girl's dreary struggle through the most sordid kind of domestic service at an age when she should have been at school. The years of malnutrition and overwork. And for the men the loneliness and nerve-strain of a life into which they had probably entered half from desperation, half from want.

But there was that hardness in Enid, that savagery in Fellowes, which seemed to prove them capable of any violent act, if violence served their turn. And though I still revolted at the thought of either of them having actually used that knife so horribly, I no longer felt that they were innocent of some part in the crime.

I felt nauseated, suddenly, with the whole affair. This relentless tracking down of the criminal seemed gruesome. Lord Simon, gently sipping his brandy, so obviously considered it all to be a most absorbing game of chess, 'something to occupy a chap', that for a moment I lost all patience with him. And the brilliant little Picon, whose humanity was more evident, he too could not help enjoying his own efforts

—and that disturbed me. Certainly I had never known Mgr. Smith actually hand a man over to the Law, but even that was partly because the criminals he discovered had a way of committing suicide before he revealed their identity.

Of course, in a way, I wanted poor Mary Thurston avenged. But as I saw the investigators with appetites obviously whetted for the cross-examination they were about to make of this handsome girl, my gusto failed, and I felt like leaving them to their questions, and going out into the air. But my curiosity, of course, got the better of me, so that I took another whisky-and-soda and leaned back in my chair to hear what questions they would put to Enid, now that they had reached the point of discovering her movements last night.

CHAPTER 16

To our surprise Sergeant Beef conceived a sudden desire to ask questions at this point.

"Could you tell me," he began ponderously, "which of the ladies and gentlemen staying in the house lit their fires last night?"

But Williams came to the rescue. "Really, Beef," he said, "while these gentlemen have important questions to ask, I think we want to waste as little time as possible."

One or two others of us joined the appeal to Beef not to hold up the cross-examination, so that, after murmuring something about "having a pretty good idea, anyway" he was silent again.

"See anything of your brother yesterday?" asked Lord Simon, returning indefatigably to his task of cross-examination.

"No. Nothing at all."

"Yet it was his free afternoon."

"Was it?"

"How did you spend the afternoon?"

Enid hesitated, and I had a curious intuition that she was going to tell a lie.

"Well," she said at last, "I'd been up late the night before—reading. And not a detective novel either," she put in tartly. "So that yesterday afternoon I felt sleepy, and went up to my room for forty winks."

"When did you first see Fellowes that day?"

"Not until just before dinner." Again, I was sure that she was lying.

"Did he have anything particular to say to you then?"

"Nothing special, no."

115

"Nothing about a rat-trap?"

"Oh, that wasn't anything particular. Whenever Mrs. Thurston wanted a talk with him, she'd tell him about the rats."

"That was an understood thing, then. Did Fellowes mention it last night?"

"Yes He just told me."

"Did you mind?"

"Mind?"

"Yes, Enid. Incredible though it may seem to you, I said 'mind'. Very gauche of me, no doubt, but I just wondered whether a man's fiancée would have an objection to his being summoned to a lady's room at eleven o'clock or so, for a 'talk'."

Enid coloured slightly, but said only, "He can take care of himself. I never worry about him."

"A very sensible attitude, I'm sure."

"Well, there was nothing in it. You know what she was. She was a bit sentimental over him, that's all. Didn't worry me."

"Do you happen to know how Mrs. Thurston spent Friday afternoon?"

"She went up for what she used to call her siesta. Don't know how long she was in her room."

"Was that a regular habit of hers?"

"Pretty regular, yes."

"Did she have a siesta on the Thursday?"

"Yes. But not for long. She'd ordered the car for two-thirty."

"And went out?"

"Yes."

"Do you know where?"

"How should I know? The chauffeur took her."

"I see. Well, let's get back to yesterday, Friday.

"Yes?"

"Did you go up to Mrs. Thurston's room when she dressed for dinner?"

"No. I'm not a lady's maid."

"When did you first go in there?"

"It wasn't long after dinner. I went to tidy up her things. She used to leave them anyhow when she dressed."

"And did you notice then whether the lights in the room were all right?"

"Only the reading-lamp came on. The big light didn't."

"That was, say, round about ten o'clock?"

"Yes."

"Were the lights all right on the previous night?"

"Yes, I think so."

"What did you do when you found there was a bulb missing?"

"Went to Mr. Stall, and asked him for one. He said he was busy and I must find it for myself."

"And did you?"

"No. Why should I have? It was his place to give it me. He kept all the stores. So I thought to myself—well, if Mrs. Thurston asks about it, I shall tell her straight."

"And did she ask about it?"

"When?"

"When she came up to bed. The cook has told us that you followed her up."

"Yes, I did, but I didn't go into her room."

"Why not?"

Enid looked rather solemn, and hesitated. "When Mrs. Thurston got to her room, I was not far behind. I saw her open her door and go to switch on the main light. Then I heard her say, 'What are you doing here?' And I stopped where I was."

"What kind of a voice did she use for that interestin' question?"

"She seemed a bit startled."

"Did she know that you were behind her?"

"I don't think she realized it. Or at any rate, finding someone in her room had upset her too much to notice."

"And did you hear any answer?"

"No."

"So you waited to see who came out?"

"No I didn't, then!" For the first time Enid sounded angry. "It was no business of mine who was there. It might have been any of the gentlemen. I didn't know."

"You know, however, that it wasn't Fellowes?"

"It wasn't him, because he came up to bed at that minute, and passed me on the landing."

"What did you do next?"

"Started doing my bedrooms. Turning back the beds, and that. I went into Mr. Townsend's room, then Mr. Williams's."

"Mr. Norris's?"

"No. I saw him going into his room when I went into Mr. Williams's. He was coming back from the bathroom. I was doing Dr. Thurston's when I heard the screams."

Lord Simon leaned back in his chair, stroking the whole length of his chin. Then suddenly he leaned forward. "Look here, Enid. You're about the nearest thing we shall get to a witness of this crime. We want the truth. Now, tell me, who *was* in Mrs. Thurston's room when she reached it that evening?"

She looked straight into his eyes. "Cross my heart, I don't know, my lord."

"And you don't know who took the bulb out of its fitting?"

"No."

At this point there was a sudden and rather violent interruption. The door was burst open, and a short dark man, with the sallow cheeks and burning brown eyes of the Mediterranean races, hurried into the room. He had a little

118

black moustache, and undeniably the appearance of an *atorante*, an *apache*, an exotic sort of savage. He crossed straight to Enid, and his voice, which was entirely English, came as a surprise to me.

"Don't say anything to them," he advised her, "until you have a solicitor. Have they been asking you questions? You shouldn't have answered. They can't make you answer."

Enid did not seem grateful for this consideration. "I've got nothing to be ashamed of,' she said.

"That's not the point. They'd get anyone mixed up in their dirty crimes. Don't you say anything, I tell you."

Lord Simon had been examining the new-comer coldly. "Mr. Miles, I presume?" he said.

"Well?" assented Miles.

"Glad you've dropped in. You may be able to help us. I take it that you've heard of our little gathering from my man Butterfield?"

Butterfield, as though in answer, walked in. "I spoke to the person, as you instructed, my lord. I find his alibi quite in order. It was, as you knew, his free evening. He spent it, not at his own hotel, but at an inn called the Red Lion. He was actually partner to the Police Sergeant in a contest at a game known as Darts, my lord."

"Darts," repeated Lord Simon disgustedly.

"That was the name of the pastime, my lord. Darts. I made quite sure of my information. At ten o'clock he remained talking with a group of persons outside this public-house, until ten-twenty, when two of them accompanied him to his hotel. It appears that the winners in this game, my lord, have their—I beg your pardon for mentioning it, my lord—their beer paid for by the losers. This person and the Police Sergeant in partnership had been almost uniformly successful in the game, and in consequence in a very ambiguous condition. However, Miles was assisted to his hotel, where the kitchen-boy, who shares his room, undressed him, and states that he was in bed and asleep before eleven, and did not stir again. The Sergeant, it appears, was summoned here."

"If I 'ad known you was interested in Miles's movements, I could 'ave told you," grumbled Sergeant Beef.

"Quite so. So you have an alibi, friend Miles. Well, well, it's a useful sort of thing. What can you tell us, though?"

"Nothing. My sister never had anything to do with it, nor yet Fellowes. So you might as well stop questioning them."

"You must admit that it's rather odd, though, Miles, that the three of you, with such interesting records, should be handy when a crime's been committed."

"Don't see what that's got to do with it. There's nothing against me since I came out. Fellowes has got a clean record for three years. And my sister's never been in any trouble. I don't think much of any detective," he added, "who suspects people, just because they once had been in quod."

"Nobody has mentioned the word suspicion, Miles. It was just the coincidence which interested me. You see, I'm not a great believer in coincidences. Who proposed that game of darts?"

"I did."

"You met Sergeant Beef at the Red Lion, perhaps?"

"No. I went to his house."

"You went and fished him out for a game?"

"Yes. What about it? He's a good player. And there was two fellows coming over from Morton Scone who are hot stuff."

"So it was for the honour of the village, as it were, that the Sergeant turned out? Thank you."

M. Picon only asked him one question. "These gentlemen from Morton Scone, did they tell you anything of what you call in English the tittle-tattle of the place? Was there any news from Morton Scone?"

Miles looked honestly puzzled. "No. Not that I can remember. We didn't have much time for talking. We were playing hard."

There was silence in the room, broken only by the gentle snoring of Mgr. Smith. I had been examining Miles. Small, slick, rather furtive—here was a man who at least psychologically, I felt, could have been considered guilty. I had heard of the treachery of these people of mixed blood, and looking at him I could believe what I had heard. His long, rather yellow hand, lying on the back of his sister's chair, could have used that knife as it had been used. And the almost feline agility of the man could, I felt, have overcome the inexplicable obstacles. But his alibi, as Butterfield had indicated, seemed unimpeachable, so that yet another suspect was abandoned in my mind.

"Anyway," he said, "I'm not going to have my sister asked any more questions. Not without she has a solicitor here. She oughtn't to have been asked any. It's not fair, in a serious case like this."

"All that we want, *mon ami*," put in M. Picon, "is the truth."

"Well, you can find that out, without ˜sking her any more. Come on, Enid."

She rose without a word, and with a defiant glance back at us, Miles escorted her from the room.

"It is of no consequence," said M. Picon. "There was nothing else she could tell us. So if she and her lover are to be believed, someone was waiting in the *chambre* of Madame Thurston when she reached it, yesterday."

"And that someone," I felt called upon to say, "could have been one of five. It could have been Norris, Strickland, Stall, or the Vicar. But it could also have been a someone of whose presence in the house we are unaware."

"Or someone of whose existence we are unaware," put in Sam Williams.

"That is, always presuming that Enid and Fellowes have not invented that person altogether," suggested M. Picon. "We have only Enid's and her lover's word that he was there."

"Yes, we don't seem to be getting very much farther, do we?" smiled Lord Simon.

"Who knows?" returned M. Picon. "A little light here, a little light there, and soon, *voilà!* the sun is up and all is day."

"It will be, too," grumbled Sergeant Beef, "if you don't get on with it."

"*Bien, bien,* my friend Bœuf. But remember the English proverb, the more you haste, the less you speed, is it not? We come now to the young Strickland."

CHAPTER 17

I WAS learning something about the effect of a crime on people, which I had never fully realized from merely reading about murder. It was the quite unexpected effect which suspicion, cross-examination, and the presence of skilled detectives, had on everyone concerned. These things had already broken down the preposterously theatrical manner of Stall, the butler, had made Fellowes, usually a cheerful young man, growl monosyllables in a threatening sort of way, and shown Enid as a girl of some character who could tell a story, or at least her own story, very well.

But I was still not prepared for the changes in my fellow-guests, least of all those in David Strickland. He had always seemed to me one of the few Englishmen to whom that expressive Americanism 'hard-boiled' might justly be applied. Even his appearance—bull neck, cheeks tanned and mapped with the red veins that are the bloom of alcohol, eyes hard and humorous—argued that he would be invulnerable to this sort of thing. I had expected to find him terse and rather gruff, perhaps, but able to answer any questions that were put to him quite satisfactorily.

Yet when he came into the room, I, who knew him well, was certain that he was actually feeling nervous. He nodded uncomfortably to the investigators and hurriedly lit a cigarette. Whether or not he had any connection with the crime, he had something to hide. I was sure of that.

"Sorry to have to ask you a lot of dam'-fool questions," said Lord Simon, then scarcely paused before beginning to do so. "Ever changed your name?" he snapped.

"Changed my name?" repeated Strickland.

If only, I thought, I had more insight! Was he really

123

surprised at the question, or was he gaining time?

"Yes. Deed poll, and all that sort of thing."

"No. I've never changed my name. Why?"

"Oh—just wondered. Known the Thurstons long?"

"A few years."

"Come here quite a lot, I suppose?"

"Yes. What's the idea of all this, Plimsoll?"

"Curiosity, old boy. Do you happen to be hard up?"

Very coldly Strickland said, "No thanks. Why, did you want me to lend you something?"

Lord Simon was quite unperturbed. "April Boy came in, then?"

Strickland half-rose. "Is it any business of yours what bets I make?"

"Awfully sorry, old man. I suppose bets should be considered sacred. Between a man and his God—or his bookmaker. But my man Butterfield did happen to hear from a gentleman of similar calling to himself that you were in a tight corner this week. And if you want to put a hundred pounds on a horse at six to one, without anyone knowing it, I suggest your not using the extension of a telephone which has a man like Butterfield glued to the main."

"I shall tell Thurston how damnable I think it, that this sort of snooping should go on in a house where one's a guest."

"Far more damnable things than that have gone on in the last twenty-four hours. There has been, for instance, a murder."

"I can't see that it justifies your hanging round listening to my conversations on the 'phone."

"Well, let's waive the point, shall we? Then perhaps you will tell me just how matters stand between you and your bookies?"

"I'm damned if I will."

"Then I must tell you. That hundred you put on this

morning was a last fling—an absolutely desperate shot. You're up to the eyes in debt, you had no means of raising the money, and you shoved this on knowing that if the horse did not win you could not find the hundred. You know only one bookie who would take the bet. Well, you've won. I congratulate you."

Strickland was calmer now, but sounded more dangerous. "Look here, Plimsoll, you're here—though God knows who asked you here—to find out who murdered Mary Thurston, not to ferret out details of my betting "

"But suppose—mind, I'm only just supposin'—that there was some sort of relationship between them?"

"What the hell do you mean? How could there be?"

"What were you doing in Mary Thurston's room before dinner last night?"

Strickland turned furiously to me. "I've never liked you, Townsend. I've always thought you a mean-natured sort of devil. But I didn't think you'd join in this sneak's game."

I was about to explain that I should have had no right to keep any information like that to myself, when Plimsoll went on. "Well," he insisted, "what were you doing there?"

"I had something to talk over with Mary Thurston."

"And couldn't she lend you the money?"

I expected Strickland to break out again—I even wondered if there would be a fight. But perhaps he was a little cowered by the fact that the investigators knew of his visit to the dead woman's room. At all events, I was surprised to hear him say, "No," in a deep voice, but quite clearly.

"So you stole her diamond pendant?"

Again no outward sign of anger. "No. She gave it to me. Or at least told me to pawn it. It would raise what I needed." After a silence he went on. "I had told her on the 'phone the day before that I was in a hole, and she had promised to help me. Now she said that she was awfully sorry,

125

something unexpected had happened, and she couldn't. I've no idea what she meant."

"It's funny," mused Lord Simon, "that when you happen to be speakin' the truth, you're so much more convincin'."

"That was the truth."

"Indeed? Then your troubles were over?"

"It seemed so."

"Until this morning—when you found that the police had charge of the pendant. Quite. Nothing that could be called 'trouble' had happened in the meanwhile, I suppose?"

"In the meanwhile Mary Thurston had been murdered."

"Ah yes. We must get back to that. You were the first, I think, to go to bed?"

"I believe I was."

"Bit unusual for you?"

"Perhaps. But I'd been up early that morning. I was dog-tired."

"Are you always dog-tired after getting up early?"

"No. I was last night."

"You had no other reason for going to bed so soon?"

"I was a bit bored. Townsend and the Vicar were rather much, in one room."

I took no notice, of course, inwardly deciding that I would not allow myself to be drawn into suspecting Strickland merely because he was attempting to be rude to me.

"And yet although you were so tired, you did not go to bed?"

"I had several letters to write."

"They must have been urgent."

"They were."

"When did you leave your room next?"

Without a moment's hesitation Strickland said—"When I heard the screams."

"Not before?"

"No."

126

"Did you hear Mary Thurston come to bed?"

"Not consciously."

"You heard no voices from her room?"

"No. The wireless was playing right underneath me."

"You did not guess that anyone was in her room that evening?"

"Certainly not."

"Was your window open?"

"I don't think so."

Lord Simon stared straight at Strickland for a moment, and then with a gesture indicated that he had no more questions to ask.

M. Picon said, "Monsieur Strickland, I have only one question to put to you. It is about those so horrifying screams. Perhaps you will be so good as to think carefully before you tell me what I want to know. It is a little matter, but so much depends on it. *Where did those screams come from?*"

I was less surprised at this ridiculous question than I would have been if I had not already heard it asked of Stall. Although I realized that I was unoriginal in doing so, and though I knew that my predecessors in the thought had always been proved ignominiously wrong, I could not help feeling that the little man had gone off the rails at last.

"Where did they come from?" repeated Strickland. "Why, from Mary Thurston's room, of course."

"You are sure of that?"

"But it never occurred to me to doubt it."

"*Précisement.* Is that why you are sure?"

"No. No, even when I first heard the screams, I knew they were from Mary Thurston's room."

M. Picon stared at him, as though he wanted even more confirmation, but apparently decided to let it go at that. Strickland walked over to the decanter and helped himself to a drink.

"I call this third degree," he said with a rather sheepish grin. "I need a good stiff drink."

"That is a sign of the cross-examination," said Sam Williams.

"But not a sign of the Cross," said Mgr. Smith, waking up for the first time in the last three-quarters of an hour.

Alec Norris, who followed, could tell us very little. His room was on the other side of the corridor, and he had heard nothing, he said, until he had heard the screams. He had seen no one after he had gone up to bed, except Enid, who had been going into Williams's room as he had come back from the bathroom

"You had a bath?"

"Yes, I always bath at night. I work afterwards, and I find that it clears the brain."

"Then you returned to your room?"

"I did. And settled down to write."

"Do you usually dress after having a bath at night?"

"Invariably, if I'm going to work."

He spoke precisely and calmly. All traces of the hysteria he had shown at first had vanished. His skull-like head was high, his cold eyes met his questioner's.

"You were the first to reach Mrs. Thurston's door. Can you remember in what order the others came?"

"I think so. Thurston first, bounding upstairs like a mad-man, followed by Williams and Townsend. Then Strickland out of his room, then I think Fellowes from upstairs, and, perhaps half a minute later, Stall, also from upstairs."

"Did you notice the girl Enid?"

"Yes. But not for some minutes. I think it was after they had broken down the door. She came out of Thurston's room as white as a sheet. Fellowes spoke to her, and she ran straight downstairs."

"You have a very accurate memory, Mr. Norris."

"I have a trained memory. I have taken a course in Pelmanism."

Rather unexpectedly Mgr. Smith turned to him. "I understand, Mr. Norris, that yesterday evening you expressed an interest in crime from what you called the psychological point of view?"

"Something of the sort."

"Presuming that the phrase means anything at all, do you find this particular crime interesting from the psychological point of view?"

Alec Norris looked at him, and for a moment I thought a shadow crossed his face.

"I do not understand this crime," he said at last.

"Nor I," said Sam Williams sadly.

CHAPTER 18

AND now for the Vicar, I thought, with some relish. For of all those who had been interrogated there had been none who, from the first, had seemed to me so likely to do or say something quite unanticipated as Mr. Rider. He had seemed to me, on the evening of the crime, the only person with any real mystery about him. There was his rather grotesque appearance, his reputation for eccentricity and fanaticism, there was his very odd question to me yesterday, and most singular and inexplicable of all, the discovery of him kneeling at Mary Thurston's bedside only twenty minutes after the murder.

Surely, I felt, after so much inconclusiveness, the investigators would extract something definite from this man. Surely now even I would begin to see some of that 'light' which was guiding M. Picon.

The Vicar smiled nervously yet civilly to us as he came in, and sat down quickly. His long fingers he kept twisting into intricate cat's cradles before his chest. He too, I was certain, was afraid of something. He waited to be questioned as though with any one of the innocent queries put to him might come disaster. And yet, I thought, he found it hard to concentrate. His nervous mind went wandering off, and his pale eyes grew vacant. One thing was certain—the man was suffering.

"Sorry to bother you, Mr. Rider," began Lord Simon. "Fact is, we're hopin' you can help us a bit."

"I'll do all I can."

"You've known the Thurstons for some time?"

"Ever since they've lived here. They have attended my church—and have been good enough to invite me to the house more frequently than I could very well accept. You see, I had no means of returning their hospitality My home . . ." He shrugged, and ceased speaking as though he had suddenly recalled that he might be saying too much.

"Was there anything in this household that—so to speak —got your goat? Any goings-on, as they say, which worried you?"

"I think not."

"Yet you asked Mr. Townsend last night if he had noticed 'anything wrong'."

The Vicar paled. "Mr. Townsend, whom I *then* took to be a young man of good sense and discretion, might have seen some evidences which had escaped me."

There was no mistaking the indignation in his glance. I realized that my role as an associate of investigators carried its penalties. I had certainly made two enemies at least.

"Evidences of what?" said Lord Simon evenly.

"Evidences of . . . something scandalous. I had heard rumours."

For the first time in my brief personal acquaintance with Lord Simon he showed unmistakable anger. "And you considered it your duty to investigate the truth of those rumours?"

"Yes."

"To go into a house to which you had been invited as a guest, and question another guest about them?"

"Yes." Then very quietly, almost meekly, he added, "Have you never felt such questioning to be your duty?"

Lord Simon did not condescend to reply. And why should he? His questions were prompted by his determination to find out the truth about a crime; the Vicar's were the merest Nosey-Parkerdom, if they were nothing worse.

"And what, exactly, were those rumours?"

"I hardly like to revive them now. *De mortuis*, you know, *de mortuis*."

"Mr. Rider, I hardly think this is a moment for you to

profess scruples about blackguardin' another person, even if that person is dead. What were those rumours?"

"It had been bruited in the village, had in fact reached my ears, that some sort of . . . understanding existed between Mrs. Thurston and the chauffeur."

To all of us, I think, came the disappointment that must be felt when a promised *bonne-bouche* of scandal turns out to be stale news. I, for one, had hoped that Mr. Rider would produce something new.

"Had you yourself seen any evidences of it?"

"Not actually."

Lord Simon spoke and looked as though there was an unpleasant smell in his nostrils. It was quite evident that he did not like the Vicar.

"And what you heard did not prevent your accepting the Thurstons' invitation to dinner last night?"

"I considered it my duty to . . ."

"Ah yes. I was forgetting your duty. Did you happen to know that it was Mrs. Thurston's habit to retire to bed at eleven o'clock?"

The Vicar stared silently at Lord Simon. "No," he said at last.

"Yet you had dined here . . . how often?"

"Oh many times, many times."

"Did you never stay to chat with Dr. Thurston after Mrs. Thurston had retired?"

"Occasionally."

"And you have never heard her make a remark to the effect that eleven o'clock was her bed-time?"

"Now that you mention it, I do seem to remember something of the sort."

"What time did you leave the house?"

"About twenty to eleven, I believe."

"So that you knew when you went that Mrs. Thurston would soon be going to bed?"

"I might have guessed it, had I thought about it."

"What had you been talking to her about? You and she were sitting alone together for some time."

"Oh, parish matters, chiefly. She told me, I remember, that Stall, the butler, who is a chorister of mine, would be leaving her shortly."

"Did she express any regret?"

"Oh yes. She had been very satisfied with him."

"And had you?"

"He had a good bass voice, I believe."

Lord Simon leaned back in his chair. I took my eyes from the pale and twitching face of the Vicar to watch his interrogator. Perhaps it was because he must now be approaching his most serious questions that Lord Simon now dropped all evidence of anger or distaste, and became his usual self—drawling and apparently effete.

"Well, Mr. Rider, you seem fond of a bit of sleuthin' yourself on the quiet. Keepin' an eye on misdemeanours, and all that. You'll appreciate the difficulties of a fellow-sleuth, won't you, and do what you can to help him out of a hole? Fact is, you can help us along quite a lot. Hope you'll do your best to answer a few more of my silly-ass questions. Here goes, anyway. When you left the house, where exactly did you go?"

It was, I was sure, this very question that the Vicar had dreaded. He swallowed as a man does who has an inflamed throat.

"I . . . I had decided to walk home through the orchard."

"Let's see, that's at this end of the house, isn't it? Not overlooked by any of the windows?"

"That's right. There is a footpath across it which leads straight into the garden of the Vicarage."

"And you took that path?"

"Yes."

"And went home?"

I thought that no question which had been asked this evening produced quite such an expectant hush as this one. The Vicar's fingers twined and untwined and his eyes had fallen. When his answer came it was scarcely audible. "No," he said.

"You didn't? Then where did you go?"

"Nowhere. I stayed in the orchard."

"Picking fruit, perhaps?"

"No. No. You must not misunderstand me. I stayed in that orchard in agony of mind. I paced up and down, up and down in torment."

"I wonder whatever was the matter? Sat on an ants' nest, or something?"

"Lord Simon, this is no joking matter. I was in great distress. When I told you just now that Mrs. Thurston and I had discussed parish matters, it was only half the truth. We had also spoken of the chauffeur. Mrs. Thurston had admitted that she was fond of him. It is true, she claimed that her affection was that of a mother for her son. But I knew—I felt that it was otherwise."

"*Honi* bally well *soit*," commented Lord Simon. "So that made you march up and down the orchard for . . . how long?"

"I was in the orchard when I heard those heart-rending screams."

"Oh, you were. You must have done about half an hour's pacin' about."

"I suppose so. I lost all count of time. And then I couldn't make up my mind what I should do. It was some minutes, I believe, before I gathered courage to return to the house. But at last I did so. I went to the front door, and rang the bell. The door was opened by Stall. I asked him what those sounds had been, and he said, 'Mrs. Thurston . . . up in her room. She's been murdered, sir.' I at once asked for Dr. Thurston, feeling my place was at his side.

Stall left me alone to find him, as he had to return to the maid, who had had an attack of hysterics. So I hurried up to the bedroom, and found the pitiful, terrible corpse of that poor woman. I did what I could—I knelt beside her and prayed. It was thus you found me."

As he finished Mr. Rider did a very embarrassing thing. He buried his face in his hands, and began violently to weep. We could hear the sound quite plainly in that silent room. And again—I trust my intuitions—I did not believe that it was for Mary Thurston that he was weeping.

Mgr. Smith's voice interrupted him. "Where did you work before you came here, Mr. Rider?" he asked.

Evidently, I thought, he wishes to relieve the poor man by persuading him to talk of himself in a more non-committal way. There could be no other explanation for a question so entirely irrelevant.

"I was a curate in a London parish."

"And you came straight to this village from that work?"

"No. I had a . . . nervous breakdown. The work in London . . . I was an invalid for a time."

"Would you mind telling us the nature of your illness?"

The Vicar gaped blankly at him. "It . . . it was nothing very serious. I was subject to certain delusions. As a matter of fact"—he made the announcement very solemnly—"I thought I was Queen Victoria. For several months I spoke exclusively in the first person plural and had an unfortunate habit of draping a scarf about my head in the form of a widow's *coiffe*. But that is all over, I am glad to say. I recovered completely seven years ago, and have never been revisited by the malady."

Certainly, if we were waiting merely for the unexpected, Mr. Rider was no disappointment. It had needed a man with the insight and imagination of Mgr. Smith, however, to discover that he had been something more than eccentric, though as I looked at him now, with his white cheeks tear-stained and his eyes glazed by a look of absence, I knew that I ought to have guessed it long ago.

M. Picon, who had seemed at a loss during the Vicar's more hysterical moments, now returned to the practical issue. "Since you were in the orchard, *m'sieu*," he said politely, "you saw no window of the house?"

"No."

"Not at all? During all the time that you were out there?"

"No."

"You could not say whether any window in the front of the house was illuminated?"

"No."

I wished that M. Picon would leave him alone. I was sure that the poor fellow was again going to break into those embarrassing sobs.

"Where, *précisement* stood you when you heard the scream?"

I was right. Instead of answering, the Vicar once more covered his face. "Oh, leave me alone now," he said. "I have done wrong. But who hasn't? Which of you is guiltless? And the wrong I have done has nothing whatever to do with you. Nothing whatever. There is nothing more I can tell you which will help you to find the murderer. So leave me alone . . ."

He stood up rather unsteadily, and made for the door. I saw the investigators exchange unwilling glances.

CHAPTER 19

"I CONSIDER that man a nosey parker of a most un-pleasant kind," commented Sam Williams, when the door had closed behind Mr. Rider.

"But let me remind you," said Mgr. Smith, "that there have been Parkers less sane and more sinister than the proverbial Nosey. There was a Thomas Parker, who was a Lord Chancellor of England and a pilferer, and a Matthew Parker, who was an Archbishop of Canterbury, and a Protestant."

"Exactly. Well, we've heard all these ladies and gentlemen, and personally I'm for a spot of shut-eye," said Lord Simon.

I was astounded, and disappointed at this announcement. I had never doubted, while the cross-examination had gone on, but that the investigators would have completed their theory by the end of it, and that we should see the expected arrest before we went to bed. They at least had seemed to know where their questions were leading them, and although I had no inkling I had put this down, conventionally enough, to my own inexperience and obtuseness.

"But . . . don't you know who is the murderer?" I asked Lord Simon rather blankly.

"Instead of tellin' you what I know," he returned, "let me remind you of a few of the things I don't know. I don't know who Mr. Sidney Sewell may be. I don't know who is Mrs. Thurston's stepson, or if the two are the same person . . ."

"Nor," I interrupted sarcastically, "do you know whether her first husband liked his eggs scrambled or boiled, nor who his great-grandmother may have been. But really, Plimsoll, if you've solved this thing, I think you might tell us."

Lord Șimon gave me a long-suffering look. "Don't get agitated, old boy. I'm doin' my best, don't you know."

"Do you know how it was done?"

"I've got some sort of an inklin'."

"And do you know who did it?"

"I've got my suspicions, as policemen say."

"Then why can't you tell us?" broke in Sam Williams. "This atmosphere of suspicion is most unpleasant."

"It's just a bit of the old professional vanity stuff. I want to complete my case, and all that. Seriously, it isn't complete yet. Not by a long chalk. Suspicion's no good to anybody. What we all want is a cert. Let me have to-morrow and I'll see what I can do. Yes, Butterfield?"

Lord Simon's man had come into the room, and had been waiting for his employer to finish speaking.

"I think I have what you require, my lord," he said, and handed over a somewhat grubby piece of paper.

Lord Simon glanced at it, whistled, and gave it to Picon. It was handed right round, and when I had it I recognized at once the rather childish calligraphy of Mary Thurston.

My dear one, (it read)

I am sorry about yesterday. I must speak to you this evening at the usual time. You must not be angry with me. I would do anything in my power to make you happy. You know I love you. Don't let anything prevent this evening.

M. T.

"From the *chambre* of Stall, of course?" said M. Picon.

"Yes, sir."

I was infected by all this reasoning and drawing of conclusions. "But," I said, "if Mary Thurston had already arranged with Fellowes by means of her rat-trap instructions, why should she send this note?"

Lord Simon's reply was good-natured, but crushing. "In the first place, how do you know that this note was addressed to Fellowes? In the second place, what makes you think it was sent last night?"

I glanced at the grubby piece of paper. "No. I suppose it is older than that."

Butterfield coughed. "I have applied the usual tests, my lord," he said, "and I find that the ink is at least a month old."

He was still speaking when he noticed that Lord Simon had allowed the ash from his cigar to fall on his jacket. Without hesitation he produced a large clothes-brush from his pocket and whisked it away.

"This, *en tout cas*," said M. Picon, holding the paper up to the light, "was the instrument of blackmail."

"Looks like it," yawned Lord Simon. "Well, I'm going to get some sleep. May have to go a long way to-morrow."

"Really? What for?" I asked, doing my part as questioner readily enough.

"To find Sidney Sewell," he replied.

"Do you think that means going a long way?" I asked, for I already had my own ideas on the subject.

"Quite likely. Well, good night, everyone." He stalked away, followed at a respectful distance by Butterfield.

"And I, too, may have to be absent a little," said M. Picon.

I was beginning to enjoy this. "You too? And where will you go, M. Picon?"

"I, *mon ami?* Who knows? Perhaps to Morton Scone, to see whether the flag is still what you call at half-mast."

He smiled happily at his droll announcement. From the hall I heard Lord Simon offer him a lift to the village, which he accepted.

"Have you thought," murmured Mgr. Smith, "how strange it was that Mr. Rider supposed himself to be Queen Victoria? I should have imagined it would have been Elizabeth. For when a man believes that he is a queen, one would think he would choose the queen who believed herself a man."

I ignored this obvious irrelevance, and turned to Williams.

"What do you think?" I asked wearily. "Are we getting any further?"

"I'm certainly not. And sometimes I wonder whether anybody else is. If we only knew one fact for certain! If there was one witness on whose word we could absolutely rely. But what happens? The servants turn out to be gaol-birds, Strickland is in debt, Rider has been off his head, if he isn't so still, Stall is a blackmailer, and as for Norris— the fellow's a writer and a neurotic, and I wouldn't trust him an inch. What is one to think?"

"We can only fall back on what we saw for ourselves."

"And that was Mary Thurston, lying murdered in a locked room, from which no one could have escaped by the window because there was no time, or by any other way, because there was no place."

"Yet time and place are a murderer's tools," said Mgr. Smith, "that is—if he's a clever murderer."

Once more I ignored him. "We've got no fact to go on. If we only knew who took out the electric light bulb, we should be progressing."

"Do you think so?" chirruped Mgr. Smith. "Because there was practised a crime on the light, I don't see why it should necessarily be a light on the crime."

"Really!" I said, for this was beginning to exasperate me.

Sergeant Beef, I noticed, was fumbling with his un-necessarily large note-book. He coughed impartially. "Now that those amateur gentlemen's gone," he said at last, "there's one or two questions as *I* should like to ask."

Williams smiled kindly. "Really, Beef? And of whom would you like to ask them?"

"Of you, sir. And of this gentleman." He indicated me.

"Fire away, then," said Williams. "Only do remember it's nearly midnight."

"Well, sir, it's not me as 'as kept you here till this hour, talking about flags and 'arf-mast, and son-in-laws, and 'eaven knows what else that's got nothing to do with the murder. I've 'ad to wait to ask my questions. First of all—" he licked his pencil, "first of all, I understand you was talking about murder mysteries before dinner last night. Do you 'appen to remember 'oo started that conversation?"

"I'm afraid I don't. Do you, Townsend?"

Waste of time though I considered it, I did my best to remember, but without success. "No. I can't think. Why? Is it important?"

"Very important," said Beef solemnly. "Very important indeed."

"I really can't see how it possibly can be," I returned, for I had an idea that Beef was only asking questions because the others had done so, and to establish his position in our eyes.

"Well, it is. And now, another thing. How long do you think these larks had been going on?"

"Really, Beef. What 'larks'?" asked Williams.

"Why, between Mrs. Thurston and Fellowes, of course."

Williams stood up. "Look here, Beef. The best thing you can do is to forget about that. We don't want it discussed in every public bar in the village. There was probably nothing in it in any case. Mrs. Thurston was a very kind-hearted and sometimes indiscreet lady. But there was nothing there to feed the local scandalmongers."

"I'm not in the 'abit," said Beef, with elephantine dignity, "of discussing matters like that in the village. And it 'appens to be needful for my enquiries that I should know."

"I can't tell you, I'm afraid," said Williams sharply. "I have said already that there was nothing in it."

"Oh yes there was," said Beef more hotly, "else what

141

about that letter? That wasn't just kind-'eartedness."

"That letter? It may have been anything, It may may have been written years ago. It may have been to her husband."

"Well, Stall was able to put the screws on with it, anyway. There was more in that than met the h'eye."

Williams turned to me. "I think it's disgusting how all sorts of things are dragged out in these cases, and made sordid. Plimsoll's largely to blame. You knew Mary Thurston, Townsend. You will bear me out when I say that she was a good woman, and that all this sort of thing was quite foreign to her?"

"Certainly I will."

"What I should like to know," said the Sergeant, "is whether the Doctor 'ad any notion of what was in the wind."

Williams was thoroughly angry. "Beef," he said, "you are using your position to try and ferret out some nastiness which does not exist. I shall certainly complain to the Chief Constable of this. It is outrageous that a man of your type should be able to come up here and try to infect a tragedy with his own dirty-mindedness. Once and for all I tell you that whoever murdered Mary Thurston, and for whatever motive, there was nothing discreditable in her life to have caused it. I have known her and her husband for many years, and they were decent, upright and devoted in a way that you could probably never realize. Now please say nothing more of that kind."

"I'm only doing my duty, sir," said Beef. And a rather awkward silence followed.

At last the Sergeant turned to me. "There is one question I would like to ask you, sir."

"Well?"

"It's about when you went to look round the grounds. 'Ow long would you say you was out there?"

"Ten minutes or so, I should say."

"And Mr. Norris and Mr. Strickland went with you?"

"Yes."

"Thank you, sir. And now I'll say good night." To our relief he closed his note-book, and took himself off.

When Mgr. Smith had gone up to bed, I faced Williams. I had sympathized deeply with him in his defence of Mary Thurston's good name. "Look here, old man," I said, "as between you and me, have you got any suspicions?"

He shook his head. I saw now, standing close to him, that he looked ill and tired.

"Once or twice it has seemed to me that you and I and Thurston are the only three who have kept sane through all this. They've all seemed a bit hysterical to-night, haven't they?"

"It was pretty gruelling. I'm glad we didn't have to go through it. But these detective fellows seem to be pretty confident."

"Oh, they'll get the right man, of course. They never fail."

"No. Not if there *is* a right man."

"Why, what on earth do you mean?"

"Well, Townsend. I've told you before. I'm the last man to start tinkering with the supernatural. But when reason ends, what are you to do? With my own eyes I saw Mary Thurston lying murdered on her bed. With my own eyes I searched the room while you stood in the doorway. I looked out of the window within ninety seconds of that last scream. And there was no one. I tell you, however you may laugh at me, I don't, I cannot believe that we're dealing with a human murderer. Or if we are, he has a means of moving which is as yet unknown to science."

If Williams had said all this last night it might have disturbed me more. But now I thought of little Mgr. Smith. And I knew that what I called in his talk 'mystic' he would call 'matter-of-fact'. And I knew, somehow, that super-stition could not live in his presence, that whatever else he did he would dissolve the uncharacteristic nonsense that Williams was talking.

"Come along," I said, "let's get some sleep."

CHAPTER 20

I SPENT a very bad night. Looking back on the whole gruesome business, I think that the worst part of it was this period in which we three, who were neither investigators nor suspects, were left in an unpleasant state of doubt, not knowing whom to suspect. Unless one is naturally malicious it is horrible to think of the people round one as potential murderers.

I woke before dawn, and after tossing about miserably for some hours, I dressed, and got downstairs to find the fires only just lit, and having that cheerless smokiness which makes even a position in front of them unencouraging. But looking out of the long windows I saw that it was a glorious morning—warm and still, as though autumn had turned back regretfully for a day. I decided at once to walk down to the hotel, and see Lord Simon. He, I felt, could put my mind at rest. He had admitted that he had suspicions, and his suspicions, I had reason to know, were as good as other people's certainties.

Stall was in the hall, and said good morning much as though this were a normal week-end, and I an ordinary guest. I knew for certain that Stall was at any rate a blackmailer, if he was nothing worse, so that it need be no mere suspicion in his case. I scarcely nodded in reply, and said that I should not be in to breakfast.

It was pleasant walking down the familiar village street in the clear morning air, and my spirits revived a little. This evening, at all events, would put an end to our mistrust, and we would be able to return to our normal lives. And in the meanwhile it was a lovely day.

The man Miles was cleaning brass at the door of the

hotel. I asked him if Lord Simon was up yet.

"Oh yessir," he replied, with none of the defiance that had been in his voice last night. "His lordship has been up some time. His man has just come down to fetch his lordship's breakfast. You'll find him in the sitting-room at the top of the stairs."

"Thank you, Miles," I returned. Again, this unpleasant doubt as to how one should behave. I had no wish to hobnob with a murderer, but the fellow was civil enough.

Against a wildly incongruous background, Lord Simon sat waiting for his breakfast. The room was crowded with a chilly miscellany of knick-knacks and ornaments, gewgaws and trumpery of every kind which had been popular towards the end of the last century. Lord Simon's head was a sober shape against an enormous case of stuffed birds, perched in a grotesque parody of naturalness on lichen-covered branches. Lace was festooned over baize along the mantelpiece, which supported an overmantel as intricate as an Oriental building. A firescreen painted with garish overgrown carnations had been laid aside, a woolly black rug was before the fire, and a bunch of pampas grass stood in a tiled urn in one corner. The table had a green and tasselled tablecloth on it, the furniture was of bloated mahogany, there were muslin curtains on great brass rings and foot-stools in unlikely places.

"Come in—if you can bear it," said Lord Simon, when I hesitated for a moment. "You see what one has to suffer in the cause of truth? Have you ever seen anything like it? It can't be true!" he said, glancing about him. "Had breakfast?"

I explained that I had not waited up at the Thurstons' house—I had been too anxious to see him as soon as possible.

"Good. We'll breakfast together." And Butterfield, entering at that moment with a tray, was sent to get another breakfast.

"I came to see you at this early hour, because I really hoped you might be able to tell me something. You know, it is most unpleasant suspecting everyone in the house in turns. I scarcely slept last night."

Lord Simon nodded, and helped me to kidney and bacon. "I know. Bally awkward. You're just going to ask someone to have a round of golf and you remember that he may be a murderer. Or someone suggests a harmless stroll and you find yourself wonderin' whether you'll ever come back from it."

"That's just it," I said. "And since you understand so well, perhaps you'll clear it all up for me. Who do you think did kill Mary Thurston?"

Lord Simon looked pained, as indeed any famous investigator might, at being faced with so flat a question, and since Butterfield returned at this point with another tray, he became very busy in serving out more breakfast.

"One thing about crime," he commented, "it gives you an appetite." And he concentrated on the kidneys.

"But look here . . ." I began again.

"Tell you what I have done," said Lord Simon cheerfully. "I've found Sidney Sewell."

"You have? Where? At the Thurstons'? Or somewhere else?"

"In the perfectly obvious reference book. Where I ought to have looked in the first place."

"You mean the *London Telephone Directory*? Or *Who's Who*?"

"No. No. In the Gazetteer."

"In the Gazetteer? You mean he . . . it's a *place*?"

"That's it. It's a village about forty miles from here. I'm going there presently. Like to come?"

"But—I don't understand. If it's not a person, but only the name of a village, what's the point in going?"

"Shouldn't ask too many questions," cautioned Lord

Simon, rather archly. "It's not done in the best detective circles. But I don't mind tellin' you this much. I think our visit would clear up another little matter that's troublin' me. This stepson. Elusive sort of bloke. I rather want a word with him."

"And you think . . ."

"That's all I think for the moment," said Lord Simon, lighting his first cigar of the day.

"Well, I'd certainly like to come, it if will elucidate things any quicker."

"That's right. And now . . ." he turned to a heap of papers beside him, "there's a sale at Hodgson's to-day. I really ought to be there. It's awkward confusin' one's interests."

He found the catalogue for which he was looking, and began to study it carefully. Then he rang for Butterfield.

"Look here, Butterfield. Run up to London, will you? One or two lots we might as well have. Nothing terribly special—but there's not much for you to do down here. I've put my limits against the books I shouldn't mind your buying. Here you are. There's the original manuscript of Chaucer's *Parlement of Fowles*. You can get that. Oh, and there's a Faust Bible—the early edition without a date, supposed to be about 1450. Interesting story to that book, Townsend. It caused the whole bag of tricks of the legend about Dr. Faustus. All he was, poor old bloke, was a rather snappy bookseller. He printed his Bibles, nipped 'em across to Paris where nobody had heard of printing, and sold them as manuscript Bibles at sixty crowns a time. This caused a strike among the Bible scribes, who couldn't copy 'em out for less than three hundred crowns, poor devils. It was thought that Dr. Faust was in league with the devil, because he could produce as many as he could sell at this price. The red lettering was supposed to be his blood. So they searched his rooms, and seized his stock. Awkward, wasn't it? And all because he palmed 'em off as manuscripts. Anyway, here's a copy of the bally thing, Butterfield, which we may as well have. *Biblia Sacra Latina Vulgata.* Then I see there's Caxton's *Chronicle of England,* the 1480 edition. Shouldn't mind that. They've got a Shakespeare first folio, too. Mm—nice tall copy, $13\frac{1}{8}$ by $8\frac{1}{2}$, so you may just as well bring it along. Not much of a sale, on the whole, after some I've attended. Still, I think it's worth your while going up, Butterfield."

Butterfield nodded gravely. "Very well, my lord," he said. "Oh, and here are the photographs you required, my lord. I trust that they are all satisfactory. The one of Mr. Townsend is particularly clear, I think."

"Of me?" I said incredulously.

"A formality, old man," said Lord Simon soothingly.

He took the large envelopes which Butterfield handed to him and drew out a number of portraits. I saw, staring unsuspectingly up at me, first Fellowes, then Miles, then Strickland, Norris, and finally an outrageously vulgar likeness of myself.

"Really, Plimsoll," I said.

"Don't worry, Townsend. We had to have snaps of everyone within the age limit. Embarrassin', of course. Have much difficulty in getting them, Butterfield?"

"None at all, my lord. I found a vantage point from which they were framed nicely, one after another, my lord, and I just waited."

Lord Simon enquired no further.

Presently I began telling him about the odd questions which Sergeant Beef had put to Williams and me last night, after he had gone. I said that we could not understand what he was getting at.

"You don't know the police as I do," chuckled Lord Simon.

"But he seems pretty certain that he knows who is guilty."

149

"Of course he does. He has to. The police are always certain, till it is proved that they're wrong."

"I wonder who it is that he suspects."

Lord Simon sighed with some *ennui*. "Probably Norris, I should say."

"Why Norris?"

"Well—one can only have dim glimpses at the official mind. But I should guess it was Norris. You see, Beef doesn't know how the murderer got out of that room. But Norris was at the door when you and Thurston and Williams reached it. He, according to Beef's point of view, was nearest to the crime. Therefore he was guilty."

"Do they really think like that?" I asked.

• "My dear chap, when you've seen as much of them as I have you'll know that they don't think at all. They just guess."

"Good heavens!" I said, with visions of all the murderers in England being arrested, tried and hanged by guesswork.

"Of course," conceded Lord Simon, "here and there in the Force you find a glimmer of intelligence. But something more than intelligence is needed in a case like this. A modicum of imagination, for one thing."

"Just so," I agreed. "I suppose you had to have imagination to know that there was a rope in the water-tank?"

"I suppose so."

I had, as a matter of fact, almost forgotten those ropes, and now that I remembered them they seemed, in the light of last night's enquiries, more mysterious than ever.

"But, Plimsoll," I said, "about those ropes. How *can* they have been used? I swear to you that it was impossible for anyone to have climbed up from Mary Thurston's room and pulled the rope after him in the time. From the moment of the last scream to the time Williams pushed the window open was scarcely a couple of minutes. You can't tell me that a man would have had time to murder Mary Thurston, cross the room, climb on to the rope, close the window, climb the rope to the window above, crawl in, and draw the rope after him? It couldn't have been done."

"I dare say not. But who said anything about climbing the rope?" asked Lord Simon.

"Well, if he dropped down it," I went on decisively, "he must have had an accomplice in the room above to haul it up after him. And even then I doubt if the two ropes together would have been long enough. Besides, what about foot-prints? There was a flower-bed under that window. Are you going to tell me he stopped to rub out his foot-prints in the soil? And if this *was* how it was done, who could it have been? Stall, Fellowes, Norris and Strickland all got to the door of the room too quickly to have come in by the front door. It only leaves the Vicar—or conceivably Miles, if his alibi was not as good as it sounded. And then he would have to have had an accomplice in the apple-room."

Lord Simon smiled. "You've got hold of the wrong end of the rope," he said.

CHAPTER 21

HE drove violently fast, of course. It was not to be supposed of him that in speed, of all things, he should show an uncharacteristic moderation. So I leaned back in the seat of the Rolls, and comforted myself with the somewhat selfish reflection that most other cars were smaller, lighter, and more easily crumpled than this one.

"Strange name for a village—Sidney Sewell," I observed.

"Not really," replied Lord Simon ; "it only seems so because when you first heard it you assumed that it was the name of a man. Almost any place with a double name would seem like that. Horton Kirby, for instance, or Dunton Green. Chalfont St. Giles might easily have been the villain of a Victorian novel, and I see no reason why Compton Abdale (a village in Gloucestershire) should be thought to be the name of a place more than Compton Mackenzie. It just depends on how you hear of them first."

"But what made you think of Sidney Sewell as a village?"

"I didn't. I just tried it in all the reference books I could lay hands on. There chanced to be an out-of-date telephone directory which I got from the post office, and a *Times* Atlas which I found at the hotel."

We purred quietly over a narrow bridge at fifty miles an hour, and ten minutes later I was relieved to catch a glimpse as we shot by, of the name Sidney Sewell on a signpost. It was something to have got as near as that without actual disaster.

The village itself was a pleasant and rather dignified one. The central street was divided from the houses on each side of it by wide grass strips, which gave the whole place an air of spaciousness. We were travelling through it at a still fairly considerable speed when Lord Simon applied his brakes with skilled force, and brought us to a standstill.

"Good Lord—look at that!" he said.

Now all I could see was the quiet village street before us, with very little traffic and scarcely a human being in sight. There was a butcher's shop over to our right, from the door of which the proprietor was watching us rather indifferently. On our left was an inn called the 'Black Falcon', and a blue saloon motor-car stood outside. Next to the inn, and nearer to us, was a garage. But nowhere in the placid and normal scene could I see anything which might have caused Lord Simon's exclamation. Unwilling, however, to admit that I was less perceptive than he was, I waited for him to reveal more.

"That car," he said at last. "Surely you know it? Thurston's."

I looked again at the blue saloon. It was a standard model of Austin make. I did not see how I could be expected to recognize it, and said so.

Lord Simon sounded quite irritable. "Have you ever heard of index numbers?" he asked. "That's Thurston's all right."

I realized what I was expected to say in order to restore Lord Simon's good humour, and the tone in which I should say it. "Then what on earth is it doing here?" I asked.

"Fairly obvious, don't you feel?" said Lord Simon, smiling amiably again.

It was, of course, far from obvious to me, but it was pleasant to have our respective roles happily restored, and I nodded.

Lord Simon, with a bold sweep of his large car, drove straight into the garage, and told a mechanic there that he wished to leave it under cover for half an hour or so. He saw that it was place in the far recesses of the corrugated iron building, out of sight of the road, and we walked out of the place.

He led the way, however, not past the windows of the inn, but into the yard at the back, and went up to a small back door. He knocked rather gently, and presently an untidy woman opened it.

"Yes?" she said unencouragingly.

"Oh, would you mind tellin' us where the gentlemen from that car may be? I mean the car standing in front of your house."

The woman eyed him curiously. "What business would it be of yours?"

"Nothing really. Just my silly curiosity," smiled Lord Simon, and handed her a ten-shilling note.

"They're in the private bar," she replied sulkily.

"How many of them?"

"Three."

"Three? That's odd. Is there another bar?"

"There's the public."

"Can it be seen from theirs?"

"No. It can't. There's glass partitions round the counter, to prevent prying and spying."

"But the same bar serves them both?"

"Yes. Anything else you want to know? Haven't you got nothing better to do than ask questions?"

"Yes. Something far better. We'll have a drink. And we'll have it in the public bar. And we won't talk there, if you don't mind. And you won't mention that we're here. That's for two whiskies. My friend likes whisky—drinks it with lobster. Keep the change. Now which is the way?"

Through an untidy kitchen in which washing was hung to dry the woman led us to a door, and left us alone with a large cat. We sat down in silence and waited.

The voices which came through from the other bar were not loud, and the words they spoke were indistinguishable. But the speakers could be identified. Fellowes—I distinctly heard him say, "Cheerio, sir!"—Strickland, who called for

"Three more!" in his rather thick, deep voice, and, to my surprise, Alec Norris, whose shrill laugh would have been recognizable anywhere.

The atmosphere was musty, the advertisements on the wall out of date and dismal, and the words of those in the other bar inaudible. I was beginning to get thoroughly impatient, when I heard some movement, and Strickland's voice raised.

"Wait here, then, Fellowes," he said, and his voice came from this side of the room. "We shan't be more than a quarter of an hour."

There was a slight tinkle in the shutting of the door, indicating that it was glass, as ours was, then a ring of feet on an iron mat at the door. Looking out of the window of our bar we could see Strickland and Norris setting off together along the road by which we had entered the village.

Lord Simon did not hesitate. He walked straight through into the private bar and confronted Fellowes. But the chauffeur, beyond putting down his drink and facing us, remained undisturbed.

"Interestin' meetin'," began Lord Simon, "I wonder what you'd happen to be doin' here?"

"Obeying orders," Fellowes returned.

"Indeed? Whose orders?"

"Dr. Thurston's. He told me to take these two gentlemen wherever they wished to go."

"Did you ask him, then?"

"Yes. Of course I did. When they said they wanted a run in the car somewhere, it wasn't for me to take them without permission. So I asked Dr. Thurston."

"And what did he say?"

"He told me not to bother him. Take them anywhere."

"So you decided to come to Sidney Sewell."

Fellowes was silent for a moment, then said, "No. I didn't choose it. They said where they wanted to go."

155

"Mm. So you've no idea why this place was chosen?"

"No."

"You had no object in coming here yourself?"

"No."

"Rather good at monosyllables, aren't you, Fellowes?'

"Don't know what you mean."

We returned to the public bar. Lord Simon seemed rather quiet, even perplexed at that moment. But very shortly we saw Strickland and Norris returning. Fellowes must have told them at once of our presence, for Strickland burst into the room, and Norris followed him.

"What the devil do you mean by trailing us about like this?" Strickland asked furiously.

"Cool down, my lad," drawled Lord Simon. "Can't a fellow have a run in a car without all this excitement?"

"Don't talk rot, Plimsoll," shouted Strickland. "You followed us here! You must have. As for you, Townsend, sneaking round with these dam' detectives—I'm disgusted. Are you trying to prove that I did this murder?"

There was a high-pitched question from behind him. "Perhaps you suspect me?" asked Alec Norris.

Lord Simon smiled to them with aloof boredom. "My dear old boys, don't work yourselves up. You'll know soon enough whom I suspect. Nice place, Sidney Sewell. Ever been here before, Strickland?"

"Oh, I'm sick of answering your silly questions, Plimsoll. Come on, Fellowes, we'll get home."

And the three of them marched out. From the window we watched Fellowes get into the driving-seat, and Strickland and Norris sit behind.

"Well, well, well," said Lord Simon.

The interview had made me uncomfortable. If Strickland turned out not to be the murderer it would be awkward when we met again, for I certainly seemed guilty of spying.

156

Detection was, after all, Plimsoll's job, but for me, it would seem, there could be little excuse.

"And now," said Lord Simon, as we walked out into the pale autumn sunset, "I have one more call to make. I wonder where we are likely to find the post office?"

I proved myself helpful by stopping a passer-by and enquiring. It was a hundred yards down the street I was told, and we set out briskly together.

"I wonder whether you'd mind awfully just waitin' outside for me a moment?" asked Lord Simon, when we had reached the little general store which combined its business with that of the G.P.O. "Sorry to be ill-mannered and all that, don't you know."

"Oh, not a bit," I said, presuming that he wished to make a private telephone call.

But it was not long before he returned, smiling broadly. I began to think that all this investigation was giving me detective habits, for I had already deduced that he must have been on the 'phone to the Thurstons', since he had not had time for a long-distance call, when he said suddenly:

"Well, that settles that."

"What?" I asked obligingly.

"The identity of the stepson."

"You know who it is?"

"Yes. I know who it is."

"Then your case is complete?"

"Remarkably complete."

"And you're not going to tell me?"

"Terribly sorry, old boy. Against all professional etiquette. You shall hear this evening, I promise you. Interestin' case, though. Very interestin' case." And he continued to smile contentedly as he drove us back at a slightly less breakneck speed.

CHAPTER 22

AFTER lunch I met M. Picon in the garden of the Thurstons' house. He was stooping to pull a weed from an almost flawless border. Knowing that one of the investigators had solved the whole problem, I felt that I could afford to speak to him quite light-heartedly, and did so.

"Well, Monsieur Picon, have you completed your theory?"

He looked up at me and said, "Ah, *mon ami*, it is you. No doubt you know everything, is it not?"

"Well, not exactly," I admitted.

"Nor, to speak the truth, do I. Last night we exhausted the enquiries here. Now we must look somewhere else."

I was amused, thinking to myself that after all Lord Simon had beaten him to the solution. But I only said, "Where will you look now?"

"In the *heart*, my friend. When the brains show no more one must look in the heart, and there, *voilà!* the truth."

"I should not have suspected you of such sentimentality," I said.

"That is not sentiment—it is logic. The heart may guide as truly as the head. And now, would you like a little *promenade?*"

"Is it far?"

"A few miles. Not too far."

"Where on earth are you going to?" I asked.

"To the village of Morton Scone."

I laughed outright. "Look here, Monsieur Picon," I said, "I don't know what you want to go there for, nor what your theory is, but I can tell you this much. You don't need to bother. I've been with Lord Simon this morning, and he's found out about Sidney Sewell. It isn't a person, as we all thought, but a place. In fact I went there with him this morning. And while we got there Fellowes and Strickland and Norris had arrived. So Lord Simon knows everything now."

"Your reasoning, *mon ami*, is a little confused. What information did Lord Simon glean from the arrival of this so indicative trio and the village of Sidney Sewell?"

"I don't know that, of course. But he told me he knew the murderer."

"And do you think that I, Amer Picon, do not know also the murderer? And what is that, to know the murderer?"

"I thought that is what we were all trying to do," I returned innocently.

"Then you are mistaken. What we have to do is not to know ourselves, but to prove to others. If we cannot, what have we accomplished? The good Bœuf would arrest his man, and the murderer would go free."

"But surely Lord Simon must realize that. After all, he's had nearly as much experience as you have."

"Maybe. But everyone his method of proof. And a part of mine is a promenade to Morton Scone. Do you accompany me?"

"I shall be delighted. Only if after this Monsignor Smith wants me to go with him to Jericho, I shan't be surprised."

"You might do worse," said M. Picon seriously. "He would know much of the ancient city. But come along. We have not too much time."

I was surprised at the brisk pace that he set. His legs were short, but his remarkable agility made it hard for me to keep up with him. However, I had set myself to see as much of the methods of all three of these great men as I could, and was willing enough to make the effort. Now that they were nearing the end of the chase, every move they made should be interesting.

"I'm afraid I haven't been able to help you much, Monsieur Picón," I said after a long silence.

"*Au contraire*, my friend, your evidence has been of the greatest service to me. You remembered something of the utmost importance, which you might well have forgotten."

"What was that?"

"You do not know? But naturally, your own part in this affair."

"*My* part?" I almost shouted.

"But yes. You, too, had a hand in it. Oh, but quite unconscious, I assure you. Still, a part."

"Good Lord. What on earth was that?"

"Did you not rise and open the door?"

"Which door? When?"

"But naturally. The door of the lounge. Just before the screams were heard."

"Well, yes. I did. But I fail to see what that could have to do with it. Unless . . ." A new and horrible idea flashed into my brain. "Unless there was some devilish mechanism in that room which I set in motion."

"Fortunately," said M. Picón, "the machine is not yet invented which will cut a lady's throat while she lies waiting for it, and throw the knife from the window, then disappear from the face of the earth."

"I suppose not," I admitted.

We marched on in the sunlight, which had begun to pale a little. I was glad of the fresh air and exercise, and glad, too, of some activity which filled in the afternoon, for my impatience to know the murderer's identity would otherwise have become feverish. To think that at last, after all this guesswork, I was to know the truth. I resolved to think no more about the murder, for otherwise I should start once again to suspect each in turn of the people at the Thurstons'.

We must have been within half a mile of Morton Scone

when M. Picon suddenly took my arm, and said, "*Vite!* This way!"

I was so much taken by surprise that for a moment I hesitated. He pulled me quite fiercely, however, to the side of the road, and almost bundled me through a hole in the hedge. He had scarcely time to follow, when a car approached. I had been aware of it a moment before, when it had been in the distance and beyond a dip which had taken it out of sight, but I had paid no attention to it. The little detective, however, seemed to be in a state of tremendous excitement.

"Observe!" he snapped, as he stared at the roadway we had left.

It was once again Dr. Thurston's dark-blue car, and since it was not travelling fast I had ample time to recognize its occupants. Fellowes was driving, and beside him sat the girl Enid, while in the rear seat, smoking a cigar, was Miles.

"You see?" said M. Picon, as soon as the car had gone past. "What I have said! Look in the heart, my friend. When the mind no longer tells tales, look in the heart!"

"But Monsieur Picon," I exclaimed, "this is too much! This morning I went to Sidney Sewell, and saw Fellowes with two of the suspects; this afternoon I come to Morton Scone, and here he is with another two!"

M. Picon laughed. "And perhaps, when you go to Jericho with the excellent Monsignor Smith you will find him there with some more!"

"But what does it mean?" I asked.

"Patience, my friend."

"But how did you know, while it was still a long way off, that that was the Thurstons' car?"

"I did not. But I thought it might be. I was expecting it."

"You were? What made you expect it?"

"Oh, but you must understand I was not expecting it

with any great confidence. But I knew it had gone this way, and I thought that possibly, possibly, mind you, it would return."

"You knew that they were going to Morton Scone, then?"

"I had an idea. no more. A small idea. But the ideas of Amer Picon at times come true, you see."

"Well, that one certainly did, though I'm hanged if I know what to make of it."

"And I wonder what the good Bœuf would make of it. His partner in the brave game of darts, is it not?"

I smiled at that.

"Yes, I wonder. Who do you think he suspects, Monsieur Picon? He seems pretty sure of himself, whoever it is."

"Probably the so skilled and expert cook, I should think," said M. Picon. "But then your English police are not of the most intelligent when it is a matter of crime."

"Not in this case," I admitted.

Suddenly I stopped short. "Monsieur Picon!" I exclaimed.

"What have you, *mon ami?*"

I burst out laughing. "What a couple of fools we are!" I said.

"For that, in your so English proverb, you must speak for yourself," he returned huffily.

"No. But don't you see? We've walked about a quarter of a mile since we saw that car. And all for nothing. You have seen what you set out to see. We could have turned back at once."

"And who knows what I set out to see?"

"Well, it was obviously the car, coming back from Morton Scone, with Fellowes and the rest of them in it."

"That was almost an accident."

"Then you still must go on to the village?"

"Naturally."

"But whatever for?"

"You have surely forgotten one all-important detail. The flag on the tower of Morton Scone church was at half-mast, is it not so?"

"Yes. But . . ."

"*Allons.*"

I obeyed. But inwardly I revolted. I began to think that M. Picon was deliberately mystifying me, or that, having absent-mindedly continued walking to Morton Scone as I suggested, he now pretended that it was necessary, in order to save his face. But as we were approaching the village I had another idea.

"I know!" I said, "you think it was a double murder. The doctor in this village died the same day. You connect the two?"

"The doctor was very old, and had a weak heart. He knew himself that he might die at any time. His death was perfectly natural."

"Then what *has* Morton Scone got to do with it?"

We had reached a point on a gentle hill-side from which most of the village was clearly visible. It was a pleasant Sussex village, whose predominant colour was that quiet red to which bricks and tiles are toned in the process of time. There were houses with plaster fronts and houses with timbered fronts, and an inn sign hung across the footpath.

"Perhaps nothing at all. Perhaps a great deal," said M. Picon very thoughtfully.

He did not move for at least a whole minute, and then only to turn and look up at me with a frankly puzzled face.

"Tell me, Monsieur Townsend," he said, "do you notice anything strange about this place?"

Strange? It seemed to be the embodiment of all things homely and familiar, all things I loved most dearly. One might have chosen it to settle in, after a vagrant life. Laughter and inn fires', I thought of, and kindly little sweet-shops kept by the sort of elderly stout women who may be called a 'body'. Even as we looked a farm-cart started on its way through the street, and the man who walked at its horse's head shouted a cheerful greeting to someone in a window. Here was friendliness and a quiet sequence of days for a number of calm and normal people, here were gardens, no doubt, and a little school muddling its children through their reading, writing and arithmetic. Here were honest folk and very English houses. Certainly nothing that I could call 'strange'.

"It may seem strange to you, Monsieur Picon," I said, "but to an Englishman I assure you this village . . ."

He interrupted me most rudely, and said, "No, no. I do not mean that. It is strange for lack of something. For see, school, inn, police station, and post office no doubt, but where do you see, my good friend, the *church?*"

And I found myself gaping back at the village, realizing the implications of its absence.

CHAPTER 20

"So Fellowes was lying?" I suggested, as we walked on, "He hadn't got an alibi at all?"

"I hope not," said M. Picon, "for in that case our walk will have been quite wasted."

I thought it best to say nothing after that, and we continued in silence till M. Picon saw an old man stacking a bonfire in a kitchen garden beside the road.

"*Pardon*," he called. "Could you please direct me to the church?"

The old man stared at him for a moment. "The church? It's the best part of a mile from here," he said. "Your shortest way is by the footpath."

"But the road also goes, *n'est-ce pas?*"

"Oh yes, you can go by the road if you want to, but it is the longest way round."

"I would like to go by the road."

"All right. Keep straight on through the village till you come to the petrol station, then turn left. It's a quarter of an hour's walk. You can't miss it."

"Thank you," said M. Picon, and strode off again, his short legs moving at considerable speed.

"Turn to the left at the petrol station," called the old man after us, as though he regretted that our chat had been so short. "You can't miss it," he repeated.

I kept at Picon's side, but not in the best of humour. "Why can't we go by the footpath?" I asked. "He said it was shorter."

Picon made absolutely no reply to this, except to turn to me with a brief but disarming smile. So that I could do nothing but hurry along with him. We passed right through the village, and I had not even a chance to stop and glance at some of the more interesting old houses. And we had left the last building behind by some five hundred yards or so, before a sudden turn in the road brought us within sight of the church. At that we stopped, and Picon stood looking intently towards its tower. I did not see why he should stare like that, for a glance would have told him that there was no longer a flag flying on it, whether at half-mast or not.

Farther down the road on our left was a cottage, the only building visible between us and the church. Towards this the extraordinary little man hurried, murmuring "*Voilà!*" "*Allons!*" "*Vite!*" "*Là, la!*" "*Mon ami!*" and others of his favourite expressions. Reaching the small wicket gate he did not hesitate, but lifted the latch, and walked up a brick path to the front door. He knocked vigorously.

"Really, Picon," I said, "what can you want at this house?"

For some time there was no reply to his knocking, but at last a woman's voice shouted from somewhere in the cottage, "Come round to the back, will you?"

Picon looked at me enquiringly, not knowing some English habits. "It's all right," I said. "This door probably won't open at all. Hasn't been moved for years."

We went obediently round to the back door, where a thin woman with straggling dark hair and very dirty clothes stood waiting for us. "Yes. What is it?" she said, eyeing us somewhat suspiciously.

"I wanted to ask you a question or two," said Picon, raising his hat with a rather foreign show of gallantry.

"Oh, you did. Well, I don't want any brushes—not however good they are. I've got enough to do my housework, thank you."

Picon turned to me. "Brushes?" he whispered enquiringly.

"She thinks you're a commercial traveller," I said in his ear.

166

He turned to her smiling. "*Mais non, madame!* I do not wish to sell you anything. It is not that. A little question, no more. Now . . ."

"Well, I never give anything, not to those what collects at the door. As my 'usband says, you never know what 'appens to the money. And goodness knows I've none to spare. You might just as well collect for me, I'm sure I need it as much as any."

"No, no!" cried Picon, "I ask for no money. It is information I should like, if you please. Perhaps you could tell me . . .'

"Why, we had the man round with the voters' list only last week," the woman said. "It's my belief you're a fraud."

"*Madame*, would you please tell me whether you noticed a blue car stop in this road on Friday afternoon?" He brought out his question in one breath, frightened that he would be interrupted again before it was finished.

The woman seemed to be impressed. She wiped her hands on her skirt, and took a step nearer to us. "Friday? That's the day Mrs. Thurston was murdered, isn't it?"

She could not yet believe that such good fortune as this had come to her—to be a person actually questioned in connection with a matter so topical, so stirring and so famous as a local murder.

"Yes," said Picon patiently.

"Have you got anything to do with it?" asked the woman eagerly. "Is it something of that that brings you here asking questions off of me?"

"Yes."

"Well!" She was spellbound. It was a great moment for her. She looked from one to the other of us. "Fancy that!" she said.

"And now perhaps you could tell me about the motor-car?" insisted Picon gently.

"Motor-car. Motor-car." She was driving her brain to its

utmost. Even now this glorious moment of importance might escape her. But her eyes lit up. "Yes!" she said shrilly, "there was a motor-car stop outside of 'ere!" Then her voice dropped. "But then it's the one that often does."

"What is it like?"

"Dark blue. Driven by a chauffeur."

"And you say it often stops here?"

"Well, yes. Pretty often. Several of them do, you know. They leave their cars here while they go for a walk through the woods. Especially when the primroses is out. We get quite a lot then. My 'usband always says he's going to put a notice 'NO PARKING' on our gate, but he never does. We don't get so many this time of year, of course. But this blue one's been more than once lately. You see"—she became conspiratorial—"you see, the young fellow what drives it brings 'is young lady, and off they goes for a walk through the woods. Well, it's famous, that footpath."

"And on Friday?" said M. Picon, not so much prompting her as keeping her relevant.

"Oh yes, they was here on Friday, because that's the afternoon I does my washing, and I remember seeing the car in the road while I was hanging it out. There was a nice breeze, too, I was thankful for, seeing that I had more than usual . . ."

"And you say they both came? The chauffeur and his girl?"

"Yes, they was both there because I 'eard 'em quarrelling."

Picon started. "You heard them quarrelling?"

"Yes, cat and dog they was when they got out of the car. Only not like anyone as is married—that's different."

"Did you hear what they said?"

"No, I didn't. And shouldn't like to of, neither. I never believe in listening to what doesn't concern me. All I know is they was on about something, and 'ard at it till they went down the footpath. I don't know what happened after that, though I can well guess."

"No doubt," said M. Picon dryly. "And when they returned?"

"Oh, it was all over then. Sunshine after the storm, as you might say. I saw them coming up the road together, arm-in-arm they was."

"And you heard nothing, absolutely nothing that passed between them?"

"Not a word. Well, I'd never listen to other people's conversation."

"What did they look like?"

The woman gave an incoherent but sufficient description of Fellowes and Enid, and M. Picon, by asking a few questions, confirmed their identity with the two whom the woman had seen.

"Eh, *bien*, I thank you, *madame*. You have been of the very greatest assistance to me."

"That's all right," said the woman. "Do you think I shall be wanted at the trial?"

"I can't tell you, I'm afraid."

"I suppose I shall 'ave my photo took, won't I?"

"That is for the newspapers to decide. But at all events you have the satisfaction of knowing that you have materially assisted me in my search for truth."

This did not seem to please the woman very much, but when M. Picon once more elaborately raised his hat she managed to smile.

"*Au revoir, madame*," said M. Picon, and we left her gazing after us.

"But, Picon," I began, scarcely able to wait until we were out of earshot of the cottage, "how did you know that you would get your information there, of all places?"

"*Mon ami*, are you really so short-sighted? Could you not see that it is the only house near a point from which one would notice that the flag on the tower was at half-mast?"

"Picon! You're a genius!" I exclaimed, and did not

grumble at the long walk home.

"And now," said Picon, "for a little I must think, and then, perhaps, all is complete. *Voyons.* Amer Picon will not be so far behind, after all. There is light now. Oh yes, my friend, plenty of light. A little thought, and I see all. A most ingenious crime. A most ingenious crime."

"Well, I wish I could see anything at all. If this visit of Fellowes and Enid's means so much, what was Fellowes doing with that other pair this morning? Perhaps it was a murder by a sort of committee, Picon?" I suggested, conscious that my guesses were getting wilder and wilder, as the evidence grew more confused. "Perhaps they were *all* in it?"

M. Picon smiled. "No. I do not think they were all in it," he said.

"Then . . . but hang it all, Picon, I don't believe you've solved it after all. You may have discovered who had the best motives, but what none of you seem to think about is that room. It was bolted, I tell you, and I never moved from the door while Williams searched it. How are you going to explain that? You may have proved that Fellowes was lying when he said he never took Enid that afternoon, but how will that help you? You've got to explain a miracle."

"No, *mon ami.* The miracle would be if Madame Thurston lived, not that she is dead. This scheme was irresistible, and it seemed undiscoverable. But it was worked out without remembering Amer Picon—the great Amer Picon. For your police—pah! It would never have been discovered. But to-night you shall see. I will tell you all you want to know. Everything shall be made plain to you. I promise."

"If you do that you're a wonder. Do you know sometimes lately I have almost begun to agree with Williams, that there was something sinister, something occult?"

"Sinister, yes. But there was no magic here," said M. Picon, as we reached the outskirts of our own village.

CHAPTER 24

M. PICON left me in the village, where he was staying, and I hurried on towards the house alone. It was dusk now and in the autumn breeze, which had risen with the evening, the trees cracked and swayed. I was thinking how pleasant it would be to warm my hands over a fire and drink some hot tea, when I noticed something in the road before me which at first seemed too shapeless for a human being, as though a sack of coals had become animated and was moving forward between the hedges. As I came nearer I recognized Mgr. Smith.

I had noticed that people who had not the advantage of a long acquaintance with him, often expressed a wholly superfluous pity for the little man who had the trick of appearing vague and ineffectual. So I was determined not to sympathize with him over the fact that both Lord Simon and M. Picon had got ahead of him, lest I should find myself looking foolish when he revealed that he had solved the problem long ago.

Besides, Dr. Tate, the local G.P., was with him, and addressed me at once. "I have been telling our friend here." he said, "of a rather curious legend connected with this village. I thought it might be rather in his line."

I could see that Mgr. Smith was smiling at that, but he made no reply and Dr. Tate continued. "The archæologists call it the story of the Angel of Death," he said, "but I don't know how that name was first used. It seems that the story itself had been handed down from mediæval times, when the house that is now called Tipton Farm House was the only habitation of any size about here, and must have been something like a small castle. It was in ruins for centuries, and rebuilt in Georgian times. If you go there any time you can see that some of the walls are three feet thick. What those walls could tell!"

"Why?" asked Mgr. Smith innocently. "Does their thickness mean that they are the kind of walls which have ears?"

Dr. Tate continued. "I forget the name of the family," he admitted, "but they were, of course, Catholics, and had all the faith of people of your religion in bogeys, and what not."

"Bogeys?" asked Mgr. Smith.

"Well, you know the sort of thing."

"I'm afraid I don't," said Mgr. Smith.

"Well, hang it, do you believe in devils?" challenged Dr. Tate.

"Do you believe in germs?" retorted Mgr. Smith.

Dr. Tate decided to leave this treacherous ground. "At all events, the members of this family were superstitious. And the head of it, Sir Giles something or other, was the most superstitious of all. For years before he finally died, he claimed to have visions of the death that awaited him. It was no ordinary death . . ."

"What is an ordinary death?" asked Mgr. Smith.

"Well—death from some illness . . . death in bed."

"I see. An ordinary death is one in which the deceased was attended by a doctor, perhaps?"

"Yes. No. I mean . . . well, whatever an ordinary death may be, the death visualized for himself by Sir Giles was very far from ordinary. He said he could see him coming— the Angel of Death himself. He came through the air on great black wings. He was clad in black from head to foot, and he held a sword in his hand.

"What was the sword for?" asked Mgr. Smith.

"To strike with."

"I see. I thought its use might be to perform an operation."

"Sir Giles saw this a number of times—always the same.

172

The Angel of Death came winging through the air from a great distance, and came to avenge himself on the unfortunate Sir Giles."

"To avenge himself? What had Sir Giles done to him, then?" asked Mgr. Smith.

"He was a very loose-living old fellow. And these visions were a good deal a source of repentance. He seemed to think that the Angel of Death would strike him for his sins. Mind you, I'm only telling you the local story."

"I know. I hope it has a happy ending."

"At last, it seemed, the Angel of Death struck. The old man had been behaving outrageously, even according to the standards of those days. And he seemed to expect that he would suffer for it. He said that he had seen the black wings beating their way nearer several times. And at last one evening he went up into a tower of his castle alone, and did not reappear for some hours. The household grew anxious, and presently one of his sons went up to look for him. He found the old man lying in his own blood on the floor of the topmost room, not quite dead, but on the point of expiry."

"And what were his last words?" asked Mgr. Smith, who seemed to be enjoying the whole story in a chuckling sort of way.

"The son raised his father's head, and the old man nodded to the window, or port-hole, or whatever they had in castles then. 'Death came on wings!' he whispered, and then expired."

"And how had he died?"

"That is the interesting part of the story," said Dr. Tate. "It was never known how he died. There had been a sentry at the foot of the stairs all the time the old man was up in his tower, and a thorough search was made of the whole building without any success. The room in which he was found was thirty feet from the ground, and no weapon was discovered. So the people in the house, being as I said, superstitious . . ."

"Oh, they were all superstitious. You did not tell us that."

"Well, what can you expect they were in those dark ages? Anyhow, they believed of course that the vision of the old man had come to pass, and the Angel of Death had struck him at last."

"I see. So his murderer was never discovered?"

"No. What do you think of the story?"

"I think that like many good stories it is a lie."

"Oh."

"But you are quite right in thinking that I should be interested in the story. Is it well known about here?"

"Very. It would be difficult for anyone to live in the parish long without hearing it. Why, I believe that our crazy Vicar even used it in one of his sermons the other day. Sort of warning to people who misbehaved themselves. But then he's an unaccountable chap. Well, I turn in here. Little girl with whooping cough. I hope you clear up this rather more urgent mystery of ours. Terrible business. I'm not an advocate of capital punishment myself, but I think that the man who killed Mary Thurston ought to be hanged. Good night to you both. Good night."

Dr. Tate turned into a narrow drive and left us to complete our walk alone. I was thinking quickly. Something in the story had caught my imagination. The idea of death coming on wings. The mystery of Mary Thurston's death was to me so baffling that nothing seemed too far-fetched. Suppose—of course I knew it was fantastic—but suppose that someone could fly like that? Even if it was only from a first-floor window to a point on the ground far enough away from the walls to leave no sign of landing. Was it, after all, so impossible? I remembered, as a boy, experimenting in jumps from the roof of a shed with an open umbrella in my hand to break the fall. The experiments had not been very successful, but still . . .

After all, it was not as though the murderer would have

had to fly *in* at the window. It was only *out* of it. Surely some contrivance, perhaps in the nature of a parachute, would have been possible. Or wings of some kind. There were such things as gliders. Was I really a fool to wonder about such possibilities?

I turned to my companion. "Don't you think that perhaps this story of murder might be relevant to our problem?"

"Any story of murder might be relevant to our problem," he replied, "from the story of Cain and Abel onwards."

"But isn't it conceivable that something of the sort might have happened here?"

Mgr. Smith turned to me. "It is hard enough to find what actually did happen without looking for all the things that might have happened. A dragon might have flown in at the window and with his tongue which is a sword have done the deed. A newly-invented balloon might have hung over the house like a cloud and lowered the murderer to the window. A man might have made a miraculous leap to the window-sill, and afterwards have projected himself into the boughs of a neighbouring elm tree. Or I might have been hiding all the evening under the bed, and have changed myself into a rat on your approach. Yet it is not very helpful either for me or for Dr. Tate to invent these sensational hypotheses."

"You do know then," I said with some relief, "what really did happen, and who is guilty?"

I was waiting breathlessly for his answer when he suddenly caught my arm, and we stopped. There was a slope of the downs above us, and its outline was as smooth and distinct as that of a dome. There was a clump of trees bent by many years of wind, and maintaining their distracted lives in spite of it. I can see their shape and the edge of the hill to this day, for there was one detail in that silhouette which made it memorable to me.

It was such a detail as my companion liked, and of the kind to which he was accustomed. Black against the oyster-blue sky of dusk were two figures, a tall and a shorter one. It was not only their position against the sky which made them look black, their clothes were black, too, and there was something fluttering about the smaller one. I started. What were those limply flapping things at the man's side, which hung now close against him, now rising flippantly in the breeze? Could they be . . .

But in a moment I told myself not to be a fool. There was nothing unnatural about the man's outline. Its flapping appearance was produced by a black Inverness cape, and having realized that, I knew that it was the Vicar.

Mgr. Smith blinked in the blank and innocent way which I knew concealed his most intelligent discoveries. He watched the two coming down the hill towards the Thurstons' house, holding the crook of his umbrella with both his hands. And as he did so, all my confidence in the solutions of Lord Simon and M. Picon evaporated. After all, where had they got me? This morning, I had, in company with Lord Simon, seen three of the suspects, and he had told me that his theory was complete. This afternoon, on my walk with M. Picon, I had observed three more, and he, too, had solved the riddle. And now, in this maddening moment, here was Mgr. Smith, blinking in his unmistakably ominous way at the remaining two. (For the other figure was recognizable by now as that of Stall.) So that really, after motoring eighty miles or so, walking eight, and standing in a chilly breeze staring at the outline of the downs, I was no nearer to the truth than I had been last night.

I scarcely needed to repeat my question to Mgr. Smith when he at last walked on. "You *do* know then?" I almost whispered.

"Yes," he said, "I know."

CHAPTER 25

ONCE more we were in the library—Williams, Lord Simon, M. Picon, Mgr. Smith, Sergeant Beef and I. Dr. Thurston had offered to come, but the investigators had agreed that since all the details were now to be revealed, it would be too painful for him. Nor was his presence necessary. He would hear of the arrest later.

I do not exaggerate when I say that my excitement was terrific, and I have no doubt that Williams was just as expectant. It was not merely that the mystery was to be elucidated, but that a human being was to be sent to a certain death—for with three such detectives to find evidence, surely no Counsel in the world would be able to exonerate him. And this may have made our interest a morbid one, but it naturally gave real point and drama to the proceedings. Someone was to be named, arrested, tried and hanged—someone we knew, someone we had conversed with to-day. I looked down at my hand and saw that it was slightly trembling.

Just as Lord Simon had been the first to interrogate each of the witnesses, he began speaking now. "I may as well outline this unfortunate affair," he said, "and then my colleagues can amplify or correct any of the details. How would that do?"

M. Picon nodded, and Mgr. Smith did not dissent, so Lord Simon began to talk. There was a silence almost uncanny in the room as he drawled out the circumstances.

"Interestin' case," he said, "but not quite as bafflin' as it looked at first. However, it has kept us guessin' for a time, so let's give it its due. Clearin' up most crimes is as simple as shellin' bally peas. This certainly wasn't that.

"First of all we must go back a little way. Remember that will? Unfortunate sort of document, when you come to think of it. Mrs. Thurston's first husband had a biggish fortune. And between that fortune and the son who felt a right to it he set only one barrier—a woman's life. There you have the foundation of the whole story. Conventional enough in essence. Motive, as usual, money.

"The stepson you remember was abroad when that will was made, and may or may not have heard of his father's death. We know from Thurston that he was the type of chappie who was always turning up without a bob, to rest on his laurels and the family honour for a spell, so that his coming home may have been just the customary sort of thing. But in the meantime he had changed his name. You know how these things happen? Half a dozen creditors, some little eccentricity in the way in which a cheque was drawn—something a trifle shady. So stepson arrives with a brand-new name, an empty pocket, and a lot of curiosity. Still conventional, you see.

"And the very first news that falls on his flappers is that his old man has kicked the bucket, and his step-mother has married again. Well, well, thinks Stepson, and pops off down to his father's solicitor to ask about the will. Unpleasant set-back. Interest left to the wife for lifetime; and only his measly allowance to go on with. He had never seen Mrs. Thurston, you remember, so that not even knowing her as the good-natured soul she was, he set about cursing roundly at scheming females who nipped in to pinch his birthright. He was a very furious young man.

"I don't know whether any of you have been reversionary legatees, and had to twiddle your thumbs while someone lives on the money which will one day be yours. I'm told it's the most demoralizin' business. The most virtuous and temperate natures grow potentially murderous. But this fellow was not exactly a born murderer. He wanted

178

money. He meant to get money. But if he thought of murder in the first place he was headed off by the penalty. The fortune involved had surprised him. The details had been given him by the solicitor, and the sum left by his father made his eyes pop. And since he knew there was so much money in question he wasn't the lad to hang back.

"So he started. more or less begging—which might have been harmless enough. He found out that Mrs. Thurston was living here, and had a car, so he ran down to a village which was just near enough to make a meeting feasible, yet not too near. And from this village, which was called Sidney Sewell, he wrote to Mrs. Thurston. That first letter, one supposes, was quite a polite and pleasant affair. Regret over his father's death. Sorry he had never met his stepmother. Usual sort of thing laid on with a trowel, perhaps, but nothing too stirring.

"However, I feel convinced that it contained one phrase which troubled Mrs. Thurston a good deal—a request that she should say nothing to her husband. What reason he gave one cannot possibly suggest now, but it is pretty certain that he found a good reason. Good enough, anyway, for as we know Mrs. Thurston never mentioned to her husband that her stepson had reappeared. More's the pity. She might have saved her life.

"Instead of that she went to see her stepson, and in her usual, easily pleased way she liked the fellow. Now I'm bein' a bit psychological and all that sort of thing. I'm goin' on the characters of both of them to get an idea of what happened. But I feel sure that in that meeting Mrs. Thurston was very much herself, the woman you all knew primarily as a hostess. She saw that her stepson would fit very well into her circle here. She had a passion for entertaining. She saw a way of fitting him in. And she planted him on her husband without tellin' Dr. Thurston who the fellow in reality was.

"How far he persuaded her into that we shall probably never know. It suited him excellently. And from that moment he began to sponge on Mrs. Thurston with an ease and a greed which seem incredible now. He never tried to blackmail or bully her. That wasn't necessary. He played the part of the poor son who had been cheated out of his rightful due by her very existence. He had the sense to play the part gently and good-humouredly. He never grumbled, but he pointed out that he never grumbled. He made her feel that it was hard luck on him, and that she must do all she could for him. And he did very nicely, thank you.

"Now so far I have reconstructed the story as it looks to me, and filled in the gaps in a fanciful sort of way. The bare facts I have confirmed. The stepson did arrive in England soon after Mrs. Thurston's second marriage, and did go to his father's solicitor to hear about the will. I've spoken on the 'phone to the solicitor myself. Charming old boy, and remembers the visit distinctly. Moreover, he did go to stay at Sidney Sewell, and Mrs. Thurston, as we know, was in touch with him there. And finally he did come to this house, was in this house at the time of the murder, and is, unless Beef has let him get away, in this house at this minute."

Lord Simon paused at this point to re-cross his legs and sip some Napoleon brandy which Butterfield had craftily put into one of Dr. Thurston's decanters so that his Lordship could enjoy his favourite beverage without ill-breeding. The pause made me so impatient and curious that I could not help saying—"And you know who it is, Lord Simon?"

"Yes. I know who it is."

"How did you find out?"

"That was really too easy. I instructed Butterfield to obtain photographs of all the men here who could, so far as age was concerned, have been the stepson. And armed with these I went, as you know, to Sidney Sewell. The public house was disappointing, for it has recently changed hands. But the post-mistress had not only been there a long time, but had an excellent memory. She instantly recognized one of the portraits as that of a young man who had stayed in the village some years ago. There is no point in keepin' the name from you. It was David Strickland. I have since confirmed it. Strickland's real name is Burroughs, and Burroughs, as you will remember, was the name of Mrs. Thurston's first husband. Strickland is in fact the stepson in question."

"Well, Sergeant," I said, rising, "you'd better arrest him."

But Sergeant Beef did not move. "I should want to know a great deal more than that before I was to arrest anyone," he said. "Very likely Mr. Strickland was Mrs. Thurston's stepson. I'm not saying he wasn't. 'E was a very generous gentleman, and always stood drinks all round when he came down to the village. So I don't see that 'is being 'er stepson makes 'im a murderer, does it?"

Lord Simon smiled. "All right, Sergeant," he said. "You shall hear the whole thing. All in good time, what?"

I was relieved, I think. Though I felt no personal animosity towards Strickland, I had no particular affection for him, and I was thankful, at least, that this continual suspecting of each person in turn was over, and I could hear the rest of the details undisturbed by doubt. Nor was I greatly surprised. The fact that Strickland's room was next door to Mary Thurston's had always seemed to me highly suspicious.

"There can be little doubt that the murder was a premeditated one. It was very carefully planned. But I think it was what you might call conditional premeditation. Strickland wanted money, as we shall see later. And if he had been given enough of it this week-end he might not have committed this highly unpleasant crime. But he had his plans ready before he came here. He knew the house well, and the people who worked in it, and those who were to be invited for the week-end. He knew, too, that if Mrs. Thurston was murdered, suspicion would certainly fall on him, for he had the strongest motive. As the stepson who had changed his name, and who would inherit a fortune on Mrs. Thurston's death, he couldn't escape suspicion. So, knowin' what he was up against he had to work things out pretty carefully.

"And, believe me, he did. I don't like to think how long it took for the plan to mature in his somewhat turgid brain. Months probably. And it wasn't a bad plan—as plans go. It had its weak spots, of course, but we must remember that this was our friend's first effort in this line. He couldn't be expected to be perfect. And I think on the whole his attempt at bein' bafflin' was creditable for an amateur. If he had been just a *little* bit cleverer he might have deceived me. But then if he had been just a little bit cleverer he wouldn't have gone in for murder at all. It's a mug's game.

"However, thus we have him, arriving for this week-end, in urgent need of money, and determined to get it from Mary Thurston, by persuasion if possible. And if that failed, he had in his brain a complete plan for murderin' her in a way which would perplex half a dozen Scotland Yards. But I don't think we should run away with the idea that, had she handed over what he wanted, it would have saved her life. It might have postponed his crime, but no more. When her first husband made that will he pretty well did for Mrs. Thurston. It should be a lesson to people who make wills on those lines.

"I have got the facts of Strickland's financial situation last week. I needn't bore you with them—tedious things, debts. But you can take it from me that he was desperate. He had to have money—snappily too. And he came here to get it."

CHAPTER 26

"You are wonderin' what this plan of his might be. Devilish cunnin' bit of intrigue. The first thing he had seen when he had begun to figure out his way of eliminatin' his stepmother, was that he would need an accomplice. And the first thing I saw, and I suppose the first thing all of us saw about this murder, was that an accomplice had been there. Hang it, short of something supernatural the murderer had to have an accomplice to escape from the room and leave the door locked, and show no sign of himself on his way of escape two minutes later. And for Strickland there was an obvious assistant all handy and willin'—the chauffeur Fellowes. But he wasn't such a fool as to speak to Fellowes till he had made up his mind that this week-end was the time.

"Mind you, he knew his ground. It is certain that this idea of murderin' his stepmother had been in his mind a long while, and on all his recent visits he had chatted with the chauffeur. He knew his story. He knew the fellow had been in gaol. He knew that his one ambition in life was to get clear of this place with enough money to buy a pub and marry Enid. He knew that he was having some sort of an *affaire* with Mrs. Thurston. And he judged him, and rightly, to be the very man to fall in with his plan."

Here Sergeant Beef interrupted loudly. "Well, I don't believe it," he said, folding his arms. "I know young Fellowes. Rough, if you like, and may 'ave got into a bit of trouble before now. Done a bit of 'ousebreaking I *dare* say. But not murder. I don't believe it. 'E could put two darts out of three in the double eighteen as often as you like, and I don't believe 'e'd ever 'ave 'ad nothink to do with cutting that lady's froat. Straight I don't. Besides, I know who did do it."

Lord Simon smiled patiently. "I'm glad to hear of Fellowes's proficiency in the pastime which seems to occupy most of your time and attention, Sergeant. But I'm afraid I can't see its relevance quite. Besides, have I asked you to believe our young friend guilty of murder? You must learn the virtue of patience, Sergeant. Useful in this job. And don't go jumpin' to conclusions. Where had we got to? Oh yes. On Friday morning we find Strickland arriving at the station after a week's racin' which might be called disastrous if you were to put it mildly. He is met by Fellowes who has been seeing a good deal of his girl lately—takin' her out in the car. That may have been disastrous, too. Judgin' from what we have seen of Enid, I don't suppose she was enjoyin' this long waitin', and savin' money, and hopin' before they could get married and own their pub. Besides, one can't imagine that she was delighted at her young man bein' whistled for like a pet dog every time their lady employer was lonely or temperamental. So that Fellowes, too, was probably approachin' breakin'-point.

"I don't think that Strickland will have said anything definite then. He knew enough to be pretty sure of Fellowes. But he may have arranged to see him after lunch, or even have asked him whether he would be prepared to come in on something that would see them on to Easy Street. Can't tell. Anyway, they had that time for a chat, alone in the car from the station.

"He had already let Mrs. Thurston know that he would need money, and she, as we know, had drawn two hundred pounds ready for him. But here was another difficulty. The man Stall had intercepted, some three weeks ago, a letter from Mrs. Thurston to Fellowes. It was a silly indiscreet letter, the sort of thing that someone as foolish and thoughtless as this lady might well have written. But he had found it

184

sufficient as a means to terrify her into parting with quite large sums of money. The truth is that Mrs. Thurston was genuinely fond of her husband, and bein' essentially an innocent soul she had imagined this silly little weakness of hers for a young chauffeur to be a far more terrible thing than it would have seemed to anyone else. At all events, when Strickland got her alone for a minute after lunch and asked her if she had the money ready for him, she had to tell him she had not. Perhaps she had not the time, or perhaps she did not wish, to tell him why she had not. I imagine that the whole thing passed between them in this very room, and in the presence of some of you. A hurried exchange of whispers.

"What had happened, probably, is that Stall had been listening at the main of the telephone, when Strickland rang her up on Thursday morning to say he would need the money. And Stall had heard her promise to have it ready for him. Or else Stall had seen the counterfoil in her cheque-book, and knew from it that she had just drawn the two hundred pounds. Or he had chosen by chance this time for a last determined blackmail campaign, knowing that he was under notice to quit. At all events he had got wind of the money, and made it clear that he was to have it.

"Finding that he was not to receive this sum, which he had intended to get doubled, Strickland went straight to the chauffeur, and told him his plan. At this point he showed a most horrifyin' sort of determination. He did not hesitate. He had his notions cut and dried and he was going to put them straight into action.'

Here Lord Simon hesitated. Full of admiration I watched him light another cigar, before revealing to us what we were now burning to know. He had told us who was the murderer, but his identity was not, I thought, as mysterious as his method, and I wanted to say "Go on! Go on!" while the young man nonchalantly applied a match to his cigar.

But he took his time, and when he began to talk again it was from a new angle.

"When you were thinking about the escape from that room, and you had an inklin' that there was a rope in it somewhere, did you wonder how that rope had been used?" He asked the question directly of me.

"Wonder? I've done nothing but wonder," I replied irritably. "Even supposing that the rope was let down from the floor above by an accomplice, I don't see how it could have been of much use. I've told you again and again that no one would have had time to climb out on to it, close the window after him, climb up it, and haul it up, before Williams opened the window again. And even if he had, he couldn't have reached us at the door as quickly as Strickland, Fellowes and Norris did."

"What about droppin' down it?" asked Lord Simon.

"The same thing applies. Suppose that there was someone upstairs to haul it in, the murderer would have had to climb out on to it, close the window, drop to the ground, and get away before Williams looked out, and the rope would have had to be hauled up after he had dropped from it. I don't think that those are possible. But even if they are, how was it he left no footprints on that soft bed which came out six feet from the wall? And how did he get in again, and upstairs to us in the time? And how did his accomplice haul in the rope and come downstairs as quickly as that? No. I don't believe it's possible. In fact," I added on a sudden inspiration, "I'm not sure that the ropes were not a blind!"

Lord Simon smiled. "You are right about the first two things," he admitted; "there wouldn't have been time for anyone to have gone up or down the rope."

"Well, then?"

"It didn't occur to you perhaps that there are other directions in which it is possible to travel?"

"What do you mean?"

"He means," put in Mgr. Smith suddenly from his arm-chair, "that a rope is not ony used to let a man climb, but also to make a man swing."

"Exactly, said Lord Simon; "swing is the word I want here and hereafter. Strickland knew that he might not have time to climb a rope, or drop down a rope, and establish that unimpeachable alibi which was necessary to him. But he would have time to swing on a rope, as comfortably as you please from outside Mary Thurston's window to out-side his own. All he had to do was to have a rope hung beforehand from the window that was *over his own*, with the end of it caught and hooked at Mrs. Thurston's ready, and his fire-escape, or escape from justice if you like, was ready. An accomplice was only necessary to haul the rope in afterwards."

I gasped. Of course! Why hadn't I thought of that? And there were Williams and I talking about the supernatural!

"But Strickland was no fool," continued Lord Simon. "He was judge enough of character to know that Fellowes would not come in on that. For one thing, Fellowes would not have enough to gain by it. There was the will made out to the servants—but Strickland didn't feel that it would be enough inducement to a man to bring him into a murder plot. I think he was right there. Fellowes was not quite such a bad hat as all that. No, Strickland went about it far more cleverly. What he was going to do, he said, was to pinch Mrs. Thurston's jewellery.

"Now that, as you can see, was right in the chauffeur's line of country. He, or Enid's brother, knew just where to plant it afterwards. And Strickland's plan was ingenious. What they had to do, he said, was to make sure that no one inside the house could be suspected. The door must be left bolted and an escape made via the window. That was where Fellowes was to come in. It was at that point that Strickland pretended to think of a snag. Mrs. Thurston's jewellery was valuable, and a safe had been let into her bedroom wall for it, and only she and the Doctor knew the combination. So Strickland did a bit of his deep thinkin' stuff. 'Tell you what,' he said, 'I'll stick a bally mask on, wear an old overcoat, and be waiting for her when she comes up to bed. I'll waggle a revolver in her face, and make her open the safe. Then, if you have the rope ready, I can escape by the window, and it will never occur to her that it was anyone in the house. And it won't occur to the police, either, when they come to investigate it. They'll think that anyone who gets *out* of the window, got *in* by the window, and if we make it clear to everyone that we were inside a few minutes before, and inside a few minutes after, she was held up, we're clear.'

"Now that plan did not sound to Fellowes as crazy as it may sound to you. In the first place, Mrs. Thurston could be relied on to go to bed at eleven. In the second place, she was obviously a woman who could be easily scared. And in the third place, by escaping out of the window, Strickland would give a pretty fair imitation of a bloke from outside. He would have to make sure of her silence, of course, till he was well away, and he would have to make certain that she did not follow him across to her window, and see him pop into his own. But neither of those would be very difficult.

"Fellowes, in any case, was not hard to convince, because his own part in the affair wasn't very difficult or incriminating. All he had to do was to haul the rope in when Strickland was safely in his window, and afterwards collect his share of the oof. That was not a hell of a job for a man who had already been to gaol for housebreaking.

"So the whole thing was arranged thus. During dinner Fellowes was to get the rope from the gymnasium, hang it out of the window of his own bedroom, which, as you know, is *over* Strickland's room, go down into Mrs.

Thurston's room, and by means of a hooked stick or something haul the end of the rope over to her window. He could fix it there by the simple expedient of pulling the end into the room, and hauling the window down on top of it. Even if anyone went into the room after him, and before Mrs. Thurston came to bed, those long curtains would hide it.

"When the rope was fixed, Fellowes was to take out the electric light bulb, so that when Strickland came the room would be in half-darkness. And after that he had nothing to do until eleven, when he was to go up to his bedroom and haul in the rope.

"Meanwhile Strickland, so far as Fellowes knew, was to go to bed early, get into Mrs. Thurston's room in his rough disguise, wait for her to come to bed, clap a hand over her mouth quickly to prevent her screaming, gag her, force her to open the safe, pocket the jewellery, tie Mary Thurston to something out of sight of the window, climb out on to the rope, let the rope swing him to his own window as it would kindly do in obeying the law of gravity, nip in, conceal the tomfoolery, and be ready to come out of his room and join the hue and cry.

"Fellowes thought it a splendid idea. He saw only one snag in it. That was his friend Miles. He knew it was Miles's day off, and that he, who would certainly be outside and not inside the house, would, as an experienced cat-burglar, be at once suspected. But this he could easily avoid by seeing Miles that afternoon, and telling him to see that he had a cast-iron alibi in the evening. So Fellowes was quite happy.

"And Strickland's own real, and rather more private plan, was now perfect, too. No paltry disguises for him. A disguise might frighten her into giving a premature scream. He would be waiting in Mrs. Thurston's room in his own charmin' and natural guise, and when she came up he would neatly slit her throat and swing home in safety. He would then step out of his room with a perfect alibi almost before

189

anyone could reach her door. Afterwards, he would have to explain it to Fellowes as necessary. And Fellowes would be too deeply involved to peach. Fascinatin' fellow—Strickland."

CHAPTER 27

"NIGHT fell, as they say," continued Lord Simon in the airy way which he customarily used for the discussion of such atrocities, "and it was a nice windy night so that goings-on at windows would not be heard. You all gathered in the lounge for cocktails. And now an odd thing happened. There was talk of murder, and of the discovery of murderers. Awkward that, and for a time it quite took the wind out of our friend's sails, or put the wind up him, whichever you please. He didn't like the sound of it. Nasty idea, that, of inevitable discovery. He flattered himself on having worked out a neat little plan, but suppose he wasn't quite as clever as he thought? Your conversation, in fact, nearly saved Mrs. Thurston's life. Perhaps Strickland even thought some-one had rumbled him, and was delicately pointin' out that it really wouldn't do.

"At all events, he so far hesitated in his ideas as to have another try for some money. If, after all, she could be persuaded to see him out of his tight corner, he privately resolved—very kindly—to refrain from killin' her. And he went to her room before dinner and pleaded again. But by that time the unhappy lady had parted with her two hundred pounds to Stall, probably during the afternoon, when she had gone to her room for her usual siesta. Stall, when I asked him when he had received the money, told an obvious lie. He said that it was just after lunch on Thursday, whereas we know from that cashier who wore that unsightly sort of plaque in his tie, that Mrs. Thurston did not draw it until three o'clock. Stall chose a time when he knew she was in her room—just after lunch on Thursday. But he didn't know that she hadn't then drawn the money. His reason for lying was obvious. He would admit when pressed that he had had the money 'as a gift' but he wasn't going to admit that he'd been in her room on the day of the murder. Well, would you? I'm hanged if I would in his place. Nasty things, murders. Best to keep away from them.

"Stall was a blackmailer of the sneerin', bullyin' sort, for he had deliberately leaned against a lady's dressin'-table and taken snuff in her face to show his independence. So that when Strickland tried again for money he was disappointed. All Mary Thurston could do for him was to give him, or lend him, her diamond pendant which he could pawn for enough to see him through, perhaps. The fact that he slipped the thing in his pocket was evidence, I think, that at that moment he had abandoned the idea of his crime. Well, vacillatin' is dangerous, and he regretted afterwards having accepted the thing.

'Townsend, he knew, saw him coming out of Mrs. Thurston's room. But when, later, he had taken up his resolution again, that did not seem to matter. Why, after all, shouldn't he have spoken to his hostess for a moment? After a drink or two he could shrug that away as unimportant. He came down to dinner, and, while making it clear that he was abnormally tired, he behaved otherwise without any of the eccentricity that might be expected of a man who was making up his mind to commit a murder. And some time before Mrs. Thurston would retire, he rose, said good night, and went up to his room.

"Fellowes, in the meantime, had done his half-unconscious part. Under the pretence of 'running in' the engine, he had gone down to the village in the afternoon and warned Miles. And Miles had ingeniously established his alibi by securing no less a person than the village sergeant as his partner in this enthrallin' game of darts of which we have heard so much, and then pretending to be so drunk that several witnesses had to help him home to a room which he shared with another witness. So he was all right.

"But when Fellowes, during dinner, had reached the gymnasium he was a trifle puzzled. Would one of those ropes be long enough? I own that I was myself perplexed at the finding of two ropes, until I realized that this question had worried Fellowes. Looking at the length of them where they hung in the gymnasium he had decided that one might not reach, and had taken both. He had left the latch of the front door up, and watching at the little window beside it until he saw Stall go into the dining-room with a tray of food which would take some time to serve, he carried them safely through the hall. You will remember that I asked you, Townsend, about that little window in the hall, and Stall said that the curtains were rarely drawn across it.

"He got his ropes up to his bedroom and secured one end of one of them. Can't say exactly what he slung it on to. In such details both he and Strickland seem to have been pretty knowin'. It may have been the beam. If so he padded it. There were no marks. And when he dropped it down he saw that it was long enough, and went downstairs to Mrs. Thurston's room. Here he looked round for something with which to reach the end of the rope, and found a couple of old parasols in the wardrobe. He tied one to the other, leaned out of the window, and hooked it. Then he dropped the end into the room, pulled the window down on it, and so left it ready for Strickland without having to make a sign or a scratch to show where it had been fastened. Oh yes, in such details they were cunning, these two.

"Then came the question of the electric light bulb. He suddenly thought, rather uncomfortably, that Strickland had given him no suggestion as to the disposal of this. Should he take it away with him? Or leave it in the room? Might its removal in any case not show that someone inside the house had been active? On the whole, he did the wisest thing. He argued that had the thief come from outside and for some reason decided to remove the bulb, he would almost certainly have thrown it out of the window; and that is just what he did with it, taking care that he threw it far on to the lawn so that its fall or explosion should not be audible to those on the ground floor.

"Then he left the room. He had, he thought, prepared for a rather cowardly robbery. Actually he had set a trap for a very vile murder. He had been careful, all the time, to wear gloves. Strickland may have recommended this, or he may have learnt it in his housebreaking days. At all events he left no fingerprints, for in such details, as I say, these two were cunning.

"When he got downstairs he found, rather to his irritation, that he had about two hours to wait before his next step, and it was then, in an excess of enthusiasm I think, that he cut the telephone wires. I don't think this had figured in Strickland's instructions, for Strickland would have seen that the sooner the police and the doctor were on the spot, the better. But Fellowes, who had experience but no finesse, just thought that in a general sort of way, it was worth while holdin' 'em off for a bit. So he snipped the jolly old communications.

"Everything, unfortunately, went to schedule. Mrs. Thurston said good night to you all, and entered her room for the last time. She found Strickland there. She did not find the strange man in the mask who, as Fellowes fondly thought, would await her. But merely her stepson. 'What do you want?' Enid heard her ask, in a rather startled, but not frantically startled, voice. He had come earlier that evening to beg—and had taken all she could give him without risking the notice of her husband. What more could he want? She found, too, that the strong light in her room was out of order. So that the man standing there in the half-darkness was a little startling.

"Meanwhile Fellowes was quietly establishing an alibi

downstairs. Whoever robbed Mrs. Thurston of her jewellery, he and Strickland had argued, would appear afterwards to have been waiting for her when she came to bed. So he said very pointedly to the cook, 'Hello, it's past eleven,' and apparently without hurry left her. That would remind her in the future that it was after, and not before, her mistress went up to bed that Fellowes followed. Only he had not the time to make it much after.

"He must have grown anxious during the next ten minutes as he leaned out of the window of his bedroom, waiting for Strickland to appear at Mrs. Thurston's window, down to his left. And it is a bit gruesome to wonder what caused that delay, and what took place in the dimly lighted room beneath. And then, when Fellowes heard those screams, a less cool type than he might have lost his head. He didn't. He waited, and almost instantly Strickland gripped his rope, pulled the window after him, swung across to his own window and was gone. In a moment the rope was hauled in, stuffed in the tank, where, probably, he had already concealed the other one which had proved to be unnecessary, so that both Strickland and Fellowes were outside Mrs. Thurston's bolted door almost as soon as you were.

"Perhaps it was not until that night that they realized their most serious blunder. They had thought of everything —finger-prints, alibis, and witnesses—but they had failed to provide for the removal of the rope. It was a stupid and an elementary mistake, but was there ever a murderer who did not make a stupid and elementary mistake? And Fellowes had the additional remorse of finding himself a party to a murder. But for obvious reasons he kept quiet.

"He wanted, however, two things. One was to dispose of those ropes. This hope was frustrated when next morning I put my hand on one of the rotten things, and Monsignor Smith came across the other. His second desire was to get hold of Strickland alone, and have a reckoning with him. He did not know, he does not know yet, that he was deliberately fooled. He has no idea that Strickland expects to gain a great deal by Mrs. Thurston's death. He probably thinks that Strickland's disguise lapsed in some way, and that Strickland murdered Mrs. Thurston to conceal his identity. While Strickland has taken great care to avoid being alone with Fellowes. Even when he asked Dr. Thurston for the use of his car, and found that Fellowes meant to drive him in it, he had the presence of mind to persuade Alec Norris to accompany them. So up to the present he has succeeded in escaping a reckoning with his accomplice, and on that, at least, I think he is to be congratulated. For though Fellowes strikes me as a roughish bird, I don't think he would have taken up murder as a hobby if he had known what he was doing, and I don't think he'll easily forgive the bloke that let him in for it.

"As for the girl Enid, I'm pretty sure she knew nothing of the idea on hand at the time, and I don't think she suspects her young man of bein' mixed up in it. She spoke the truth when we asked her questions, except when we asked her if she had been out with Fellowes in the car that afternoon, and a lie in answer to that was natural enough. Perhaps someone else"—he glanced at Mgr. Smith—"may have reason to think she knew everything. I'm inclined to think not.

"As for Miles—all he knew was that there was a little scheme afoot to grab the tomfoolery . . .

"'E means the jewellery," put in Sergeant Beef, seeing me looking puzzled by Lord Simon's second use of this queer word.

"He may even have known the way it was to be done. But he had nothing to do with it. Not he. And Mr. Miles went in for the very best quality alibis, as you see. He invited the Sergeant to hurl the honest javelin with him.

"And what about Stall, say you. What about him, say I, remembering Ben Gunn and all that sort of thing. Stall was a nasty sort of blackmailer, but he regrets this unfortunate affair as much as you do, if for rather different reasons. In another fortnight he would have gone. Jolly old swallow, Stall would have been. With his nest pretty well feathered. Do swallows feather their nests? Let's hope so, it sounds well. And now this untimely bit of murderin' has turned up, and let the whole tribe of cats out of his unpleasant carpet-bag, and he faces a stiffish sentence. Well, well, the best-laid schemes of mice and men, and all that. Aren't we getting zoological, Butterfield?"

"Your lordship's phraseology has certainly taken an almost biological turn," assented Butterfield gravely, from his place near the door.

"Then the Vicar. In deference to Butterfield, I won't say he had bats in the belfry. But that's about what it comes to. He had purity on the brain. And when, that evening, Mrs. Thurston, quite unconscious that he was on the snoop for such details, told him that she was very fond of young Fellowes, it set the feller's brain spinnin' like a top. No wonder he walked about that orchard for half an hour. If he hadn't heard the screams he might have been there all night.

"As for Norris—there is no reason to doubt his perfectly simple story. That mild attack of hysterics of which you all make so much, was natural enough to a feller of his type. It must have been disconcertin' for him to have been interrupted in the middle of writin' one of his fearfully intense novels by something as vulgar as a murder, and we must sympathize with him.

"And there you have it—lock, stock and jolly old barrel. I expect Monsieur Picon will hang a few more trimmin's on it, and I look forward to hearin' him. Meanwhile . . . yes, Butterfield. Another brandy, I think."

CHAPTER 28

I HAD guessed that one of the 'trimmin's' which M. Picon would add to Lord Simon's brilliant reconstruction of the crime would concern the parlourmaid Enid, in whose movements he had shown such a keen and sleuthy interest. But I could not see what more there was to be said. Lord Simon had been so thorough and so complete, forgetting not the most trivial point, and accounting for every known fact, that there seemed little left for M. Picon to divulge. However, the little man seemed eager to talk, and excited over something he had to communicate to us, so that we all leaned back and prepared to hear him.

"That,' he said to Lord Simon, "was an interesting theory. Very ingenious, *mon ami*. I have listened with *plaisir* to every word of it. Unfortunately, however, it is incorrect, right from its *commencement*. The gentleman called Strickland, so genial and so *sportif*, as the good Bœuf has told us, is as innocent of the murder as you or I."

I cannot exaggerate the effect of this startling declaration. Lord Simon was, of course, the least concerned, and sipped his brandy imperturbably. But his man Butterfield gave a visible start, and turned pale. It was evident that never before had he heard his employer's theories questioned by anyone but police inspectors, unintelligent spectators, or criminals. That the celebrated M. Picon should make such a blunder seemed incredible to him. Williams and I sat up violently, and even Mgr. Smith showed a mild interest.

"But have no fear," continued the foreign detective, "I, Amer Picon, will reveal everything to you. Everything. Are you ready? *Allez . . . hoop!*

"I have told you, have I not, that when there seems to

be no motive in the brain, one must look in the heart. This was no murder of the intellect—though by its very simplicity it was difficult to reconstruct, but a crime of passion. You are surprised, is it not? *Eh bien*, my friends, I also have had my surprises in this case.

"Let us examine, if you please, this household as it was before this violent occurrence. We have the genial Doctor Thurston, an English gentleman who, like so many of your English gentlemen, sees no farther than his nose. We have Madame Thurston—very kind, very easy-going, and a little, one must say, stupid. We have the butler, Stall, what you call in English 'a sly dog', eh? And the so competent cook. Then we have the young man Fellowes, who knows what it is to be inside a prison, and the girl Enid, of mixed blood and rather unfortunate antecedents. *Voilà*—the caste.

"Now what goes on? There is here the eternal triangle, *n'est-ce pas?* Madame Thurston is attached to the young chauffeur, who in his turn is in love with Enid, who is much enamoured of him. And there you have the beginning of the trouble. My friends—beware of that little triangle. He is dangerous.

"All is secret. The good Doctor must know nothing, nothing at all. Madame Thurston may take the automobile ride in order to chat with the young man she adores, but it must be surreptitious. Enid may know all, for her lover assures her that she had no need to doubt, but she must not let Madame Thurston see that she knows anything. And when the butler, Stall, has stolen the so fateful and incriminating letter from Madame Thurston to the chauffeur and uses it to blackmail the lady, she herself must be silent to Fellowes, and conceal from him what is going on, lest he attacks the butler, and all is exposed, all is ended. You see what secrets were here?

"Two people besides the sly Stall are suspicious of Madame and her chauffeur—the cook and the Vicar. But the cook is quite satisfied with her situation, and very sensibly decides that it is no business of hers, though, as she told us, there were things of which she did not approve. And the Vicar, he is not sure. He is fond of espionage, the good Vicar, and presently he will know more.

"Meanwhile, like many households, this household goes on. Underneath the routine, Madame Thurston conceals her love, and the torture of being blackmailed. Enid conceals the furious fire of her jealousy, which persists in spite of all her lover says. The chauffeur conceals from the middle-aged lady who loves him his real love for the girl. The blackmailer conceals his activities from all, save from Madame Thurston. And everyone conceals everything from Doctor Thurston. *Voilà*—an atmosphere! All have secrets. But the household goes on like any other.

"And why does it so? Because, my friends, there is money. For the servants there are good wages now, exceptionally good. And there is the will which shall make all of them rich one day. And for money much can be endured. So it goes on, and the time draws near to this fatal week-end, in which matters must reach a climax.

"Now everyone is approaching what you call the breaking point. But most of all the chauffeur. Three years he has worked here, and is not yet married to Enid. He wants to take a little inn. He has some money saved, but not enough. Enid, too, wants to go with him. But how can they? If they leave this situation they may not find another where they would be together. When we are in love we are slaves. They must stay here and work, and he must be pleasant with madame, and she must endure her pangs of jealousy. There is no escape, it seems.

"But there is the will. Are we not forgetting the will, the little trick which Madame Thurston has played on her servants? *Voilà*—a chance! If madame now were to die suddenly, of cancer or consumption, say, all is settled, all is solved. They would be rich, they could buy their little inn, there would be no more jealousy for Enid, and no more cleaning the car for Fellowes. If only . . . but why dream? Madame is strong. Madame may live for thirty years. Why dream?

"Yet, why not? If anything were to *happen* to madame, now. That would help. An accident—a fatal accident. Already the ideas are alive. Already the beginning of a plot. And as for time, when better than this week-end, when so many guests are here? All that must be found is the way. That is most important—the way to cause that so regrettable fatal accident, without any possibility of the stupid police interfering afterwards. That is the great question.

"And, *messieurs*, we who know something of these matters know only too well that when all else is determined, a way can be found. Only too soon. So we find Fellowes the chauffeur determined that Madame Thurston shall meet with this accident and the week-end approaching. It was into the atmosphere of this potential crime that you came for your week-end.

"The chauffeur had been a sailor. When I first perceived that among the tattoo marks on his arm was a representation of the Southern Cross, I was convinced of that, and he has since admitted it. And to me came the idea, the little plain idea, that a sailor might climb a rope. It was of the simplest, this idea, such as a little child might have. But beware always of the complicated. The idea was correct. It might have been otherwise, but as you will see it was correct."

At this point Sam Williams broke in rather impatiently. "But, Monsieur Picon," he said, "we've already discussed over and over again the possibility of anyone having climbed out of that window, and it has been proved that it was not possible in the time . . ."

"Patience, if you please," said M. Picon; "step by step, if you will listen. I, Amer Picon, will tell you all. *Eh bien*,

201

here we are with a chauffeur who can climb a rope. But of what use is that? He must have an alibi. No amusement to commit a murder, and be caught escaping by means of a rope. *Pas du tout.* It must be done better. How? Ah, then comes the great idea. The chauffeur sees just how the *pauvre* Madame Thurston may meet her accident, how he and Enid may inherit some of her money, and escape without ever being suspected. A big idea, this time! And one to deceive nearly all detectives. All but Picon. For Picon, too, has an idea sometimes.

"The room must be a little dark, and the chauffeur must go to see *madame*. That, we are told, was not so unusual. He must bolt the door. That, too, may have happened before. His rope hangs at the window, suspended firmly from the apple-room the window of which is directly over the opening of Madame Thurston's room. All is prepared. He must advance to *madame*. That, also, he has done before. Then, not the embrace, but *vite*, the knife. Tcchhk! It must be done. In silence and swiftly he must sever the jugular vein. Then, hoop! On to the rope. The sailor's climb to the apple-room. The concealment of the rope. The descent to the kitchen. The conversation with the cook. *Voilà un menu!*

"Meanwhile, the young woman, Enid, does her part. She is in the room of Dr. Thurston, which is divided from that of Madame Thurston by a wall. Near this wall she stands. She waits until her lover has descended to the kitchen, and the murder is done. Then Ow! Ow! she screams. It is Madame Thurston being murdered. For who can distinguish the screams of two women? One may know the voice of each very well, but the scream, that is different. No one can tell. So near to the wall, too, it must seem to come from the poor lady's room. Then—all will arrive. The door will be burst open, the crime discovered. Who has done it? Certainly not the chauffeur, for was he not

202

talking with the cook? Certainly not Enid, for does she not arrive at the door immediately? Certainly not Miles, for was he not with Bœuf? Such was the plot, Intelligent, *n'est-ce pas*? But not quite intelligent enough for Amer Picon.

"And now we see what came of that plot. *Allons! Voyons! A la gloire!*"

CHAPTER 29

"FIRST arrives Monsieur Strickland who, as *milord* Plimsoll had taken such pains to show us, was Mrs. Thurston's stepson. He is what you call in your so expressive idiom, 'broke to the wide'. He has written to his stepmother in advance that he will need some money, but urgently. And she, who is generous and good, has arranged to overdraw yet another two hundred pounds for him. But *hélas!* what says the bank manager? Without security no more, Madame. She takes the two hundred pounds, and returns home.

"Then he arrives. 'It is all right,' perhaps she tells him, 'I can give you the money!' And he is relieved of his troubles. But sshh! She has spoken too loud. The butler has discovered that she has this sum. He has already blackmailed Madame Thurston with the letter that she wrote to Fellowes, and now determines to obtain also this money. During the afternoon he sees her and she has to give him the two hundred pounds. It is a pity.

"Then, after that so intelligent discussion of the literature of crime, you go to dress for dinner. Madame Thurston sends for Fellowes and tells him to set the trap for the rat. That is good for Fellowes. It is not necessary, but it is good. And Monsieur Townsend perceives Monsieur Strickland emerging from Madame Thurston's room. She has given him her pendant to help him through his troubles. She is kind, this Madame Thurston.

"During dinner the chauffeur, just as Lord Simon has explained, fetches the ropes. Lord Simon has obliged me by perceiving how he brought them into the house unobserved. I had myself wondered at that. But it is simple. He used the front door. He goes to the *chambre des pommes*. He suspends the rope. He goes to Madame Thurston's room and removes the light. Why? She must foresee no danger. It is necessary that she should be silent. The semi-darkness will assist him. All upstairs is now ready. He descends, and *sneep!* the telephone wire is cut. Why? The Doctor must not come too soon, or the fact may be discovered that she was murdered earlier than the screams.

"He goes now to the kitchen. Dinner is over. Presently the guests begin to go to bed, or to go home. The door of the kitchen is ajar. Why? Because one must know when Madame Thurston goes to bed. Eleven o'clock draws near. Ah! At last! Madame has left the lounge. Enid rises at once and follows her mistress to her room. She explains that she cannot get another light bulb. She is sorry. Does Madame require her further? *Mais non*, madame is secretly expecting the chauffeur and requires no one. Enid says good night, with a smile. It is also good-bye.

"Once more the chauffeur ascends. He takes the rat-trap with him. He enters madame's room. She awaits him. All is well. There is very little light. He remains with her a little while. Why? Ah, that is no matter for the detective, that delay. It is for the priest to understand. Perhaps the crime seems at last too terrible. Perhaps he wishes her to be at a disadvantage. Who can say now? But at last he can delay no more. He has brought his weapon. He strikes. *Voilà!* It is done. Quite silent. She had no time to cry out. She is dead.

"And now he is nervous. He crosses quickly to the window. He throws it up. He is on the rope. And he can climb. *Parbleu!* But can he climb, this man who was once a sailor? He pulls down the window, and climbs swift, swift, to the window of the apple-room. He enters. He commences to draw in the rope.

"So far, all has gone *à merveille*. But now occurs a little disaster for the murderer. Downstairs there is a conversation between Dr. Thurston, Monsieur Williams and Monsieur Townsend. The wireless plays. What does Monsieur Townsend? See, he rises. He will fetch something from his overcoat. He goes to the door and opens it. But no. Monsieur Williams addresses him. He is interested. He forgets the something in his overcoat, and returns to the other *messieurs*.

"But what is the effect? The poor Enid! She has been waiting for ten minutes for her lover to descend from the apple-room, so that she may do her part. But still he has not come. And now she hears the noise of the wireless suddenly increase as the door is opened. Someone comes, she thinks. Someone will find her. She is discovered. Her lover will be hanged. But wait—there is yet time. He has surely climbed in now? Quick, to the door. Ah, *bien*, he is there. He descends. She returns to the room of Dr. Thurston and she screams. She has saved his life, she thinks. But she could not foresee that Amer Picon, the great Amer Picon, would investigate!

"The chauffeur is what you call nonplussed. Why has she screamed too soon? In a panic he runs into his own room. Then, in a moment he realizes that he must show himself at once, as soon as possible. He joins you at the door. He is relieved. His alibi, though not as good as if he had been with the cook, is still perfect. He will escape.

"What is there more to do? He offers himself now to those who seek' the criminal. He is calm, and confident. He fetches the doctor and the policeman. Why not? The doctor may now examine the body, but it is more than half an hour since the murder. It cannot be possible for him to tell that she died just four or five minutes before the scream. And the policeman—but he is acquainted with our honest Bœuf. He is *enchanté* that he should investigate. So he goes willingly.

"Nor is he troubled that the ropes should remain concealed in the tank. Why should he be? He has seen that the screams of Enid have been taken by all to be the screams of the murdered woman, so that his alibi is perfect. No rope in the world can convict him, he thinks, not having foreseen the intervention of Amer Picon.

"He made, however, one stupid blunder, this so longsighted young man. He arranged to meet the girl on the afternoon before he committed his crime. And he tried to conceal that afterwards. Then when I wanted to find out what his movements had been that day, he fell plop into the trap, and was caught as surely as the little rats in the apple-room. Figure to yourself—he has decided on Friday to carry out the scheme he has planned. Already, as we know, he has in view the public-house he will take when he has received the money. He has made up his mind. He wants, of course, to meet his accomplice. This he effects so secretly that none see them go away in the car together. Perhaps the girl is hidden in the back. Perhaps she waits for him beyond the village. At all events their meeting was concealed. They drive to their customary place, where it is unlikely that they will be observed. They leave the car where they have always left it, and where it will arouse no comment, since a car may often be left near to a lovers' lane. They are quarrelling. The girl, perhaps, is impatient with so much waiting, and with her lover's attentions to madame. He must pacify her. He tells her of his decision—that the day they have awaited is here. They complete their plans. They smile again. They return to the car, and drive to the house —unseen.

"But then, *quel dommage!* I put my little question. I want to be sure that he was not in the village, I say. Can he tell me something which will prove him to have been elsewhere? And he, the poor fool, who does not know Amer Picon, tells me of the flag that was at half-mast. He leaves me then only one thing to do. It is a hope, a chance, that he stopped the car at a point from which that tower is to be seen. And *voilà!* it comes true! I discover that he went there with his accomplice.

"Then worse, they both deny that they were out together. How foolish! Had they been innocent, why should they conceal it? A little scolding for an offence in the routine of the house, what is that? Nothing. And by denying it, they make it guilty. Oh yes, even this young man had his blunders.

"That then, *mes amis,* is the explanation of this mystery. You, unfortunately, all of you who tried to solve it, sought the impossible. You thought, as the murderer intended that you should think, about the manner in which someone could have escaped from the room after the screams and before your entry. That was foolish. It should have been evident at once to you that nobody could have escaped in that time. Then either he was still there, or the screaming had not been done at the time of the murder. And since he was not still there, *voilà!* the certainty was the latter. You see how simple, how logical, now that *Papa* Picon explains? But no—you do not reason so. You begin to think of the unnatural, of creatures with wings. You should have known that always, my friends, always in such cases of a murder behind locked doors the explanation is a matter not of the means of escape, but of the time at which the crime was done. Ah, if we all drew the conclusions which murderers mean us to draw, what a happy time for murderers! But fortunately there are some who have a sense of logic!

"This man had, as you say, all the luck. Everything conspired to shift the blame on to other shoulders, and to confuse the investigators. There was Monsieur Strickland, the stepson, who would benefit so much, who had been in trouble and changed his name, who slept next door. There was the butler, already guilty of blackmail. There was the *curé*, who was not quite well in the head, and who arrives at the bedside so soon after the murder. And there was Monsieur Norris who was also upstairs at the time. So many to be suspected! So much confusion. Surely he is lucky. But no—fortunately there arrives Amer Picon, with his sense of logic. He is lucky no more. He and his accomplice are discovered. *Voilà! C'est tout!*"

Looking back on the moment at which M. Picon finished, I think that my first emotion was one of sympathy with Lord Simon. It must have been galiing to him to see his card-castle collapse, and the iron-clad edifice of M. Picon take its place. He had worked so hard and conscientiously, that he deserved to have been successful. But no. The little foreigner was obviously congratulating himself. All doubt was now removed.

CHAPTER 30

M. PICON had scarcely finished speaking, and was still smiling in self-congratulation, when Mgr. Smith unexpectedly began.

"What you all seem to forget," he said, "is that a man who can be a spy, can also be a spider "

At once I remembered all his mystic references to King Bruce, and things of people or facts that hang on threads, and I asked myself what abstruse wonders were now to be revealed as commonplace.

"You, too, have discovered the murderer?" I asked; not, I must own, taking the little cleric very seriously, but willing enough to be diverted by his account.

"I have discovered the murderer," he replied, "by a rope, a phrase, and by the way in which a man killed flies. It is very simple, but it has the terror and the power and the immensity of all simple tnings."

He paused for a moment, as though wondering whether he should tell us. Then he went on. "There was a woman murdered in a locked room, from which the only escape was by the window, and the only manner of exit from the window was by a rope. So without beginning to talk in that superstitious way of unnatural happenings, it was necessary to discover how that rope had been used. It cou!d have been neither climbed nor used for descent, so we came to Lord Simon's explanation—that a rope may swing, and a man may swing on it. But what I think Lord Simon failed to see, was that when a rope can swing from left to right, another may swing from right to left.

"In Mrs. Thurston's room there were two windows, one which was made to open, and one, constructed without frame or hinges, which would not open. And both had stone ledges at least a foot wide. And you were all observant of the window which opened. But what about the window which did not open? It could have let in lovely things, fresh air and moonbeams, the scent of flowers, and truth. For the truth of this matter was behind the window which did not open, waiting to be admitted.

"To escape from the room a man had to swing on a rope. But he did not swing to the right to the window of Strickland's room, but to the left, to the unopening window, for the rope to which he clung was let down *not* from Fellowes's room, but from the box-room. And there he stood on that ledge, gripping the stonework above him, while you were searching the room. He could not watch you clearly, for the window is of stained glass, but he could see when you had gone. And then he returned. For another rope was hung from the window of the apple-room, on which he could swing back to the window which did open. It was simple to discover this. One only had to remember that no pendulum goes only one way, that an action has its reaction, that black, in fact, is opposed to white.

"But who had done it? Whoever had swung on the ropes had had an accomplice who hung them. Or should one say that whoever had hung the ropes had had an accomplice who swung on them? At all events there were two people concerned.

"And while we sat at lunch on Friday a spider appeared on the table. The butler came into the room and picked it up carefully in his fingers. I was watching, and I thought that the man who shrank from killing an insect would probably hesitate to kill an employer. But suddenly I saw a very horrible thing. The butler had not shrunk from killing the spider because he loved spiders, but because he hated flies. He took the creature and carefully set it on the window-ledge where several sleepy flies were crawling. And he turned away regretfully, as though he wanted to wait and watch the results. It was appalling, but like many appalling things it showed the truth. The man who had set a spider to kill a fly had set a man to kill a woman.

"But what man? It had been a weak man who was persuaded into it, a guilty man who was blackmailed into it, or a devil to whom it had to be no more than suggested. It could have been no one who came to the door of the room or was present at the search. And that afternoon I set off for the village church. At first I thought that I should have to look elsewhere, for Mr. Rider was neither a weak, nor a guilty, nor a bad man. But when he showed me a fine *piscīna* in the chancel of his church and referred to it as a wash-basin, I perceived the terrifying truth. He was not himself a devil, he was possessed of devils, he was insane. And this madman was the instrument which the real murder had chosen.

"But only one rope had been found. If it had happened as I thought there must be two. I hoped, as I thrust my hand into the tank, that there would be nothing in it but water. The crime as it appeared to me then seemed too vile. But no—it was there. Two ropes had been used.

"You see, this butler here was a very wicked and very clever man. He had been a butler for twenty years or more, and as he said, he had excellent references. But imagine what had gone to the making of those references, what innumerable subservient humilities, what civil grins, what concealment of personal emotion! He was a man given to hatred and jealousy, who had been forced for two decades to show complaisance and satisfaction.

"At last he is employed by a woman who thinks she can trick her servants into loyalty. But loyalty comes with trial, not with trickery. A man may call a June evening New Year's Eve, but we shan't sing *Auld Lang Syne*. A man may put a crown upon his head, but we shan't sing

God Save the King. A woman may make a will, but we shan't sing *For She's a Jolly Good Fellow.* And when Mrs. Thurston signed this will she was not securing for herself any service—except unfortunately the Burial Service. It was her death warrant.

"For the wicked and clever man of whom we are speaking was too wicked and not quite clever enough for success. He was wicked enough to see that if he could get Mrs. Thurston murdered he would inherit her money, but not clever enough to know that there was no money to inherit. He was wicked enough to plan her murder, but not clever enough to find out that she had only a life interest in her first husband's money. So that the trick has worked twice—on the murderer as well as on the murdered woman.

"He saw a way of escaping from all service, of achieving what all his life he had most ardently craved—his independence. If he could eliminate this woman he would not only leave the house, from which he had already been dismissed by her husband, without danger of the blackmail he had practised being discovered, but he would also inherit his share of her money. He would be comparatively well off for the rest of his life, for we may presume that he had already saved a certain sum.

"But how? He had not even the courage necessary to murder this woman. But what he lacked in courage he had in guile. He looked about him for someone to do the thing for him. And it was probably not for some time that he found this agent in the unlikeliest place—the local vicarage. Something like a sardonic smile must have come to him when he first thought of that. For who would look for violence in a vicarage? Who would expect to find a murderer in a manse?

"Stall sang bass in the choir, and made himself useful to the Vicar. At first, while the weak brain of the latter had still enough health to ape normality, he was satisfied with that. But gradually he came to exert more and more influence over the wretched man, until he had only to suggest something to the poor lunatic brain of the other, and he could persuade him to take any course of action that he chose—always providing. of course, that the Vicar was convinced that it was his duty Quite early in their sinister relationship, Stall must have learnt that this was his easiest way to accession—he had to prove to the Vicar that such and such a thing was his duty, and the thing was done. When I think of it I see the stars turn awry with nausea. He was an unusual criminal, and I thank God for it.

"Then, drawing nearer to his final object, Stall began to suggest to Rider that there was evil in the relationship between Mrs. Thurston and young Strickland. The Vicar, with his mania for what he called purity but what I should call puritanism, needed very little instigation on this point. His mental disorder took the form of an abnormal hatred for even the happiest and most innocent love, and when Stall began to fill him with suggestions of this scandal, he was quickly and insanely alert, and doubtless saw many things which did not exist.

"Then slowly the butler must have begun to suggest the horrible idea that it was Rider's duty to assassinate the woman he had represented as guilty He had found a weapon which had hitherto been the prerogative of political plotters—a madman who could be made to commit an act of violence for the sake of an imaginary virtue, a man who would undertake a crime as though it were a crusade. It was here, probably, that he used that absurd story of the avenging angel striking at the old man in the tower. He led him on with a legend, fanned his anger with a fable, lured him with a lie. Until at last Mr. Rider was ready.

"I wondered at first that he should have troubled to extort that last sum of two hundred pounds from Mrs. Thurston at that point. But I underestimated Stall's gift for calculation. He had a very vile fault—a love of scoring off his fellows. By manipulating the murder of Mrs. Thurston, he felt, he would be scoring off the whole series of his employers. By securing this two hundred pounds, which should rightly have been divided with the rest of the estate, he would be scoring off his fellow-servants. How he will have to wipe off those scores, it is not for us to say.

"When at last the unfortunate Vicar arrived on Friday evening he knew what he must do, and had been schooled into the method he must follow. No wonder he questioned Mr. Townsend before dinner, as though he sought some final confirmation of the facts to influence his diseased brain. And it is possible that even then he might have escaped the domination of Stall, and gone home an innocent man, if it had not been for that unlucky conversation with Mrs. Thurston before he took his leave. But she ingenuously told him that she was fond of the young chauffeur, as indeed, and inoffensively enough, she was. He left the room with his crazy conscience quiet, determined to set about the dreadful work which he believed to be his duty.

"Stall, meanwhile, had everything ready. There was the rope hung from the window of the box-room and caught at the opening window of Mrs. Thurston's room, on which he was to escape, and the rope hung from the window of the apple-room to the unopening window of Mrs. Thurston's room, on which he was to return. If one could have seen them there they would have appeared to make a great X on the side of the house, marking it out for its doom, a sinister parody of that ink-mark by which 'our window' is designated on post-cards from the seaside.

"But unfortunately no one did see them. It was a dark night, and you were all indoors. So that when Mr. Rider went upstairs to wait in Mary Thurston's room for his victim, no one suspected that he was not on his way home, except Stall, who had shown him there.

"She went up to bed. At her door she hesitated, startled, not unnaturally, to find Mr. Rider awaiting her in a room which had been partially darkened by Stall in the hope that the murder might be committed before the murderer's intention was apparent to the victim, and the alarm raised.

"What crazy appeal the poor man made in those ten minutes we shall never know, or what were the unhappy lady's answers. But at last the thing was done, and thereafter the Vicar followed Stall's instructions minutely. He seized the rope, pulled down the window, and swung, a giant spider on his thread, to the window which did not open. There he stood, gripping the masonry above him while Stall pulled in that first rope, and descended to the door to prove his alibi.

"You all came, you broke in, you searched, you left the room, and Stall, on the plea of fetching brandy for the hysterical girl, went to draw in the second rope, on which Mr. Rider had now swung back to the open window. He said afterwards that he had gone to the front door in answer to the bell, to admit Mr. Rider. At first, I thought that, had that bell rung, it would have been a peal of joy, for it would have proved this unfortunate man's innocence. But then I found that all the bell-pushes of the house, including those of the front door and Mrs. Thurston's room, operated on the same bell, so that had it sounded it might have been a summons to Stall from Mr. Rider in the bedroom as well as Mr. Rider at the front door. It might, as I said at the time, have shown that someone was not outside the front door, as well as that someone was there.

"You know the rest. You came upstairs and found the murderer, who, I prefer to think, was but the weapon of the murderer, in the room beside the dead woman."

"So you think," I asked breathlessly, "that he cut her throat because he thought it was a duty?"

"I think," said Mgr. Smith, blinking at me, "that he cut her throat because he thought it was a canker."

CHAPTER 31

It was at this difficult moment that Dr. Thurston came into the room.

"I hope," he said quietly, "that you have finished your deliberations. You haven't yet made your arrest, Sergeant?"

"Not yet, sir."

"The truth is, Thurston," said Sam Williams, "that there is a little difference of opinion among these gentlemen."

Thurston looked puzzled. He evidently found this hard to understand or credit. "But . . . but haven't you discovered who is guilty?" he asked wearily.

"Yes, Well, that is . . ." Williams was in an uncomfortable predicament. At last he turned to Sergeant Beef. "Look here, Sergeant, you, after all, represent the police, and it is your duty to make an arrest. You have heard all these gentlemen. What do you think about it?"

Sergeant Beef looked from one to the other of the three investigators with evident appreciation. "Wot do I think about it? I think wot these gentlemen 'ave told us is remarkable. Remarkable! I shouldn't never 'ave believed it possible that anyone could 'ave been so ingeenyus. And the details they thought of! It was wonderful, sir, and a treat to 'ear them. I shan't never forget to-day. It will be something to tell my grandchildren. To think that I've been privileged to 'ear all that!" His eyes, usually a trifle glazed, glowed now with honest admiration.

"That's scarcely the point," said Williams coldly. "What we have to do is to decide who is guilty, and arrest him."

"Oh yes," admitted Sergeant Beef, "I was forgetting that. I know 'oo done it, of course. But that ain't nothink—not finding out 'oo done it isn't. Why, I could never 'ave made up them stories if you'd paid me, sir. Wonderful, they was."

"Well, Sergeant, you've been saying for a long time that you know who was guilty. Suppose you tell us your theory?"

"I 'aven't got no theory, sir. I wouldn't presume to 'ave, not in front of these gentlemen. I couldn't express myself like that, wotever you was to give me."

"You have no theory? But I thought you said you knew who had done it?"

"So I do. But that's nothink, sir. Not after 'earing wot I 'ave to-night."

"Well, for heaven's sake, man, tell us what you know."

"Well, it's really too simple, sir. I don't 'ardly like to disappoint you now."

"Come along. Did the murderer have an accomplice?"

"Yus. 'E did. He 'ad two."

"Two? Are you going to arrest these accomplices?"

"Can't do that, sir."

"Why not?"

"Because one of 'em's dead and the other didn't know wot would come of it."

"One's dead?"

"Yus. See, it began really when you wos talking about murder stories, before you 'ad your supper." Lord Simon shivered at the word. "And I wouldn't 'arf like to know 'oo started that conversation."

Suddenly I remembered. It had been opened by Thurston. "As a matter of fact," I said, "though of course it's of no importance, I remember now." I turned to Dr. Thurston. "You probably remember, Doctor? You turned to me and asked me whether I had read any good murder stories lately. Of course the whole thing is ridiculous, but I just happen to remember that."

Dr Thurston smiled patiently. "Did I? Very likely. I can't remember."

"Anyway, what has that to do with it?" asked Williams.

"You'll see in a minute. Well, Dr. Thurston starts you talking about murderers, and whether they gets copped. And Mr. Norris says 'e doesn't 'old wiv crime stories and that, because they aren't true to life. And so on. It was just 'ow anyone might go on."

"Well?"

"Well. When Mrs. Thurston goes upstairs, Dr. Thurston goes to 'is own room and gets dressed. Then, after Mr. Strickland 'ad come out of 'er room, 'e slips in. 'Ere,' 'e says, 'I 'aven't 'arf got a good idea for a lark,' 'e says. 'Wot say we bamboozle 'em to-night wiv a murder, and see whether they can find out 'ow it's done?' 'Wot you mean, dear?' she asks. She was always a bit silly like and ready to be persuaded into anything."

At this point Williams stood up. "This is preposterous," he said. "Beef, we'll have no more of this nonsense. It is too painful for Dr. Thurston. Now . . ."

"*Mais non!*" said M. Picon. "Let the good Bœuf continue! He begins to become interesting!"

Beef went on. "The long and short of it was, 'e persuaded 'er. 'Now I'll tell you wot to do,' 'e said. 'When you go up to bed, don't undress, but lock your door, and shut your window. Then take this 'ere bottle of red ink, and pour it on your pillow. Get 'old of your lipstick, and paint a 'ell of a great scar across your froat. Then scream like blazes as 'ard as you can, see? We'll come and break down the door, and then we'll see whether these people wot says you can' commit a murder without being found out can see 'ow the murderer escaped! Got it?' 'e says, and she says it's O.K. Then 'e says, 'Tell you wot,' 'e says, 'I better take this bulb out of the light, otherwise they'll be able to see you 'avn't really been murdered.' And 'e does so, and chucks it out of the window."

"Then why weren't there any finger-prints on the glass?" I asked. I thought that would squash him, since obviously

220

Thurston could not have put on a glove to do it.

"Why not? Because the light 'ad just been burning, of course. It was still 'ot. So naturally he pulls out 'is 'andkerchief to 'andle it with. See?"

I saw. I began to feel a little nervous. Suppose this blundering policeman had got together enough nonsense to look like evidence? It would be uncomfortable for Thurston to have the inconvenience of defending himself.

"Well, to go on with what 'e said to Mrs. Thurston. 'When we've got 'em on a string,' 'e says, 'we'll tell 'em it was only a joke, see? Only don't you move,' 'e says, 'till I give you the wink. We don't want to let it out too soon.' And she agrees. I knew the lady myself. She was always a bit childish, like. Anything like a bit of acting an' that would 'ave got 'er easy. She was game for what she thought would be just a lark, poor lady.

"Then p'raps it was 'er 'oo thought of the next thing. 'Suppose someone was to run downstairs and 'phone the p'lice,' she says 'that wouldn't do, would it?' And 'e says, 'No more it wouldn't. I'll tell you wot,' 'e says, 'I'll run down an' cut the telephone wire, then no one can't 'phone,' 'e says, and off 'e goes to do it, like wot we know it was done.

"Then down you all comes to 'ave your grub, and Mrs. Thurston's in 'igh spirits, because although she's been blackmailed a bit by that Stall, 'oo I'm going to run in presently, she knows 'e's got the sack, an'll be gone in a couple of weeks, and besides, there's this 'ere joke on, and she's like a kid with a joke. She probably kep' looking across knowing-like to 'er 'usband, and thinking of 'ow you was all going to be took in.

"Well, then, Mr. Strickland goes off to bed, and soon after 'im Mr. Norris, and then the Vicar. We'll come to 'im later. And at eleven o'clock, as per usual, Mrs. Thurston gets up to go to bed. When she opens 'er door, she finds

221

Stall standing there, leaning on 'er dressing-table, 'elping 'imself to snuff. 'What are you doing 'ere?' she asks, though she knows very well 'e's come for 'is two 'undred quid. But she doesn't waste a lot of time arguing, she gives 'im the notes to get rid of 'im, and when 'e's gone she starts getting ready for 'er lark.

"Poor lady! She must 'ave been laughing to 'erself, little knowing what she was letting 'erself in for. She takes the bottle of red ink and pours it over 'er pillow (same as a schoolboy 'oo wants to get out of class pours some on 'is 'andkerchief and says 'is nose is bleeding). Then she paints 'erself 'orrid round the froat, and bolts the door top and bottom. Now she thinks everything's ready, and she lays down on the bed, and lets out three screams, as blood-curdling as she can make 'em. Then she shuts 'er eyes, and waits for wotever's going to 'appen.

"You know wot did 'appen. The first on the scene is Mr. Norris, because 'e's got nothink to delay 'im. Then up comes Dr. Thurston, calling out 'er name, and Mr. Williams and Mr. Townsend, and start breaking the door in. Wot's 'appened to the others you may well ask. Two of them's got something to 'ide before they puts their noses out of their doors. There's Mr. Strickland, with the diamond pendant, wot Mrs. Thurston 'ad giv' 'im before dinner, lying on his dressing-table as bold as brass. 'E 'as to conceal that before 'e dares open 'is door. And there's Stall with two 'undred of the best in his room, 'e can't come running down before they're away. Then there was the chauffeur. Well, don't forget 'e 'ad been sent for to Mrs. Thurston's room that evening. I shouldn't be surprised if e'd been on 'is way down the stairs when 'e 'eard those screams, and got a narsty turn, and run back to 'is own room for a minute. Somethink of that, anyway.

"Then you breaks the panels of the door, and look in. "Ullo,' you say, 'murdered, is she?' For there she lies in a

222

pool of blood, you think. And Dr. Thurston, 'e walks across to 'er and examines 'er, and says she's dead. And you start searching the room like mad, thinking that someone's been in there a-murdering of 'er, just as you was meant to think. And all the while the poor lady's smiling to 'erself, thinking she's 'aving a rare joke on you. So she was, up to then.

"So you looks 'igh and low, up the chimney, out of the winder, and under the carpet, not knowing as you know now, that no one 'adn't been in there since Stall was there, and 'im only for a couple of minutes. But at last you've finished, and leave the lady alone. Mr. Townsend and Mr. Strickland and Mr. Norris go out in the gardens, while the chauffeur comes for me.

"Then, with no one else there, and an alibi established, it ain't no trouble to slip back in the room, murder the poor lady, and drop the knife out of the window in time for Mr. Townsend to find it on the ground. See? I told you it was simple. 'Ardly worth telling. But you seemed to want to know how it was done."

"But good heavens, Beef," I said, really appalled by the story which sounded uncomfortably true, "what proof have you got?"

"Proof?" repeated Beef. "I got plenty of proof. D'you know 'ow I got on to this? Why, examining those bloodstains you was all so sarcastic about. You see, in that sort of way I've got a bit of an advantage over these gentlemen. I mean, I can't work out theories like what they can, I only wish I could. Only we're taught things in the police, see? And one of the first jobs in a case like this is to 'ave a good look at the bloodstains. Well, I done that, and found something funny about 'em. It was a clean pillowslip, or 'ad been before the blood was on it. And the stains on the pillow-slip *was* blood, *real* blood. But when I came to look at the pillow itself inside, what d'you think I found?

223

Not only blood, but red ink! That taught me a thing or two. Oh, I says, so that was it, was it. Acting dead, was she? And the pillow-slip with the inkstains on been took away after the real murder, was it? Only there wasn't a chance to take the 'ole pillow, wasn't there? I see. That's 'ow I come to discover it. Of course, I got the pillow and the pillow-slip. Exhibits A and B, them. That's proof enough, isn't it? And not circumstantial, wot's more."

CHAPTER 32

So at last we knew who was guilty. As Sergeant Beef said,
the evidence of the pillow and pillow-slip was not circumstantial, but was hard and certain proof. I cannot pretend
that 1 had suspected Dr. Thurston, because it had seemed
to me impossible that he, who had been with us from the
time that Mrs. Thurston went to bed until we had found her
apparently murdered, could have had anything to do with
it. Who could even have suspected that his accomplice, his
unfortunate and unconscious accomplice, had been none
other than the murdered woman! It seemed very horrible,
but even as I realized it, it seemed diabolically clever.

But there was one man who had evidently decided to
remain loyal to Thurston. The Doctor was about to speak
in answer to Sergeant Beef, when Williams placed a hand
on his arm. "Doctor, as your lawyer I forbid you to say
anything in answer to this at present. The whole thing is
outrageous, and we shall be able to prove that this
blundering fool of a policeman has made some fantastic
mistake."

Lord Simon leaned back easily. "Not this time, Williams,"
he said, "I am not one to get excited about the jolly old
police, but I'm climbin' down a peg." Then he added,
"Lord, what a relief it is to have been wrong for once!
You don't know the monotony of infallibility!"

"I also, the great Amer Picon, shall rest contented. At
last I have made the *faux pas*. Hooray, as you say in English,
it is a great change for me!"

And Mgr. Smith murmured softly, "I am so pleased.
So pleased."

"At all events," said Williams fiercely, "say nothing,

Doctor, till we have conferred." Then he turned to Beef. "I take it that there is no objection to Dr. Thurston coming with me to the study for a while before you . . . take any more steps?"

"None at all, sir. There are police in the grounds and no one can leave. I will give you ten minutes."

The two went out of the room and Sergeant Beef made an unpleasant noise as though he were sucking his teeth, as indeed he probably was doing. Then suddenly he rose heavily to his feet.

"I don't know whether I ought to leave them . . ." he began.

But his words were rudely interrupted. There was the sound of a revolver shot which seemed to shake the house, and sang deafeningly in my ears for some seconds. We jumped up, and ran out into the hall. The study door was open, and full length on the ground lay the weighty bulk of Dr. Thurston, while in his right hand was still clasped his revolver. Williams stooped over him, and Beef followed.

"I'm afraid there can be no doubt about death in *this* case," Williams said. "It must have been instantaneous."

"How did it happen?" I asked.

"He led me in here, then asked if I would leave him alone for a moment. He said he wanted to collect himself before conferring with me. And foolishly I agreed. For some reason it never occurred to me that this was his intention. I had scarcely opened the door when I heard the shot behind me."

"Let's go back to the other room," I said, for the body of the dead man was gruesome. There was an expression of startled horror on Thurston's dead face which was unendurable. Before we left him, however, a rug was laid over the corpse, and Beef took care to lock the door when we were all out of the room.

"Well, that seems pretty well to prove your theory,

226

Sergeant," said Williams, when we had got back to the more natural atmosphere of the lounge.

And indeed if further proof was necessary I felt that her it was. What could be more conclusive than the suicide of the protagonist? But it appeared that Beef was modest.

"Wot theory?" he said. "I 'adn't got no theory."

"Oh yes, you had," said Williams, "and a very brilliant one, and as it now turns out amazingly true. Poor Mary! I wonder what Thurston's motive was? I expect we shall see when we come to go through her papers. It was a fiendishly clever idea, though, for Thurston to persuade her into that pretence, and then, with his alibi established, for him to go back and murder her."

Sergeant Beef was standing between us and the door.

"'Oo said anythink about Dr. Thurston going back and murdering 'er?" he asked suddenly.

For a moment I did not understand the implications of this extraordinary question, then I was horrified to see that the Sergeant had pulled out a pair of handcuffs and drawn himself up to his full height.

"Samuel James Williams," he said, "it is my duty to arrest you. You are charged with the murder of Mary Thurston. You will be further charged with the murder of Dr. Alexander Thurston. It is also my duty to warn you that anythink you say may be used in evidence against you."

Before I had recovered from my surprise I saw that he had slipped his handcuffs over the lawyer's wrists.

"But . . . but . . ." I said. "You've just been proving it was Dr. Thurston . . ."

"I beg your pardon, sir, I 'aven't been proving nothink of the sort. I knowed it was 'im all through."

Sergeant Beef then did a very commponlace thing. He blew loudly on a whistle.

"Really!" said Lord Simon, whose sensibilities were touched by the sound.

Two policemen entered.

"Take 'im along," said Sergeant Beef. "'E won't say nothink, being a lawyer. But 'e's for it, oright. 'Anged by the neck till 'e's dead, 'e'll be."

The Sergeant thereupon helped himself to a glass of beer, and after thoroughly sucking the ends of his straggling ginger moustache, he said, "You see, gents, I 'adn't got no theories, not like yours. I still think they was remarkable. But I did 'appen to know 'oo done it. It was simple enough. What I told you about the lark was true. That was Dr. Thurston's idea—for a joke like. He never 'ad no intention but a joke, if you get my meaning. 'E took that bulb out to 'elp the joke, not wanting anyone to see she was still alive and spoil it, and he snipped the telephone wire in case anyone should ring up the p'lice and 'im get into trouble for giving us unnecessary trouble. Then it all 'appened just as I said it did. Only when Williams was searching the room 'e notices out of the corner of 'is eye that Mrs. Thurston's no more dead than 'e is. Or p'raps he 'ears 'er chuckling. And 'is brain's quick. 'E thinks, "Ullo, 'ere's a chance to do 'er in.' 'E gets rid of you all out of the way like. Dr. Thurston 'as to act as though 'e's cut up, for the sake of the joke, see? So the Doctor stays downstairs. Then this 'ere Williams who'd said 'e was going to 'ave another try at telephoning, slips up and cuts 'er froat while you're going out to search the grounds. He throws the knife out of the window, like I said. It couldn't of been there many seconds when you found it, Mr. Townsend. No wonder the blood was still wet.

"You see, this 'ere Williams was the cleverest kind of a murderer, the one 'oo knows 'ow to take advantage of an opportunity. That's 'arf the game. I'm of the opinion that anyone could be murdered, and no one found out, if every murderer did it just at the right moment. That's wot this Williams was thinking when 'e was pretending to search the room. 'E knew that Dr. Thurston was in the game with 'er, but he knew very well that when the Doctor found she was really dead, 'e'd never dare let on to that, because 'e'd of been 'anged himself—for certain. All 'e 'ad to be sure of was that the Doctor went upstairs alone, and made the discovery on 'is own, too.

"I don't suppose that was difficult. 'E knew the Doctor was downstairs alone in the lounge. All 'e 'ad to do was to suggest to 'im something that would send 'im upstairs again. P'raps 'e-pretended to 'ear a sound from the room. P'raps 'e didn't 'ave to suggest nothing, because the Doctor would want to go and 'ave a smile with 'is wife over the joke, when you was all out of the way. We shan't never know. But at all events, Williams comes back into the lounge, says it's no good, 'e can't get an answer on the telephone, as though 'e'd never left the receiver.

"Then Dr. Thurston goes up to 'is wife. But when 'e gets into the room, 'e finds she really 'as been murdered. 'E's just going to shout out, when 'e sees that it's going to look bad for 'im. He's innocent, but after all 'e suggested that dam' silly game. He made 'er pretend. And when anyone sees 'ow it was done 'e'll be suspected. Especially with 'im up 'ere alone now. So 'e says nothink, and comes downstairs, just as Williams 'opes 'e will.

"At the bottom of the stairs 'e meets Mr. Townsend, Mr. Strickland and Mr. Norris, coming in from their search of the grounds. 'E knows someone's done it, since you all left the room upstairs, and 'e doesn't know 'oo to suspect. So 'e asks you chaps where you've been. Then 'e sees that it 'ud look funny for 'im to be asking questions now, so 'e drops it. From that moment, though, 'e's 'oping that the murderer'll be discovered. 'E doesn't like keeping the secret, but 'e 'as the sense to see 'e might 'ang if 'e was to tell then 'ole story of the joke."

The Sergeant paused to drink again. "There's not much more to tell, except that I didn't ought never to've let them go in the other room together. See, Dr. Thurston was just going to come out with it that 'e 'ad planned that lark with 'is wife, but never 'ad nothink to do with the murder, when Williams, as you know, stopped 'im. Dr. Thurston didn't know 'oo to suspect, but 'e'd never suspected Williams. 'E was led off like a lamb to the other room. Tell you the truth, I wouldn't never 'ave let him, only I was hoping that we might get a bit more evidence if Williams was to tell 'im not to say anything, and 'e got suspicious of Williams. But that's wot comes of trying to make your case too cast-iron. As soon as 'e got 'im out there Williams shot 'im, stuck the revolver in 'is 'and and opened the door, with a story ready of 'ow 'e'd just turned 'is back and Dr. Thurston shot himself. If that 'ad of come off 'e'd 'ave been clea., see?

"Williams must 'ave thought I really suspected Dr. Thurston. But I didn't. I knew it was Williams."

"How?" I asked. "After all, it *was* Thurston who had arranged the so-called joke. It was Thurston who had said she was dead. How did you know it was Williams who went back in that room and killed Mrs. Thurston?"

"Simple, sir. I've told you I 'aven't got no theories. I'm no good at anythink like that. I'm just an ordinary policeman, as you might say. I found out 'ow the murder was done by them bloodstains and inkstains. And I found out 'oo done the murder by bloodstains and inkstains, too. See, I 'ave to use these regulation methods. Never do for me to get up to any fanciful tricks like 'arf-mast flags, and spiders wiv' flies, and Sidney Sewells, and that. You gentlemen understand all that. I jist 'ave to follow instructions for procedure in a case of crime. So when I'd found them stains, I 'ad a look at the clothes you'd all been wearing that night. And on the left breast of Williams' shirt, off of the 'ard part and quite near the armpit, I found a very faint pink mark. And I knew it was red ink. See when 'e'd picked

up the first pillow-slip wot the red ink 'ad been on, 'e'd
stuffed it inside of 'is waistcoat to take away and burn later.
And although it 'ad been almost dry then, it 'ad just made
that faint smudge. Then again on the outside underneath
part of 'is cuff what should I find but another little stain.
This 'un was red, too, on'y it wasn't ink, it was blood. Very
likely there'd been some more on 'is jacket, but 'e'd seen
that an' washed it orf. Only no one couldn't 'ardly 'ave
seen this. It was only small, right on the edge of the cuff.
That's 'ow I knew it was 'im.

"But we'll 'ave plenty more evidence. 'E never left a
finger-print anywhere, 'aving plenty of time. But when 'e
came to shooting Dr. Thurston I should think it's more
than likely 'e left 'em on the revolver, gambling on being
able to get back later and wipe 'em. So we'll 'ave 'im there.
Besides, when it comes to the inquest on Dr. Thurston,
ten to one you'll find that the shot wot killed 'im couldn't
of been self-inflicted. They can pretty well always tell nowadays, and you see if 'e wasn't shot from three or four feet
away instead of close to the head.

"But there's one more important of evidence against 'im.
In the grate of 'is room I found a bit of charred linen, wot
I sent up to the Yard to be examined. It turns out to be the
same stuff as wot the rest of the pillow-cases was made of.
Well, that might not of been conclusive, if I 'adn't found
out from the girl about the fires. You remember 'ow 'e shut
me up when I started to arst 'er about that? And, not
wishing to rub it in, you gentlemen joined in wiv 'im? Well,
I 'ad to see 'er later. She said Mr. Williams never liked a
fire in 'is room. It was laid, same as fires 'ad to be laid
everywhere, in case anyone wanted to light one. But
Williams 'ad never lit 'is before. And when she come to do
the grate it must 'ave been nine o'clock, because I'd examined it soon after I got 'ere that morning and found the bit
of charred linen. I thought then the coals was still 'ot and

she says when she come to do 'em she could feel 'em warm still. There was only a very small scuttle of coal there, and it wasn't all burnt. So 'e couldn't 'ave lighted 'is fire till the small hours, to burn that pillow-case. So no one else couldn't of gone into 'is room to burn it there."

"But what was his motive?" I asked. I wasn't sceptical now, but curious.

"Motive? 'E 'ad more motive than anyone. First thing I did was to go froo Mrs. Thurston's papers. 'E'd 'ad all 'er money. All 'er own money that is, to invest. 'Adn't you thought it a bit odd as a lady with two or three thousand a year, 'oo'd never lived extravagant, should be overdrawn so far she couldn't overdraw no farther, even if she was being blackmailed? Well, that's the reason. All she 'adn't spent of 'er i..come she'd been 'anding over to this 'ere Williams for years to invest for 'er. And 'e'd been living on it—'andsome. And now she was being pressed by Stall, and begged from by Strickland, she wanted a bit. And of course it wasn't there. Only when 'e came down this week-end 'e never thought 'e'd get as good a chance as that to do 'er in without being copped!"

CHAPTER 33

Now though it looked as though there was nothing more to be said, I for one was determined to clear up every point I could think of. I did not mean to be caught again by someone else who would come along with a theory that would supersede this one. So although Sergeant Beef had anxiously consulted a large silver watch several times, as though afraid that he was going to be late for some urgent appointment, I continued to question him.

"What about the ropes?" I said.

"Oh them, well, in the night 'e thought it all over, and it seemed a pretty neat crime to 'im. 'E knew by then that Dr. Thurston 'ad decided to keep quiet about this game of 'is and 'is wife's, in case 'e should be suspected. Come to that it's more than likely that Dr. Thurston had actually told 'im about it, as 'is lawyer. In fact, now I come to think of it, I should think he had. And Williams, of course, 'ad advised 'im to keep quiet till 'e saw what you gentlemen made of it. There might never be no need to mention the game, if you'd found the murderer without that. But whether or not 'e'd actually told Williams, Williams knew 'e would tell 'im before 'e told anyone else, if 'e was going to mention it. So Williams thought 'e'd got things pretty well set, a mystery as no one couldn't solve. Well then, 'e began to wonder if it wasn't *too* much of a mystery. Left as it was, the only solution to it would 'ave to be the true solution, and that wouldn't suit 'im at all. So 'e thinks 'ow 'e could show up some other possibility. And some time in the small hours 'e gets up, goes down to the gymnasium, finds a ladder, 'auls them ropes across, and 'ides 'em in the tanks. 'E 'ad nerve. But it wasn't so dangerous as it looked.

233

If 'e was caught with them anywhere 'e could 'ave said 'e was up to detective work and 'ad just found 'em, and show 'ow the murderer 'ad used 'em. But 'e wasn't caught. 'E got 'em in the tank safe enough. 'E brought the two, in case it should be proved afterwards that one 'adn't been long enough, and all 'is work wasted."

"But what about Strickland—and the pendant?"

"Wot about 'im? 'Is Lordship was right enough. He is the stepson. 'E got into a bit of trouble over racing, and changed 'is name: But 'e's oright. 'E didn't put 'is 'undred quid on that 'orse until Mrs. Thurston 'ad giv' 'im the pendant which 'e could pop for more than that, to cover 'im if the 'orse didn't win. 'E's oright, I tell you, I'm glad 'is 'orse did come in. It'll be drinks round to-night—if I get down there in time. Course he told one or two lies. Well, 'e wasn't going to let on about changing 'is name. Why should 'e? 'E didn't want all that raked up. As for 'is going to Sidney Sewell, well, what could be more natural? A run in the car was what anyone 'ud want, cooped up 'ere for a murder enquiry. It's not everyone 'oo enjoys 'em, you know. And of course 'e chose Sidney Sewell, that being the place 'e'd stayed at. But there was no secret about it, or 'e wouldn't of took Norris and Fellowes with 'im."

I was determined to find out whether the Sergeant's case was complete. "But the chauffeur?" I asked. "And the girl? And her ex-convict brother?"

The Sergeant smiled. "That's where I had the advantage, sir. See, being sergeant in a place like this, you gets to know people and what they're up to. I mean, we know 'oo might be doing a bit of poaching, and 'oo's liable to get tight. I knew this chap Fellowes pretty well—played darts with 'im a good many times. Always starts on the double eighteen, 'e does. Never misses. Well, I knew 'e 'ad a bit saved up, and 'ad been looking for the right pub for 'im and Enid for a long time. And I also knew that 'e'd just

234

settled to take over the Red Lion. Money was paid a week ago before any of this came along. And the brother, Miles, was to go and work for 'em. Pleased as punch they was about it. 'E wouldn't of wanted to go doing anyone in Not 'im. 'E was getting married and everythink. 'E may 'ave 'ad a bit of a row with the girl over not 'aving give in 'is notice. But ten to one 'e told 'er when they was out together on Friday afternoon that 'e'd tell Mrs. Thurston that night. And that settled it with Enid, so that when they got back to their car that afternoon their tiff was over. Then, as you remember, Mrs. Thurston sent for 'im, before dinner, to tell 'im about the rat-traps, which meant to tell him she wanted to see 'im later. And he came out with it then and there in the 'all, that 'e wanted to leave at the end of the week. No wonder you noticed 'er looking a bit upset when you were on your way up to change. She was upset, but she'd persuaded 'im to 'ave a word with 'er later. Well, at eleven o'clock 'e and Enid 'ears Mrs. Thurston go up to bed. 'E wants to see 'er at once and get it over, but 'e mustn't appear to be following 'em upstairs. So wot does 'e do? Wot would anyone do? Look at the clock of course and sez 'Why, it's past eleven', as though it was later than wot 'e thought it was, to explain 'is 'urrying off.

"So 'e went to go in 'er room. Only 'e couldn't because Stall was in there, after 'is two 'undred. Not that Fellowes knew 'oo it was, only 'e 'eard someone talking. And it's my belief, as I've told you, that 'e was just coming down-stairs to 'ave another try, when 'e 'eard those screams, and doubled back up again. The girl 'ad a nasty experience, though. She was in the Doctor's room, right opposite to Mrs. Thurston's, when those screams started. No wonder she couldn't move for a minute. It must 'ave turned 'er up, coming sudden like that with no noise first. Enough to give any girl a turn, especially when she 'arf thinks 'er lover's in there. She stays where she is a minute, till she

235

'ears you battering at the door, then she comes out and must 'ave been relieved to see Fellowes with the rest of you. 'E tells 'er to run downstairs, which she does, as we know from the cook.

"Mind you, it may of been lucky for Miles that 'e 'ad that alibi. It might easily 'ave appeared that someone would 'ave mixed 'im up in this, and brought out all about 'is past, which wouldn't 'ave done 'im any good in the village, when 'e goes to 'elp at the Red Lion. But fortunately nobody knows anythink about it, except you gentlemen and me, so 'e's oright. 'E'll go straight enough now. 'E never chizzles on the dart-board, and that's a good sign. Why, only the other night I was playing against 'im and I thought one of 'is darts was in the sixty. 'One ton,' I says, but he says, 'No sixty. It wasn't there.' 'E could of 'ad it as easy as wink, an' I shouldn't 'ave known any different. But 'e didn't, see! Honest 'e was. We shan't 'ave no more trouble with 'im!"

It was just then, I think, that Mgr. Smith got up to leave us. He bore no grudge against the Sergeant, and like the good sportsman he was enjoyed being wrong at last. "You see," he explained, "by the very nature of things it has never been possible for me to be mistaken before. And while there is error in a man, a man may be in error."

He beamed round on us and picked up his parasol.

"Where are you off to?" I asked.

"I must go to the Vicarage," he said, and scuttled out. We heard that it was several hours before he returned from the gloomy Vicarage, but what had passed in that time it was not our business to enquire.

When we had left the room I was seized by yet another doubt. "But, Sergeant," I said, "there is one matter which you haven't explained. And now I come to think of it, it is a serious one. What about the Vicar? You cannot account for all his movements so simply. They were really most peculiar. First of all his questions to me. Then all that time when he said he was out in the orchard, then his being by the side of the corpse so soon after the murder, and finally his saying that he had sinned. What does it all mean? Was he really mad?"

"Mad? No!" said Sergeant Beef. "'E isn't mad. That was just 'is way of trying to get out of it—defend 'imself, like."

"Defend himself? Then he did have something to do with the murder?"

"No. Not that. But 'aven't you really guessed, sir, what it was 'e was ashamed of? It's as plain as the nose on your face."

"I can't say I have—unless it was this interfering puritanism of his."

"No, not that. Though it's all part of it. You see the kind of man he was? Always seeing something wrong when there was nothing to see. Well, you know what goes with that, don't you? A nasty mind, that's what! No wonder 'e was ashamed of 'imself. When he left here that night, where did he go? Out in the orchard, pacing up and down? Not he! 'E knew Mrs. Thurston would be going to bed in a minute, and p'raps didn't trouble to draw the blinds. And out 'e goes in the garden to see whether 'e could see anything 'e shouldn't. That's how he came to 'ear the screams, and that's why he was guilty afterwards."

"In fact," drawled Lord Simon, "as Monsignor Smith would say if he were here, he was not only a Nosey Parker, but a Peeping Tom."

EPILOGUE

THE public bar of the Red Lion was brightly lit, and the beer glowed happily in glass tankards. Enid, behind the bar, watched placidly, while Sergeant Beef and I attempted with zeal to win a game of darts against Fellowes and Miles.

"Police versus criminals, you might call it," Enid had observed when we started, with pointed reference to my efforts of some months ago to assist investigation of the Thurston Mystery and not without recollection of how we had disinterred the unfortunate past history of the two men who were now our opponents. 'Criminals', in this contest anyway, were on top, for the publican, whom I had met as a chauffeur, and his brother-in-law were, as Beef put it, 'mustard at this game'.

Williams had been hanged a week before. When his trial had come on, the amount of evidence which had been collected against him was enormous, and I suspected that the prosecution had received some kindly hints from two at least of the investigators who had been concerned in the case. They had rallied good-naturedly to the Sergeant, who never lost his admiration for them. He was wont to wonder even to-day at their inventiveness, and envy their remarkable gifts.

Our game was finishing. Fellowes needed a hundred and fifty-seven to get out. Jealously I watched him throw his three darts, treble nineteen, treble twenty, double top—a brilliant bit of work. And when the well-merited beer was brought, we returned, not unnaturally, to talk of the tragedy which had first brought us together.

"It was a funny business, altogether," commented Fellowes, not, as you will gather, imputing any comedy to the affair, but referring to the element of unexpectedness which had been noticeable in it.

"Wasn't it?" said Enid, as she crunched potato crisps. "You could have knocked me down with a feather when I knew it was that Williams who had done it. I never liked him, though. Too 'igh and mighty for anyone, he was. But you wouldn't have thought he was the one to do a person in, would you? Still, there you are. You never know, as they say."

"I reckon it was a blarsted shame, though," said Miles. "To go and cut her throat like that. She'd never done anyone any harm."

"Ah," said Fellowes, "but when they gets in a mess over money they'll do anything. How much was it he'd had off of 'er? Six thousand quid, wasn't it? And nothing to show for it. He had to do something to keep her quiet."

"I dare say, but that's no reason to go on like 'e did," observed Enid. "And then shooting the Doctor as well. No one can't say he didn't deserve all he got. What was it that lawyer called him? A 'homicidal opportunist', wasn't it? He certainly took his opportunity all right."

"That's what made it so hard to get him," I ventured to observe. I have learnt not to give my opinion too freely of late.

"Yes. And what I say now," said Enid, "is what I've said all along—it was really clever of Sergeant Beef to have spotted him. Really clever, it was!"

"Hear, hear!" said Fellowes.

The Sergeant sucked his moustache. "Oh, I don't know," he said, "there was nothink in it. I just went a'ead and carried out ordin'ry instructions. 'Ad a look at the blood-stains, and the rest followed. That's where it came in. I told those gentlemen 'oo came down to investigate right from the start that it was too simple a case for them."

"Unfortunately, Sergeant, they have been told that so

239

many times by the police that they couldn't be expected to believe you."

"Well, but it was. What was there to it? Them inkstains, and then the stains on Williams's shirt, and that bit of pillow-case wot 'e'd been burning. That's all it was, and the rest came on top of it as easy as wink. It wasn't the case for them at all. I mean, wot they want is something complicated. This was just a police business—not even worth bringing the Yard down. There's things of this sort 'appening every day. And all you 'ave to do is carry out the ordin'ry instructions, take your notes, and there you are. Only I wish to gawd I could make up a story like they can. Genius I call *that*. Well, wot about another game of darts?"

THE END